THE
FLOURISHING
OF
FLORALIE LAUREL

The FLOURISHING OF FLORALIE LAUREL

Fiadhnait Moser

Illustrations by Vivien Mildenberger

 **YELLOW JACKET**

YELLOW JACKET
an imprint of Bonnier Publishing USA

251 Park Avenue South, New York, NY 10010

Copyright © 2018 by Rachel Moser-Hardy

Illustrations copyright © 2018 by Bonnier Publishing USA

Illustrations by Vivien Mildenberger

All rights reserved, including the right of reproduction in whole or in part in any form.

Yellow Jacket is a trademark of Bonnier Publishing USA, and associated colophon is a trademark of Bonnier Publishing USA.

Manufactured in the United States of America   BVG 0418

First Edition

10 9 8 7 6 5 4 3 2 1

Library of Congress Control Number: 2017038871

ISBN 978-1-4998-0668-7

yellowjacketbooks.com

bonnierpublishingusa.com

FOR JANET KARMAN AND JANET ARMENTANO

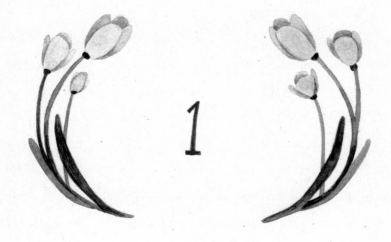

1

June 30, 1927

If you were to walk through Whitterly End, somewhere along the Here and There Bridge, you would find a little twig of a girl with flowers tucked in her hair and love letters inked on her hands. Her name was Floralie Alice Laurel, and the flowers were for sale, but the letters, well, no one asked about those. Floralie supposed nobody noticed them—or if they did, they were too polite to ask. Except, apparently, for *that* boy.

He stood just in front of Floralie, a scraggly thing he was, with untidy walnut hair and chapped lips, even though it was summer.

If he were a pet cat, Floralie might have named him "Scruffy" or "Smudge." He stared at Floralie for a good long minute before Floralie finally said, "Er—G'morning."

The boy simply stared.

Floralie fiddled with the two-inches-too-small sleeve of her school uniform—former uniform, to be precise. "Would you like to buy one?" she said, offering her basket of roses and tulips for the boy to peruse.

He stared some more.

Floralie bit the inside of her lip, and then the boy did something quite strange. He slipped his hand into his pocket and pulled from it a fountain pen and a tattered leather notebook. He flipped open the book and scrawled something on the page. *How much?*

Floralie eyed him quizzically, then took the pen and leaned over his notebook. *For a tulip or a rose?*

The boy took the pen. *For a poem.*

Floralie laughed and quickly covered her mouth to hide the gap in her teeth. *We don't sell those.*

The boy took back the pen. *It's okay,* he wrote, *you don't have to write. I can hear fine.*

"Oh," said Floralie. "I thought—" She averted her eyes. "I thought you were deaf."

The boy shrugged. *No. I can hear okay. I just don't like to talk.*

Floralie opened her mouth to speak, but instead took back the pen. *I don't mind paper, though,* she wrote. *I don't really like to talk either.* In the corner, she sketched a sprout of mugwort—dimpled blossoms and sun-stretching leaves—short, like baby arms. There was just something about mugwort flowers that felt *happy.*

As the boy read, a crooked smile broke his chapped lips. They bled a little, but he didn't seem to mind. He took the pen again and then began to write something a bit longer. When he finished, he turned it over to Floralie. *I saw your hands and there are poems on them. I like poetry, and I'd like one of yours, please. I'll give you whatever I've got in my pocket.*

Floralie gazed down to the love letters on her hands. They were written in black ink across her palms and had become a bit smudged in the late-afternoon heat. They were not the romantic sort of love letters, though. These were for the sort of person you love so much that it hurts to say the word "love." Indeed, Floralie's words wandered and rambled, but nowhere on her hands would one find the word "love." Instead, words like "missing you" and "needing you" and "leaving you" and "forgetting you" snaked up and down the lines of her palms.

It didn't matter, though, because that person would never see Floralie's words, even if they were written on paper instead of skin, and even if Floralie knew the address, and even if Floralie were back safe and sound at her old home in France. Because some words are too precious to give away, even if they're meant for someone else. And sometimes, words hurt so much that you've got to keep them somewhere outside of your head, or they might gobble you up from the inside out. That was what Mama used to say, before she disappeared.

Floralie tilted her hand so the boy could not read the letters, then took the pen. *Sorry, they're not poems. They're letters, and I don't sell those, only the flowers. I'm sorry.*

The boy took the book and scanned her words. He glanced up and twitched his mouth with disappointment, then took off into the crowd.

"Wait—" Floralie cried, and she chased after him, forgetting all the ladylike manners she had been taught at Mrs. Coffrey's School for Young Girls. She barreled through the crowds of shoppers and vendors, children and mothers. "Hey—come back!"

His disheveled hair bobbed just beyond a tall man in a tweed suit. Floralie stumbled past the man, flowers flying out of her basket. Finally, she caught the boy's shoulder. He turned, wide-eyed, as the crowd swirled around them like daisies caught in a dust storm.

Immediately, the boy knelt down on patchworked knees and began to gather the fallen tulips. Floralie bent down as well, and what she noticed about the flowers were their colors. Shadowed in the boy's hands, perhaps the tulips would seem pretty as babies' smiles or flamingo wings. But Floralie knew better. Colors were a mysterious business, and Floralie just so happened to know all their keen tricks. She was, after all, a painter—which was more to say she was a *seer*—because, really, all painting was, was learning how to see properly.

The tulips' highlights, colors like ballet slippers, Floralie would paint with a pleasant mixture of titanium white and alizarin red. Their shadows, though, she would paint a muddy swamp of a color—alizarin mixed with viridian green and a hint of cadmium orange. But the shadows, however ugly, were what gave the flowers life. Floralie's mother used to say the same about people. Broken pasts and shattered presents, uncertain futures without half a chance of happiness, those stories were what made people human. Mama knew that stories made people dance. That dance made people feel, and feeling made people fear, and fear was ugly. She knew fear was ugly. But fear, like shadows, looked up to beautiful, wonderful things. That was one of the things Floralie missed most about Mama.

As the boy handed Floralie the tulips, his cheeks blushed the same colors as the petals. Floralie took the flowers, but as the two stood, she also took the boy's book and pen, and wrote:

I'm Floralie.

Most people were too polite to laugh when they learned her name—but Floralie could always tell when they wanted to. Laughs hid in the nooks and crannies of noses and cheeks, turning ears the color of holly berries. They could not hide from Floralie.

But this boy hadn't a drop of manners in his body. He didn't even try to hold back his laughter; he simply cracked another off-kilter smile and laughed. But it was not an ordinary sort of laugh. It was a quiet laugh, a whispery laugh, a laugh sprung from joy instead of cruelty. Floralie couldn't help herself from joining in.

The boy's eyes wrinkled with his smile, and Floralie noticed they were the same honey color as the ramshackle cottages that lined the streets of Lower Whitterly End. And when his laughter settled, he stared for a moment as if memorizing Floralie. Then, he gave her a nod and disappeared into the bustle.

Floralie stood there for a while, wishing the boy had told her his name. Perhaps he would be back around. Or perhaps not. He was a slippery sort of boy, the kind Mrs. Coffrey would have called a "street rat." But Floralie thought he looked more like a mouse, which, of course, Mrs. Coffrey would have thought an odd thing to say, but it was *true.* The boy really did look like a mouse— not in a bad way, just in a mouse-ish sort of way. It was then that Floralie realized she, too, was like a mouse. She was like the boy, and though she knew hardly anything about him, she was sure of this: They both knew how to disappear.

A haze of perfume hung like storm clouds over a field of lavender and cornflowers, pretty blues and periwinkle pinpricks. The perfume shop was one they visited only on special occasions. The occasion on this day happened to be the most beautiful sunrise Mama and Floralie had seen in a long while. Mama and Floralie wove through the rows of glass bottles filled with magic liquid. They glittered under crystal chandeliers, the light following Mama like a spotlight down a stage. She glowed like a lightning bug, daisy-blond hair swept over her shoulder and pale skin stretched smooth over pink-blushed cheekbones.

Floralie stopped at a clear bottle labeled LA DANSE DE MINUIT. Mama kneeled down to Floralie's level and whispered, "These are fairy potions, my wildflower. Bottled unicorn tears, mermaid scales, and phoenix breath."

Floralie dabbed a bit of the perfume onto her finger and sniffed the soft, flowery scent, a scent so strong and sweet it seemed to take her by the hand into a fairyland far, far away.

"It smells pretty," Floralie said. She looked into Mama's garden-green eyes. "It smells like you." And though Floralie didn't say it, she believed her mother must be brewed of all the magic around her. Her mother must be part fairy, part enchantress, part angel. Floralie could hardly imagine anyone on the earth meeting Mama and not falling in love with her. She was perfect.

Mama tucked an angelica flower on the shelf behind the Danse de Minuit perfume and said, "That one's for inspiration."

2

Hot summer fog rolled down hills and through alleyways, into Floralie's shoes, between her aching toes. There were no happy couples strolling about tonight for Floralie to sell flowers to, nor were there street performers to sing merry tunes and draw crowds. So Floralie, basket of coins jingling slightly less noisily than usual, ambled down the cobblestones toward her brother's shop. But as she walked, she thought about the gray surrounding her, and how it wasn't really gray at all, because if Floralie were to paint the fog, she would paint it cobalt blue and ultramarine violet and viridian green and even a fleck of yellow ochre here and there.

The roads were thin and twisty, quiet but for the shopkeepers flipping their door signs from OPEN to CLOSED. Floralie had become accustomed to counting lampposts to guide her home when it was rainy or foggy, which happened to be most of the time in Whitterly End. Back when Floralie lived in France, she would count fireflies on her way home, watch them glint along walls of ivy and peek out from behind rosebuds. She hardly ever had to walk in the rain then. Everything was different then.

Just past Floralie's twenty-second lamppost, nestled between the cobbler and the Whitterly Library, was the flower shop. The top half of the Dutch door was swung open, and a figure, somehow caught between boy and man, was silhouetted in the frame. Slender built and long legged, he leaned over the front desk, elbow on the desk, head in his palm. As a car rattled by, headlights blazing through the mist, a fleck of light winked across his thin-rimmed glasses, lighting his furrowed brow.

Nerves zipped through Floralie's arms and legs as she neared the door. Nevertheless, when she came upon it, she creaked open the lower half and slunk inside. The shop was a small speck of a thing with pots toppling over pots and flowers tucked into nooks and crannies. It smelled of perfume and ballet, of things lost but never found.

The ceiling drooped low in places, and though Floralie could stand beneath it without problem, her twenty-year-old brother, Tom, had to hunch. He reminded Floralie of a camel, the way his shoulders crouched, and Floralie could almost see him promenading through the desert. He was a lonely creature. He stood there now, the figure at the desk, hunched over his papers beneath a bluebell-shaped table lamp.

As a breeze blew in, a small slip of paper fluttered to Tom's fancy leather shoes, the kind of shoes with pointed tips and soft-as-snow footsteps that he could hardly afford. Sometimes, Floralie thought he wore them only to pretend he was a university student instead of a shopkeeper. To pretend he had chosen university instead of Floralie, to pretend that the money he had been saving since he was five years old had gone to his own studies rather than Floralie's upbringing. To pretend that Floralie hadn't gotten expelled from Mrs. Coffrey's finishing school but months ago, and to pretend that all was well and shiny, sleek and smooth. He shook the paper off without a care, taking no notice of Floralie's presence.

He was making a sound. What was it? It was a jagged, whimpering sort of noise one might expect from a puppy or a baby. Was Tom *crying*? Floralie treaded in slowly, then quietly, gently, she breathed, "*Tom?*"

Tom's head snapped up as if struck by lightning. He cleared his throat, spared a quick glance in Floralie's direction, and spoke in what Floralie gathered to be an attempt of a dignified tone, "Floralie. Lovely to see you—er—just drop the basket by the daffodils, will you? Best be off to bed now."

"Tom . . . ," said Floralie again. "What's on the desk?" Her voice was low, and her words barely sounded like a question.

Tom sighed. "Nothing you need to worry about. Now off to bed." He wouldn't even look at her.

"They're debts, aren't they? We're running out of money."

"Floralie, please, this is no matter for children—"

"I'm nearly twelve—"

"Precisely."

Floralie inched closer to Tom and reached a gentle hand up to his shoulder. "You don't have to protect me so much—I can handle things, Tom; you don't have to keep it all inside—"

"ENOUGH." Tom banged his fists on the desk and lowered his head as Floralie leaped back. "Go to bed, Flory. Please. I love you."

Floralie felt a jab in the pit of her stomach; her throat tightened and tears welled behind her eyes. "I know you do."

Tom pursed his lips, then muttered, "Grandmama's coming tomorrow."

"What?" breathed Floralie. "Why—what for?"

"She telephoned today saying she wishes to 'inspect' you."

"Oh," said Floralie. "*Inspect.*" The word tasted like prunes.

"You must behave yourself tomorrow. That means no daydreaming, no skipping or hopping about, no paint on your dress, and no writing on your hands." He sighed, and then added, "You know what this means, don't you, Flory? You do *know*?"

Floralie tipped on her heels, feeling dizzy all of a sudden. She knew exactly what it meant. If Grandmama didn't like what she saw, she would stop funding Tom and Floralie, and Floralie had a sneaking feeling she wasn't going to like what she saw. Guilt swelled in Floralie's stomach as she swallowed the visions of her expulsion letter she had received that sunny May morning. How it turned her world gray. "Y-you're right. I think I should be getting to bed." She dropped the basket full of coins on the counter, then turned for the door and hurried down the street.

They sat in silence on the train ride back to Whitterly End. Tom clasped his fingers together so hard his knuckles turned white, and Floralie watched him bite away his tears in the reflection of the train's window. She had said she was sorry. Tom was not angry. But sadness was an affliction Tom knew only too well.

Floralie leaned back in her seat, next to Tom. "You've really messed this up," said Tom, but he wrapped his arms around Floralie anyway, lying her head in his lap and stroking her curls. "We'll be just fine, you and me," he whispered. "We'll be okay."

3

When Floralie arrived at the ramshackle cottage at the very end of Whitterly End, just down the block from the flower shop, she scurried up the rickety stairs and into her little bedroom with slanted walls and a sagging cot. Tom and Floralie had moved into this cottage after Mama was sent away and after Papa died in France, so it could be just the two of them, with Tom looking after Floralie. Tom had dreamed of going to university, but instead had decided to care for Floralie so she wouldn't have to live with Grandmama at her orphanage—the Adelaide Laurel Orphanage for Unfortunate Children. Grandmama collected children the way some people collect buttons. She used to tell Floralie that she lost her son, Floralie's papa, after he went and married Mama. She said Mama stole him from her. But Floralie was little then. She hadn't understood the way some wounds heal quick and some wounds leave scars.

When Floralie and Tom first moved in, Floralie's room had been bare. But she painted flowers upon flowers all over her wallpaper, and her room quickly turned into a beautiful enchanted forest. After moving from France to England, this wonderland was the closest thing Floralie had to *home*.

The room was small to begin with, with nothing but a brass-rimmed cot and a raggedy pink blanket, a wardrobe, and a wooden desk piled high with books Grandmama had given Floralie. All the books were about table manners and needlepoint and other things that didn't interest Floralie very much. However, they did come in handy when she was painting. This was because her paints and brushes were kept high up in a secret compartment of her wardrobe, and whenever she needed them, Floralie would pile up the books on her desk chair and climb up to reach the compartment (which would explain the muddy footprint on *A Tidy House Is a Happy House* by Mildred Grenshaw). Yes, the room was quite plain indeed, and now so were the walls. It was unnerving.

Today, as Floralie kneeled by the wall, she painted bluebells, the saddest of flowers. And somewhere along the periwinkle petals, the peridot stem's curve, Floralie lost herself in a world completely her own. She had visited this forest a thousand times. The flowers stretched tall, and the grass tickled her ankles. Sunshine warmed her scalp and danced in her hair. The hummingbirds flitted past, the foxes scampered by, and Floralie swore she heard the melodies of a chickadee in the top of an oak tree. In one blink, Floralie sat in the highest branch beside it, singing along in harmony: *"Chick-a-dee-dee-dee."*

From the top of the oak tree, Floralie could see her entire forest, blooming with colors. Reds, violets, greens, and blues. She could even see the invisible spectrum of colors that Tom had once told her only butterflies could see. But up in her oak tree, Floralie could be a butterfly. She could be anything she wanted to be.

When her wrist grew sore, Floralie dropped her paintbrush and lay upon the cot. But she did not sleep. She simply watched the sun set and the moon rise, the stars twinkle and the moths flutter. She watched the window lights across the street flick off one by one until finally, hers was the only one left lit.

As time passed, ivy slowly snaked up the legs of her cot, and again, Floralie was transported to her enchanted forest. Eagles soared among the clouds, and flowers bloomed with her every footstep. A great willow tree came into view, and Floralie ducked under and sat against its cool, dark trunk. Her back fit perfectly in the wood, as if it had been molded of clay for her. In the corner of her eye, a figure weaved in and out of the willow's leaves. This figure, barely a shadow and never quite visible, so often appeared in Floralie's forest that she had begun to refer to it as the gardener.

The figure bent down, pulled a watering can from its cloak, and gently poured some water onto a patch of fragile purple flowers beneath the willow. It patted down the earth around the flowers, then disappeared, as always.

Under that willow, with the purple flowers blooming around her, Floralie spent the night writing letters on her paper-white skin to Mama. And this time they came out in poems. When she ran out of skin, she counted words, each one bleeding out a different memory.

And all night long, across the hall, like listening to someone from the other side of a window, the other side of a dream, Floralie could hear Tom's whispering: *"One thousand twenty-one, one thousand twenty-two, one thousand twenty-three . . ."* Floralie wasn't the only one counting ghosts that night.

"Hey!" Tom shouted, crossing his arms and pouting his lips. *"Papa, she's splashing again."*

"Floralie, stop splashing," said Papa.

"I can't help where the water goes," said Floralie as she dove down to touch the bottom of the Mediterranean Sea.

"She's right," said Mama, as Floralie resurfaced. "Water's a creature of its own being. And it loves to dance," and Mama swung Tom around in a water waltz, before perching him onto her bony, though strong, shoulder. That was before Tom shot up, tall, like a beanstalk.

Papa looked on in disapproval, but said nothing. Mama smiled and stood on tiptoes in the white sand to kiss Papa's nose. "I love you," she said, and Papa said, "I love you, too."

Mama put a London pride flower in the ocean. "Perhaps it will go to Africa," Mama said. "Perhaps it will go to America; or maybe, it will go to Wonderland."

4

There was much hustle-bustle the next morning as Floralie made her way to the bridge, basket full of tulips and roses in hand. Shouts of shopkeepers and vendors swirled in Floralie's head—"Get yer bread, get yer eggs," "Newspaper, newspaper!" "Line up, folks, fresh pastries." Floralie laced through the crowds of businessmen off to catch the train to Canterbury and farmers setting up their vegetable stands.

Though Floralie stood in the heart of the English village, her own heart still felt stuck in France. She was always thinking of her little village of Giverny, which sounded of children's laughter and smelled of fields of tulips and Claude Monet's oil paint and

Mama's perfume. Floralie missed that perfume. The bittersweet of it wafted around her now, as if she were back in their kitchen watching Mama pirouette around wooden chairs, then twirling Floralie around and lifting her up into the air so Floralie could fly. And, oh, how she would fly! But that was before Mama started to act different. Before she started pulling out clumps of her hair and pouring orange juice on flowers. That was before Grandmama sent Mama away, and before Papa died. Floralie didn't even know if Mama was still in France. She could be anywhere. All anyone had told Floralie about the whole ordeal was, "It's better this way."

Floralie tried to stifle the memories and went about her work. She waved flowers under tweed-suited men, lilting, "Flower for your wife, sir?" and skipped around the skirts of women, saying, "Pretty rose for your hair, ma'am?" Some stopped and exchanged a coin for a flower, most out of pity, while the majority stuck up their noses and shooed her away.

Gossip flitted through the air like cherry blossoms in the wind. Today, the villagers chattered of the new romance between the baker and the local journalist. They talked of rumors of the bicycle repairman closing his shop, and they talked of a child who went missing from Floralie's grandmother's orphanage. That, of course, only increased the number of butterflies batting their wings in Floralie's stomach; she dreaded the scent of Grandmama's perfume, her feathery hats, and perpetual scowl of disapproval.

As Floralie wandered through thick crowds, images of a mess of shaggy brown hair and twinkling honey-colored eyes flickered in Floralie's mind. But every time she looked, all she saw were the baskets of shoppers and the briefcases of businessmen weaving between one another like tightly knitted knots. No poem-loving boy that she couldn't get out of her mind.

Three hours of waving about flowers and collecting coins later, Floralie ducked behind a woman in a straw cloche hat and made her way out of the crowd. As she neared the bridge's wall, however, someone grabbed her wrist.

Floralie whirled around, flowers falling to the cobbles.

Tom loomed over her. "What is the meaning of this?"

"Stop, Tom—that hurts!" cried Floralie. Immediately, Tom pulled away.

"I'm sorry." He flinched, and repeated, "I'm sorry . . . But, honestly? You've been writing on your hands again?" Tom's jaw tensed and he closed his eyes, which was something he did whenever he was really angry but trying not to make a fuss about it. "Oh, *Floralie.*"

Oh, Floralie. Those were the worst words. They wormed into her brain, chewed at the edges of her heart.

"You *know* Grandmama's coming today." He sighed and rubbed his brow with an almost-free hand. Curled inside of his palm was a tiny glass box of black tea leaves. He always went shopping for nice things when Grandmama came, as if to mimic her extravagant lifestyle for but an hour or two. "I can't trust you with anything, not even yourself." Floralie stared up into Tom's eyes. They were the beige of quicksand with big dark circles underneath and wrinkles at the edges—not from smiles, though. Tom's wrinkles were from tiredness. And a few from sadness.

"I'm sorry," murmured Floralie.

Tom's jaw slackened for a moment, a trace of guilt on his face. "No," he whispered, "no, I'm sorry. I've overreacted. Come on, we'd better get home." He turned, and Floralie followed him through the streets. She felt a sinking sensation in her stomach as she walked; she hated disappointing Tom.

It was hardly afternoon (Floralie knew because the fishers in the river below hadn't put on their sun hats yet). As they walked, the Upper Enders—which was what everyone called the wealthy people of Whitterly End—looked on in disdain at Floralie's raggedy uniform (smuggled out of Mrs. Coffrey's school) and scrunched their noses like they had caught a whiff of something rotten. The Lower Enders—the paupers and the farmers—on the other hand, smiled weakly at Floralie.

News traveled quick as winks in Whitterly End, and nearly everyone knew about the "unstable" child who had lost her mother, then lost her father, then lost her home. Nearly everyone knew of her being expelled from school, and nearly everyone, in some way or another, kept Floralie at a distance from them. But what no one seemed to agree on was whether to shame her or to pity her; Floralie wasn't sure which was worse.

When they reached their house, Tom led Floralie through the door and said, "Now wash that off"—he steered her through the kitchen and into the bathroom—"and don't even think about coming out till that hand sparkles." At first Floralie believed Tom to be angry, but when she looked into his eyes, all she saw was fear. He half closed the door, then paused and opened it again. "And, Floralie . . ."

Floralie looked up. A hint of softness smoothed the veins in Tom's neck, and Floralie was reminded of the face of a thirteen-year-old boy she knew long ago, laughing at one of Mama's more "unrefined" jokes and Papa's scowl—just a ghost of it.

"I won't let anything happen to you," said Tom. "I promise you that."

Floralie narrowed her eyes, unsure of what Tom was on about. She didn't exactly know how to reply to such out-of-place gallantry, so she simply said, "Sure," and closed the door.

Shouts echoed from the kitchen below. Papa had come home from work, and Mama had come home from rehearsal. Floralie never figured out

what made them so furious that night, but she did remember Tom sneaking into Floralie's bedroom late at night and stroking her hair. "He's angry," said Tom, "But we'll be just fine."

In the morning, a fumitory flower appeared in the crack under Floralie's door.

5

Once alone in the bathroom, Floralie skipped across the checkerboard floor to the sink, careful to avoid the white tiles. She didn't know why she avoided certain tiles—all she knew was that Mama had, too, and Mama had called it a dance. Mama loved to dance. This was one of those habits of which both Tom and Mrs. Coffrey disapproved. Floralie couldn't fathom why; it was a most pleasurable of games, much more so than the who-can-hold-books-on-her-head-the-longest game she had played in her etiquette lessons.

Floralie reached the sink and flicked on the faucet, icy water shocking her sweaty hands. She took the bar of soap and began to scrub at the ink, which, mind you, did not come off easily at all.

These love letters were particularly stubborn, just like the person they were for—Mama. So Floralie scrubbed her hands until the skin went red and her fingers shriveled to prunes and the words crawled back into her head because they had nowhere else to go. They exploded like cannons in there, and Floralie splashed some water on her face to quiet them.

She then combed through her tumbleweed of blond curls and emerged to the sitting room. Tom was there, changing the curtains from the yellowed lace ones to the fancy ones they only used when Grandmama visited. They were velvet, the color of red wine, and probably the most expensive things they owned.

As Tom fixed the last curtain onto the window, the doorbell rang.

Tom jumped. "The tea!" he yelped, his voice boyishly high-pitched. "I haven't made the tea!" He scurried out to the kitchen, and Floralie rushed to the front door.

"Remember like I said this morning, Floralie—curtsy, sitting room, tea. That's all—please, please, *please* do not make a mess of this," called Tom from the kitchen.

Floralie took a breath and peeked through the window. Sure enough, there was Grandmama. She was a lavish sort of person, wearing long jewel-toned gowns that never showed her shoes. She could have been barefoot for all Floralie knew. In her right hand, she clutched a ruby-studded cane. Her silver hair was swirled up in a bun topped with an extravagant feather hat more suited for Mardi Gras, and her lips were covered in tulip-pink lipstick. Floralie opened the door, a waft of prunes and sour lemons and old lady soap filling Floralie's nostrils.

"Grandmama," she said. "Er—wonderful to see you." Remembering Tom's words, she belatedly added a curtsy—a most ridiculous practice in Floralie's opinion. Curtsies were meant for ballets, not grandmothers.

"Well, well," said Grandmama. She looked Floralie up and down. "My, how you've grown, Floralie." Grandmama traced a ring-cluttered finger along Floralie's chin, then fiddled with Floralie's threadbare collar. "But I suppose it's what's on the inside that counts."

Floralie's ears burned. There was a distant rattling, and then Tom's voice leaped out from behind. "Grandmama! Come in!"

Tom whizzed toward the door and ushered Grandmama in. He twirled around her (tripping over her cane on the way) to remove her coat and hat, then tossed them into Floralie's arms.

"Thank you, Thomas," said Grandmama, and she followed him down the hall.

Floralie wrestled the frilly coat and hat onto the rack, smoothed down her curls, and then hurried after Tom and Grandmama. They sat on the flower-patterned sofa. It was old and tattered and didn't match the curtains at all, which, by the shifting of his eyes, Tom seemed terribly conscious of. Grandmama settled into herself, and then turned her stony gaze toward Tom and Floralie. Before she could speak however, Tom sprang up. "Oh! The tea!"

But Grandmama put up her hand. "No, no, Thomas. No time for tea. Actually, I would like to speak to you alone. If you please, Floralie."

"Oh—oh, of course, Grandmama." Floralie nodded and edged out of the sitting room into the back hall and closed the door behind her. She hovered outside the door, then knelt down and pressed her eye up to the keyhole. She held her breath and listened.

"I see no reason to beat around the bush," said Grandmama, turning to Tom, whose mouth twitched. "I fear Floralie is becoming corrupted."

Tom's face paled calla-lily white; he gulped. "Oh?" His voice cracked, and he coughed to cover it.

"I am *concerned*, Thomas," pressed Grandmama, "for her well-being. I fear after . . . recent events . . ."

No one spoke of Floralie's expulsion. Not even Grandmama, who was notorious for gossip.

"I fear that she will end up like that mother of hers. A starving artist slipping into madness. You can see why, can't you? She's practically a *mirror image* of Viscaria."

"She's not like Mama," whispered Tom. He looked like a feral cat being backed into a cage. "She's nothing like her."

Melancholy flitted about Floralie's head like a particularly irritating moth. All she'd ever wanted to be was like Mama.

"And what about her father?" Grandmama flourished a handkerchief and blew her nose into it. "A worse fate I can't imagine! Poor thing died of a broken heart."

That was what they always said, but Floralie knew the truth. She knew all about the alcohol. She knew about the nights Papa would come home late, red faced and angry, screaming, *"Honey, you better mop this floor,"* and *"Darling, go get the broom this instant,"* and then, finally, as the alcohol began to wear off, *"Dearest, come home,"* even though, by then, Mama had already disappeared.

"There's bad blood in this family," continued Grandmama. "But *I* can straighten her out, just as I do all those ragamuffins who come groveling at my doorstep. Just as I turned your father and you into gentlemen, I can turn her into a lady—"

"Now, this is not 1887 anymore, let's be reasonable here," cut in Tom. "Things are different from when Papa was a boy, and even me. I don't know how you run things at your place nowadays, but if it's anything like when I was there, I doubt it's going to change Floralie into something she's not. You don't know her like I do; she's stubborn."

Grandmama smirked. "Never underestimate the power of a

missed meal and a good whopping."

"Things are *changing*, Grandmama," pushed Tom. "And while I don't condone Floralie's actions, that finishing school you sent her to, well, I can't imagine it not being dead and gone in two, three years' time. And when she comes of age, Floralie could be a—a typist, a nurse—even an art teacher or illustrator if she wants to—"

Despite the smile creeping over Floralie's mouth, Grandmama tut-tutted. "*Don't* encourage her—"

But Tom ignored her. "And with all due respect, that place of yours is heading for the drain as well. Believe me, that runaway child is doing nothing for your reputation. It's not only the talk of Whitterly End, but all across Kent."

Grandmama pursed her lips. "Leave that boy out of this. What happened was indeed tragic, but inevitable. He was disturbed." She huffed and added, "If all goes the way I plan, Floralie will never have to work a day in her life. No man will be able to turn her down; she'll be a proper wife in no time, money galore." A hunger took grip of Grandmama's eyes, making Floralie's stomach flop. "Let me take her, Thomas . . . for her sake and our family's. Please."

Floralie leaped back and clutched her heart. She couldn't possibly leave Tom—at least not to become a *lady*. The thought itself left a bitter taste in her mouth.

Floralie took a breath and pressed her eye up to the keyhole again.

"She's growing up, you know," said Grandmama. "Have not you noticed?"

"She's still a child," said Tom, teeth gritted.

"Coddle her as you will, but my word is final. I expect her at my home in one week. The more we drag this out, the more ill Floralie will get. Just like her mother."

A chill scuttled down Floralie's spine. When Grandmama wanted something, most always she got it.

Tom's mouth dropped, and he began to stutter. "It—it's only been two years since . . . since Papa, and—and Floralie's still *adjusting*, you've got to understand . . ." Then Tom's voice regained its hardness, and he barked, "This isn't about manners or money; this is about you. This is about you wanting the child that my mother stole from you. This is about you and Papa, not me, not Floralie."

Grandmama puffed. "Look, Thomas. We can do this the easy way or the hard way. You do not have the financial means to support Floralie. Either you hand her over willingly, or I will, unfortunately, but ethically, be forced to stop funding both you and Floralie all together."

"You can't!" cried Floralie as she threw open the door violently and dove into the sitting room.

"Oh my." Grandmama huffed, straightening out her dress, as if Floralie's presence had put a wrinkle in it.

Floralie looked from Grandmama to Tom, then back to Grandmama. And when she spoke, her voice grew soft, like her breath was clinging for dear life to her throat. "You just can't."

Grandmama gave no sign of emotion. "Clearly, things have got worse since I've seen her last, Thomas. Far worse."

"But you can't just take me!" pleaded Floralie. "I'll never be happy. I—I'll run away."

Floralie looked to Tom, whose face had gone an even paler shade of white. His lips parted, but no words came from them. After a moment, he whispered tentatively, "Floralie . . . that's enough."

Tom's eyes were hollow, and somehow, so different from the eyes Floralie knew. Like a stranger's. "You want me to leave?"

Tom clenched his jaw. "I said *enough*. Go to your room."

"But—"

"*Go*," he repeated, an edge to his voice this time. "I will be up shortly."

Floralie gaped at Tom, then shook her head and turned for the door. As her fingers traced the brass doorknob, Grandmama's voice sounded from behind. "In time, you will come to thank me, Floralie."

Floralie squeezed shut her eyes, hand wavering on the

doorknob. She did not feel—would never feel—any gratitude toward Grandmama. Not Grandmama who sent away her mother, not Grandmama who surely would take her away from her wonderland. Without a glance back, Floralie crossed the hall to the staircase. Before ascending, however, Floralie wiped a blanket of dust from the nearest window and gazed out at her soon-to-be home.

It loomed in the distance, a thundercloud of a thing at the edge of the hillside. Gray and built of unforgiving stone, this was the home of unwanteds and lonelies, lost-hopers and dreamless-sleepers. This could hardly be called a home at all. This was the Adelaide Laurel Orphanage for Unfortunate Children.

The coffin rested at the front of the chapel. The service ended, and the guests meandered off to eat chocolate-covered strawberries; the preacher went to his daughter's violin concert, and the organist smoked a cigar outside the church. Floralie and Tom stood at the double doors at the back of the gold-gilded chapel, watching Grandmama crumble over the coffin laced with white lilies. "My baby," she wept. "My baby boy." No one understood her except Floralie and Tom of course; everyone else at the funeral spoke only French.

The man who had taken Mama away came that day with a

bouquet of bay leaves apparently from Mama—the first and only time Floralie had heard from Mama since she left. The leaves came with a note: "You change only in death." The flower arrangers threw the leaves away.

6

Three minutes later and two staircases up, Floralie sat in the corner of her room painting her wallpaper. Today she painted forget-me-nots, shy and soft, and just a little scared. In Floralie's mind's eye, blue jay feathers floated down to rest upon the tiny petals, like silk against Floralie's gentle touch. She breathed out fear, breathed in love. She remembered how it felt to be loved. How it felt to be cradled in Mama's arms, how small, how safe, how close she had felt. Somehow, the forget-me-nots let her feel that way again, and she flew to her wonderland for but just a moment, catching a glimpse of the shadowy gardener lurking behind a bush of azaleas.

BANG.

Floralie dropped her paintbrush, spiraling back to reality.

"Tom!" she gasped, whirling around.

"*This* is the problem. This is it, Floralie," sighed Tom, shaking his head. "This is the reason for everything. Your obsession with paint and flowers and fantastical nonsense!" His voice grew into a roar, but then crept back into its softness. "This is what got you kicked out of Mrs. Coffrey's school. This is what's getting you kicked out of your very own home. I've *tried*, Floralie." His voice broke on a sneaking tear. "You know I didn't raise you like this, and neither did Papa."

"Mama did."

Tom closed his eyes and said, "This has gone too far. I have entertained your imagination for too long, and look what it's done."

Floralie's stomach dropped. "No . . . no, you can't . . ."

Tom's face scrunched into a pained expression. "I have no choice. If, someday, you can find a way to make this whole painting thing work without succumbing to the same fate as Mama, by all means, do it. But right now, it's destroying our family. It's destroying us, and it's destroying you."

Tears stung at the back of Floralie's eyes. She could barely speak. "You said nothing bad would happen." She coughed away the lump in her throat and fired, "You were *there*—you lived at her orphanage for eight years before I was born. You know how horrible it is; how can you let her take me there? Last time, you said no to her. Last time, you made sure I didn't end up there. And this time, you promised!"

"Luck saved us last time," said Tom, sighing. "If I hadn't turned eighteen the day after Papa died, you would've been sent off to Grandmama then. But I can't count on luck this time, and to be perfectly honest, I think we've run dry." Tom twirled a finger through Floralie's curls. "I care about you," he whispered, but then he stepped back and tensed the muscles in his neck. "I'm tearing down this wallpaper, and—and"—he straightened up, though weakly, as if trying to muster up the anger both Floralie and Tom had seen in Papa so many times—"for as long as you live under this roof—whether one week or one decade—I forbid you to paint."

And Tom began. The wallpaper fell like withered rose petals. By five o'clock, the little room had become an island of shredded paper, and Floralie was in the middle of it. She sat cross-legged on the wood floor, breathing in the dust. She uncurled one of the wallpaper scraps and laid it flat on the floor. It had a painting on it—or rather, part of a painting now. Floralie had painted this one a year ago after finding a cherry tree still in bloom, even though it had been nearly July. Usually, the wind swept away all the cherry blossoms in mid-May.

A great *tear* crackled from the wall as another wallpaper scrap fell to the floor. Tom shook a piece off his fancy leather shoe. And then Floralie's eyes trailed up to Tom's fingers.

"Not that one," said Floralie at once. Her voice snagged at the back of her throat.

Tom's fingers were pinched over the corner of Floralie's most treasured painting. It was of a saffron flower from a bouquet Mama had received after a performance with Le Ballet Royale de Paris. It was also the first flower Floralie had ever painted on the wall.

Floralie's heartbeat quickened. "Tom." She stared at his hands. The hands that had written her secret letters just so she would have mail when she was five. The hands that had held her own as they skipped through puddles one rainy day in Paris when she was seven. The hands that had stroked her hair as she knelt by Mama, whispering good-byes when she was eight. The hands that had carried her through the door of their new home when she was ten, even though she was far too big to carry. The hands that had squeezed hers tight when she was dropped off at Mrs. Coffrey's but a few weeks later. Floralie closed her eyes. *"Please."*

Tom sighed. "It's for your own good, Floralie." His voice was stern, but steeped in regret.

Floralie watched his fingers. Part of her wanted to grab them away from her paintings, but another part of her didn't want to touch them at all.

"Grandmama's right. You can't be a child forever," continued Tom, "You've got to start getting used to the real world." He peeled the saffron flower from the wall.

Floralie's heart sank as she let the cherry blossom fragment slip from her fingers and curl up like a roly-poly bug.

Tom crossed the room. "It's about time you grew up. Later, we'll clean up, together, and it will all be past. But for now, I expect you down in the village, tidy and *pleasant*. There's a new batch of tulips to sell, so be sure to pick those up at the shop. Twenty minutes." He cracked open the door, but paused before stepping through. "I'm sorry," and the door swished behind him.

Floralie swallowed her tears and gazed around. Her room looked a little like the way it had when they had first moved into the cottage. Actually, it looked a little like the way her heart had felt that day. Stripped bare, nothing but scars where there used to be flowers. The floor had once felt like sun-kissed soil against the soles of Floralie's feet, but now it was like London pavement. The cold and callous numb of it slithered from the floorboards through her toes, up her calves, shivering her knees.

But Floralie did not blame Tom. How could she, when it was she who had—who had . . . Floralie bit her lip at the memory. It was *she* who had gotten herself expelled. Daydreamed, doodled, painted at odd hours in the night, then slept during class. Floralie brushed away the thoughts. She still felt nauseated just remembering the disappointment in Tom's eyes as he led her out the front door of Mrs. Coffrey's school for the last time.

It simply was all her fault. She was the destroyer of her own wonderland. In fact, it had been the very tools that had built her wonderland that tore it down. Imagination. Daydreams. Beauty. They were the wonders of the world to which she had gotten too attached. And as those wonders dwindled, so did Floralie. She was the undoing of her own heart.

Floralie felt a sudden thankfulness that her paints were hidden away; she didn't want to look at them. It was over, done with. All of it. And now she had to go to work. She had to be a good girl, like Tom said. Today was the day she would finally grow up. Tom would be happy. Grandmama would be happy. Everyone would be happy. At least, almost everyone.

Floralie got to her feet and tiptoed to her wardrobe, careful not to step on any of the wallpaper scraps. She pulled open the wardrobe doors, took the brush from a shelf inside, then turned to her mirror and combed through her hair. She had the sort of hair Tom would call "difficult" and Mrs. Coffrey would call a "rat's nest." So, Floralie kept to tying it at the nape of her neck with a blue satin ribbon.

Floralie then reached for her lacy white dress, which she normally reserved for Sundays (her former uniform was now soggy with tearstains), but her hand lingered over the hanger. Something in the mirror had caught her eye. Something that hadn't been there before. Reflected in the mirror was a small, dark mouse hole in the corner of the wall, precisely where a painting of irises had been an hour ago.

Floralie turned and crept over to the hole, a most ingenious idea sprouting inside her. She brushed aside a few wallpaper scraps, laid her head on the floor, and peered inside. Yes. It would work splendidly.

Floralie sat back up and unrolled one of the wallpaper scraps from the floor. It was the gardenias she had painted on her tenth birthday over Easter break. She rolled it back up, carefully slid it into the hole, and then nudged it over to the left so it was perfectly concealed.

As Floralie withdrew her hand, she glanced to her door, half expecting Tom to be standing there, arms crossed, eyes solemn. She took a breath, and her fingers trailed along the saffron painting.

One last childish whim, and then that would be it. Forever.

Floralie's excitement tingled down her fingers as she sifted through her wallpaper for her favorite pieces. Within minutes, she had hidden away her twelve favorite paintings into the wall.

The cherry blossoms were the last to go in, and she had to stretch her arm all the way into the hole to make the painting fit without being visible.

"Floralie! Are you almost ready?" called Tom from downstairs.

Floralie caught her breath and dropped the cherry blossom painting. "Oh yes, just a minute," she called back.

Now, it was just as Floralie was about to withdraw her arm from the hole that her hand brushed against something cold and oddly smooth compared with the rest of the splintery wood.

She ran her fingers along it, stretched her hand, and pulled it out. It was a box, mahogany wood and about half the size of a loaf of oat bread from Mr. Pottridge's bakery. In one quick breath, Floralie blew off the dust and examined the inscription. It was not written in elegant, swirly script but, rather, childlike letters carved haphazardly into the wood.

If you want my secrets.
—V.A.C.

Floralie didn't recognize the initials, but assumed they belonged to the room's previous occupant. She pulled on the top, but it wouldn't open. Floralie frowned as her fingers traced a small keyhole on the side.

"Floralie, it's time to *go*," called Tom.

Floralie sighed, tucked the box under her cot, and hurried out of the room.

Mama made daisy chains, wrapped them round Floralie's head like a crown, and called her queen of the universe. "The stars are yours, the moon is yours, the trees are yours, the rivers, yours, the rain, yours, the sunshine, yours." Mama laughed, but Floralie took off the crown, wrapped it round her wrist thrice as a bracelet instead, and said, "I lose things too easily. I'd rather be a peasant."

And Mama said, "Your innocence is beautiful."

7

Five minutes later, Floralie arrived at the flower shop, the aroma of perfume filling her nostrils and the dulcet lilt of sparrows' twittering soothing her ears. As the sunshine filtered in, specks of dust lit up like fairies waltzing through a bog. Floralie could see them now, wings beating slow, and carrying baskets of sweet-smelling fairy fruit . . . *No, I've got to grow up*, she thought. *Grow up, grow up, grow up.* And the daydream wilted.

Tom appeared from beneath the counter with a large wooden box labeled LES TULIPES VIRIDIFLORAS on all sides. He placed the box on the counter, pulled open the latch, and flipped back the cover. Immediately, Tom sprang back, three flowerpots from a shelf behind him smashing to the ground. "Ugh!" he cried, face scrunched like a shriveled-up carnation.

"What?" said Floralie, and she peeked inside the box, and then leaped back, too. For inside was a graveyard of viridiflora tulips, all chewed up and rotting, covered in a colony of spiders, caterpillars, and slugs.

"It's like Pandora's box in there!" exclaimed Tom, and he peered into the box again. "Dead." He breathed a sigh of relief. "All those bugs, dead, dead, dead, thank the heavens. Floralie, carry this up to the attic," instructed Tom, shoving the box to the edge of the counter, "and then pick out some tulips from a *different* box for your basket and sell at the bridge. Be back in an hour. All right?"

Floralie nodded. "Okay," she said, but then added, "The attic? We never go in the attic. Someone lives there, don't they?"

"Not anymore. Didn't I tell you? The hospital came to retrieve the body weeks ago," said Tom, grabbing a broom and sweeping the broken flowerpots to a corner.

"Oh," said Floralie. "All right, then." She shivered with the thought of the bugs, but heaved up the box anyway and disappeared into the dim back room. She crossed the room to a door at the back left-hand corner with a staircase inside. In the pitch-blackness, Floralie's foot found the first step, and she climbed.

With each step, the floorboards creaked, and for some reason, Floralie thought she heard scurrying above her. Her head filled with visions of ghosts, floating like feathers overhead, mist trailing behind their translucent skirts—but she built a stone wall in her mind's eye. *They're echoes of my footsteps, nothing more;* she forced the thought to the forefront of her brain.

When she reached the top, Floralie pushed open the attic door and pulled on the light string. As her eyes adjusted, the room came into view. It was small, bare, and—

Floralie gasped and dropped the tulip box. As it landed with a thud, a yelp escaped Floralie's mouth.

Kneeling behind a stack of old iris boxes was a boy. Floralie's hand zoomed for the doorknob, but the boy leaped up and took her hand with gentle (though admittedly grimy) fingers. Floralie turned back, and the boy held up a note: *Wait.* A shuffling echoed from below, and Tom's voice sounded: "Floralie, are you all right?"

"Oh—yes. Perfect!" called Floralie. "Just—er—stubbed my toe." Then she turned to the boy. "You've got thirty seconds to explain to me—" But as her eyes adjusted to the light, she took in the boy's features. Tattered clothes, disheveled hair, crooked smile. "You're the poem boy I met on the bridge yesterday," she breathed. "What are you doing here?"

The boy eyed her, and then carefully let loose her hand. He

disappeared behind the iris boxes and emerged with his pen and notebook.

I live here, wrote the boy. *What are you doing here?*

Floralie took the pen. *It's my flower shop. I thought George Duncan lived here—or at least until he died a few weeks ago. But it's mine now, or it was mine—I mean, it will be "was" in a few weeks when Grandmama—*but Floralie scratched out the words—*Never mind.* It was all terribly confusing. *What are you doing here?*

Saw the obituary in the paper. Moved in after Mr. Duncan, wrote the boy. *Been hopping around the library, some churches, and the like. But this place was unlocked and empty so . . .*

You live here alone?

The boy nodded.

What's your name? wrote Floralie.

The boy's mouth twitched. *Can I trust you?*

Floralie nodded. *Yes.*

Konstantinos. Nino, for short. And then he quickly added, *But you can't tell anyone.*

Why not?

Can't say. But you said I could trust you.

Floralie nodded. *I won't say a word. Nino.* Floralie liked the way the name looked on paper. *Where are you from?*

Nino's mouth twitched. *Everywhere. At the moment, anyway. My* real home, I can never go back to. I used to live in Greece. I had a family there. It was just us: me, Ma, and Pa. Nino paused for a minute, and neither he nor Floralie wrote a word. At last, Nino wrote, *That was a long time ago.* The words were faint, as if someone had blown them out of a tobacco pipe.

Floralie felt a flutter in her heart, and dizziness washed over her as she wrote, *My real home is far away, too.*

Nino grinned, but then his smile fell. *You look different from before,* he wrote. *Sadder.*

Floralie looked away. "I'm fine," she whispered, the words slipping out of her mouth before her fingers could catch them onto paper.

"I'm fine" is a cloak, and there are too many hidden pockets in those words for me to trust them anymore, wrote Nino.

That's a funny way of putting it, wrote Floralie. She giggled, careful to cover the gap in her teeth. *I don't really want to talk about it. I'll be fine. Honest.*

Will you write me a poem about it?

Floralie considered this. *Maybe someday. Will you help me find a box of tulips? I've got to sell them in a bit—not that box there, though,* and she pointed to the viridiflora box. *That one's filled with bugs like Pandora's box.*

Nino nodded, and the two set to searching for a new box of tulips, and eventually they found one labeled LES TULIPES FOSTERIANAS.

"Strange," breathed Floralie as her fingers traced the latch of the wooden box.

Nino tilted his head.

"It's the address," said Floralie.

The words *84 Rue Claude Monet, Giverny, France* were scrawled on the top of the box.

"I used to live in France—that very village, actually. *Giverny.*" She yearned for those winding roads of hyacinth-laced doorways and catching glimpses of the famous artist Monet behind the green-shuttered windows. She yearned for real croissants and she yearned for Mama's homemade whipped cream—even if Papa always complained that it was too sweet. Floralie shook her head. "Never mind. Doesn't matter anymore."

After opening the new box, Floralie took a handful of tulips, and then said, "I've got to go—maybe I'll see you later."

Nino's hand shot for his notebook, and he scrawled, *Remember—you promised me earlier you'd write me a poem.*

Did not! wrote Floralie.

Well, then promise me now.

Floralie sighed. *Fine. I promise,* and she turned and left the attic.

"Dare you," said Mama one hot August evening. They sat in the soil amidst the flowers of Mama's garden sipping tea with three spoonfuls of sugar.

"Dare me what?"

Mama's eyes sparkled in that impish way Floralie knew all too well, and then said, "I dare you to do something that scares you."

"Like what?"

"Like . . . the next passerby you see, go right on up and give him or her a flower. We know nearly everyone in this town. Turn one into a friend."

Floralie's stomach squirmed, but in a good way. "What kind of flower?"

"A tulip."

Floralie sighed. Mama often played these games with her. Mama was full of bravery like that. Overflowing with it, at times. Floralie wished she could be that way, full of life and love and not a drop of fear. "Okay," said Floralie, but there were no passersby that evening.

So Mama said, "Let's go out and find someone," and she pulled Floralie to her feet, Floralie wobbling with nervousness. "We'll give them a tulip."

Floralie and Mama went into the village and found the young woman who worked at the bakery, the one who always gave Floralie a spoon of frosting when she visited, and Floralie gave her a tulip. The woman smiled and said thank you, and Floralie felt lighter. When Floralie came out of the bakery, Mama greeted her with a blackthorn flower and said, "This one's for your courage."

8

The next day, Tom cleared out the wallpaper from Floralie's room, and Floralie spent the day selling tulips on the bridge. However, all day long, passersby said to her, "Is everything quite all right, dear?" and, "Are you still with us, love?" and (the grumpier ones), "What's the matter with you? I said I wanted *tulips*, not two lilies!"

The trouble was, Floralie simply couldn't help but feel preoccupied not only by the loss of her wallpaper, but by the curious box she had found inside her wall and the curious boy she had found inside her attic.

It was only by evening that she remembered she had promised to write a poem. Poems were so much more complicated than paintings. Paintings were like buttercups, popping up out of nowhere in broad daylight. But poems, poems were like violets. They grew in shadowed corners and secret hideaways, hard to come by and sneaky by nature. The ones she had written on her hands the night before had just fallen out of her like loose change out of a hole in a pocket. She hadn't *intentionally* tried to make a poem, and now she felt the true impossibility of it all rise in her chest. And besides that, there was no way she was showing that poem to a boy she just met. It clung too close to her heart. After four dismal tries, Floralie finally scribbled down a halfhearted attempt on a scrap of paper and snuck into the flower shop attic.

Nino lay in the corner, feet crisscrossed in the air, leaning over a book. As soon as he saw Floralie, he shot upright.

You're here! he wrote.

Floralie nodded and weaved in and out between the boxes, slung her shoulder bag down (with a rather loud thud), and sat beside Nino.

What are you carrying in there, bricks? wrote Nino, as Floralie flipped open her bag and dug through the contents. A train ticket here, a wadded-up handkerchief there . . . at last, she pulled from it a loaf of bread and three linty apples, along with a pen. *Food,* she wrote in the notebook, pushing the bread and apples to Nino.

Nino's eyes were alight, and he took the food with haste, tearing bread like a lion would a gazelle. He chewed ravenously, biting apples and bread simultaneously. Apple juice dribbled down his chin and crumbs speckled his shirt, the sound of his crunching echoed around the attic. It was the loudest sound Nino had made since Floralie had met him. When he was finally satisfied, he wiped his chin with his sleeve and wrote, *Thank you. Do you have the poem?*

Floralie shrugged. *Kind of,* she scrawled on the back of her poem.

Let's see, then.

Floralie handed her poem to Nino, and together, they read:

Stuck
By Floralie Alice Laurel

Nothing comes to mind
Blank page staring back at me
Poetry is hard.

It's a haiku, wrote Floralie.

Nino tilted his head. *Write me a real poem.*

This is a real poem, wrote Floralie, blushing. And then she added, *I'm a painter. I don't write poems.*

Write me one anyway.

Floralie frowned. *I did, and you didn't like it.*

Please, wrote Nino.

Floralie sighed. *About what?*

Nino pondered this, and then wrote, *Something simple. Meeting you, maybe. Or meeting me. Whichever.*

Fine, I'll bring one tomorrow.

No—right now.

Floralie's heart fluttered. She felt as if she were standing on tiptoes at the edge of a canyon, staring into the abyss. Something wonderful glittered on the other side, a jewel, perhaps—no—a flower—but jumping, jumping was not a practice to which Floralie was accustomed. She couldn't help but feel the cold wind slapping her face and the nauseating vertigo settling in the pit of her stomach. Her hair catching on her lips, dress tangling around her knees. An army of geese flew overhead, honking in harmony, urging her closer and closer to the edge.

Yes, perhaps she could write a better poem than "Stuck" . . . but what if she couldn't? Floralie had never had a friend before, unless Wilma Jacobson from Mrs. Coffrey's school counted. But even though Wilma had lent Floralie shoes that sparkled and sat with her at supper, she had also pulled Floralie's hair and spread nasty rumors and cheated off her French tests. But Nino, Nino could be a friend. Perhaps, though, only if she could muster up a better poem. Floralie looked to his honey-colored eyes. Certainly, she decided, he wouldn't want to be friends if she didn't even try.

And so, tentatively, Floralie wrote, *Okay.*

The words did not flow easily like oil paint, but with a topic this time, Floralie at least had *something* to go from. The two sat

in silence—seconds knitting into minutes knitting into hours—
until Floralie finally revealed her new poem.

Meeting You
By Floralie Alice Laurel

One:
There are some rules I know
About meeting someone new.
Like, a first impression is a last impression
Stand tall and stand straight
The way you wish to be painted
> *Like this, be lovely*
> *They are painting you.*
Two:
Listen twice as much as you speak
Words are useless things in
Situations like these
So keep them simple, short, and sweet
> *Like this, be lovely*
> *They are painting you.*
Three:
There are some rules I own
About leaving someone old.
Like curtsying
Or hand shaking
Or kissing on the cheek
> *Like this, be lovely*
> *They are painting you.*

That's beautiful, wrote Nino. *But it's missing something.*

Floralie huffed and crumpled up the poem. *Well, if you think
you can do better, go ahead.*

Nino cracked a smile, then leaned over his notebook. He spun words the way spiders spin webs. Floralie watched his fingertips closely—dancers on the old notepaper. And when he finished, Floralie read:

Meeting You
By Konstantinos

One:
I'll say my name, and you will say yours,
You become mine and I become yours
Lost in a simple hello,
Inventing our turn-of-a-century breakthrough
Floralie, it's lovely to meet you.
Two:
I catch your thoughts
Drifting like dandelion clocks
You reach for my hand, but slowly withdraw
You see me, not only my flaws
We'll weave a dandelion crown, just you and I
My Floralie, it's lovely to meet you.
Three:
Some people toss coins into angel-guarded fountains
For wishes, for love, for more coins, for luck,
Mine landed on you
My Floralie, my Floralie, I'm lucky to meet you.

Nino was grinning when Floralie looked up. And in spite of herself, Floralie's own mouth had melted into a smile as well. Floralie bit her lip to force her mouth shut as her tongue flicked against her teeth. Smiles, she thought, were no good for making friends when all anyone saw was the gap in her teeth.

Nino turned over the page and scrawled, *Your turn.*

Floralie sighed. *No, I'm useless at this. Where'd you learn to write like that anyway?*

Nino shrugged. *An old poet. I mean, a* really *old poet.*

Oh, wrote Floralie. *Well, can't we do something else?*

Nino shook his head. *There's nothing wrong with your poem. It's just unfinished, is all. Try again. One more time.*

Floralie uncrumpled her "Meeting You" poem and reread. She stared at it for a long time, and Nino waited, simply, patiently, and then Floralie began to write. When she finished, she handed the page to Nino, and they read:

> Meeting You
> By Floralie Alice Laurel
>
> One:
> There are some rules I know
> About meeting someone new.
> Like, a first impression is a last impression
> Stand tall and stand straight
> The way you wish to be painted
>   Like this, be lovely
>   They are painting you.
> Two:
> Listen twice as much as you speak
> Words are useless things in
> Situations like these
> So keep them simple, short, and sweet

Like this, be lovely
They are painting you.
Three:
There are some rules I own
About leaving someone old.
Like curtsying
Or hand shaking
Or kissing on the cheek
     Like this, be lovely
     They are painting you.
Another One:
Half-finished paintings are worthless
     In galleries
But lucky
     In house fires.
Those one half meets
Are easy to leave behind.
Strangers hurt less than the ones you love.
So like this, be lovely
They've only started painting you
     Like this, be lucky
     And nothing will hurt you.

Better, wrote Nino, grinning. *Much better. You told your truth.*

A smile pulled at Floralie's mouth, but she looked away. *Yeah, well, I don't get to tell "my" truth much anymore.*

Nino's grin fell. *Why not?*

Got expelled from school for it. They said I was a chronic daydreamer and a horrendously hopeless case. So they sent me back to my brother, Tom. Now my grandmother's going to take me away to turn me into a proper lady. Tom tore down my paintings. I used to paint all over my walls; it used to be my wonderland, but not anymore. Painting is my poetry, I suppose.

Nino's eyes grew stony. *That's wrong—they can't do that!* His handwriting had gone dark and heavy like a thunderstorm was brewing beneath the ink. The words almost tore the paper. *Won't your father stop her? Or your mother?*

*No, I—*her hand hovered over the paper—*I haven't got them around anymore.*

Oh, wrote Nino, softer this time. *I'm sorry.* He paused, and then added, *Me neither.*

Floralie chanced a look at Nino; he didn't look back. *I'm sorry, too,* she wrote.

So, it's just Tom looking after you, then?

Floralie nodded. *He thinks he knows everything. He thinks he's my father, but he's not. I wish he would just leave me alone.*

Nino twitched his mouth, and a pang of guilt hit Floralie in the gut. *I'm sorry—that was insensitive. I should be grateful I've still got someone taking care of me. And Tom's not always so bad.*

Nino shook his head. *No, don't worry. I was just thinking. We've got to stop them—your grandmother and brother. They can't just take you away. And they certainly have no right to take away your painting.*

Floralie shrugged. *They're completely set on it. Besides, it's my fault. We spent all our money on my finishing school instead of Tom's university. And I ruined it. All I want is for my daydreams to leave me alone. But they keep sneaking up on me.*

Nino stared at Floralie for a moment before taking the paper and writing for a few minutes. When he finished, he handed the page to Floralie.

Ivy
By Konstantinos

I see your stone walls
The more you build,
The more ivy crawls.

And longing looks like vines
Fingers outstretched,
Hands forming waiting lines.

Every single vein is reaching,
Every single vein is yearning.

Let in the ivy
Through the cracks in your stone
All they want
Is for you not to feel so alone.

Floralie half smiled at the poem, and then quickly covered her mouth. *You're different, Nino,* she wrote. *But I think in a good way.*

Neither Floralie nor Nino wrote anything for a few minutes. Floralie simply wasn't sure what to think about the daydreams anymore. About the ivy. As they sat, Floralie became aware of how silent the attic was. When writing with Nino, it was as if the attic was filled with swirling melodies, twirling dancers, when really all it was, was silence.

Finally, Floralie wrote, *Can I keep this?*

Nino nodded, and Floralie tore off the ivy poem and tucked it into her bag. And then she wrote, *Nino?*

Yeah?

I brought something I want to show you. I found it yesterday in my wall. She had been debating whether or not to show Nino. He had been, after all, a stranger not a day ago. But he was different now. Now, they had met, and he was no longer strange—at least not to Floralie.

So, she pulled from her bag the small wooden box with its peculiar engraving on the top. *Found this in my wall the other day,* she wrote.

In your wall?

Floralie nodded. *After Tom took down my wallpaper—my paintings, I mean.*

Well, what's in it?

Don't know. It's locked.

Nino's eyes grew wide, and he scrawled in excited, flourishing letters, A mystery! And then he added, smaller this time, *You know, mysteries are a lot like poems. May I see it?*

Floralie handed him the box.

V.A.C., wrote Nino, lost in thought. The letters mirrored the initials on the box below the "If you want my secrets." *Do you know a V.A.C.?*

Floralie shook her head no.

Nino began to fiddle with the lock; a light clattering bounced around the attic—

And then something skittered past Floralie's foot.

Floralie leaped back, tumbling into an empty crate, and was about to scream when Nino launched himself over her and clasped her mouth. He eyed her carefully and removed his hand.

"What on *earth*?" said Floralie, clutching her heart.

But Nino simply crouched down and walked his fingers along the floorboards like spiders until he found something. He then held it up to his chest in one palm. Floralie squinted in the dim light and almost yelped again, but Nino put his pointer finger to his lips to quiet her.

This is Philomenos, wrote Nino with his free hand.

Floralie crept toward the puff of chestnut fur curled up in Nino's palm.

Rather mighty name for a mouse, wrote Floralie, still not getting too close. The mouse chattered its teeth in a way that reminded Floralie of a baby lion learning how to roar.

Yes. He's my friend, wrote Nino, and then added quickly, *and to be precise, he's a hazel dormouse. He likes the sound of boxes opening—*

he thinks it means food. Or paper. He collects everything—shiny things like buttons, thimbles, but especially paper for some reason.

Philomenos squeaked and poked his nose up from Nino's hand. Nino pulled a few blackberries from his pocket and held them out for Philomenos, but the mouse did not take them (perhaps because, as Floralie noticed the tiny chew marks on the leftover bread, he had already had his share of supper), and instead, started to wriggle. Nino let go of Philomenos, eyebrows high in surprise, and the mouse went scuttling toward Floralie.

"*Nino!*" yelped Floralie, unable to keep the panic from her voice. However, the mouse did not crawl onto Floralie, but rather, the box, sticking his whiskery nose into the keyhole.

He's not terribly bright, scrawled Nino, still holding out the blackberries for Philomenos, but the little mouse was far too preoccupied by the box. *But he is loyal.*

Philomenos started squeaking again and scurried around the edge of the box, nosing the left-hand side.

"*What!*" breathed Floralie.

Floralie and Nino leaned over the side of the box. There was a tiny knob there engraved with the letters *E.F.T.*, and pulled out from inside was a tiny corner of parchment.

Floralie gasped. *You don't think . . .*

Only one way to find out.

Floralie confessed to Tom, "I don't want them to stay together." But when Papa said Mama was destroying their marriage, all Floralie wanted was to be small. Two years later, Floralie discovered that Papa had been threatening to leave Mama for fifteen years. But the day Papa accused Mama, Floralie found a sprig of asphodel on Papa's side of the bed with a note that read, My sorrow will follow you to the grave.

"It's his fault," said Tom, "not yours, Flory."

Floralie would rather it have been hers.

9

Floralie pinched the end of the knob. Her heart sped double time, the steady waltz of it turning into a quick-footed Charleston dance; the knob turned against the wood, *scritch-scratch, scritch-scratch.*

Floralie read Nino's eyes. They said, *Impossible.* Gently, Floralie pulled out a compartment in the side of the box.

The scent of fine French perfume filled Floralie's nostrils. *"Flowers."*

Inside the box was indeed a collection of flowers—piles of different sorts. Blues, violets, reds, pinks, large and flamboyant, small and ghostlike. But the most curious thing of all was not their colors, shapes, or sizes, but their *age*. The flowers were pressed flat so they looked more like paintings of flowers than flowers themselves. Most were wrinkled, but all had somehow retained at least most of their original color.

There was something mesmerizing about the dried flowers. They weren't dead, but they weren't alive either. Floralie's fingers traced the edge of the box and slipped inside. The flowers were rough to the touch, crinkled, like the pages of an ancient storybook. And there was something else about them that was like a storybook, too. They had a certain air of *story* to them—a mystery, a secret, a bittersweetness, a memory filled with melancholy—a *je ne sais quoi*. That was what Mama had described her ballet costumes as having. *Je ne sais quoi*. That was what Mama would have called the flowers.

Floralie's fingertips brushed against something smooth. She bent closer, flicked away a leaf, and found a yellowed piece of paper folded into quarters. As Floralie pulled the paper out, however, Philomenos hopped up and snatched it with his teeth. Nino snapped his fingers at the mouse, and it twitched its mouth, then sheepishly dropped the paper.

Sorry, wrote Nino. *Like I said, he likes to steal paper. My poems disappear all the time.*

Nino handed Floralie back the paper, and she unfolded it one quarter at a time, then laid it flat on the floor between her and

Nino. And together, they read what was written there in Indian ink and sorrow and ghosts.

My Dearest Wildflower,

Many years will pass before you find this, but I have gathered these flowers for you. Let them be your compass. Anything you wish to know about me, you will find in them. All you need is the flower dictionary, *La Floriographie Complète*, by, yes, the one and only Sylvestre Tullier. It will translate these flowers into their meanings. As much as you may or may not get along with him, you should know that Sylvestre was a great friend to me. Disagreeable, perhaps, but I still have faith that he is, deep down, a good man. You must trust him with all your heart. And my wish for you, Wildflower, is that you find me inside these petals and leaves, and the gaps between them. But more important, I hope you find yourself in them, if even just a fragment.

Remember me,

Viscaria

"She found them," whispered Floralie.

What? wrote Nino.

Floralie shook her head. *Nothing.*

The truth was, though, that it wasn't "nothing" at all. And Nino, of course, knew it. *Nothing,* he wrote, *is almost as bad as "I'm fine."*

It's just . . . , started Floralie, and it took her a minute to finish her thought. *It's like she's written back. To my letters, without ever even getting them.*

Nino eyed her. *You said you wrote letters on your hands. I remember that from when I met you.*

Floralie nodded. *They're to my mother.*

Your mother? I thought you said you didn't have parents.

I don't—not really. We left her three years ago. I didn't want to . . . it was complicated. Anyway, the letters—I never send them. I don't even know where she lives anymore. All I've wanted to do since— Floralie could not bring herself to write the words, to write out in permanent ink the fate of Mama—*since things changed, is find her. And to be honest, I'd rather have had her die than disappear. Because now I feel so unfinished. I feel like there is a piece of myself missing, but it's out there, taunting me. I want to find it before it disappears completely. Before I disappear. And this box of flowers and this letter are from her. I know it. She used to call me her wildflower. Her name was Viscaria. I don't understand the other letters though—A.C. My mother was simply Viscaria Laurel. V.L. No middle name, or anything. And then, E.F.T.—that makes no sense at all.*

Your mother's name was Viscaria?

Floralie nodded.

I like that, wrote Nino. *It's a poetry word.*

It's a type of flower, wrote Floralie. *I'm not sure what it looks like. But my mother used to say it meant "dance with me" in the language of flowers. She was a ballerina, and she loved flowers. Funny, the way she grew into her name like that.* Floralie paused. "Nino?"

Nino looked up, startled by Floralie's voice.

"Will you help me?" Floralie's words choked at the back of her throat. "I think . . . I think I've got to find out the meaning of these flowers. Before Grandmama takes me away. Away from my paints, away from Tom, away from you. She'll lock me up like a prisoner in that ridiculous orphanage of hers, force curtsies and 'Yes, sir. Yes, madam' down my throat."

Orphanage? wrote Nino. There was a hollowed-out look to his eyes that unnerved Floralie.

She runs the Adelaide Laurel Orphanage for Unfortunate Children atop the farthest hill of Whitterly End, wrote Floralie. *I just can't go there. Mrs. Coffrey's was bad enough.*

No, you can't go there. Absolutely not. His letters were jagged, sharpened like knives. Floralie vaguely wondered where this sudden passion had come from.

"I've got to find out my mother's message," Floralie said aloud. "This could be my last chance to find her." And then she added on paper, for the words wouldn't dare touch her lips, *She's the only one who ever cared for me—really cared for me, besides maybe Tom, who just doesn't know how. She's the only one who never, not once, tried to change me. I've never fit anyone's ideals, anyone's except for hers.*

Floralie stared at Nino, noticing for the first time the shadows beneath his eyes, hardly any lighter than the letter's Indian ink. His eyes had ghosts, too.

Nino picked up the pen again. *I will help you however I can. Cross my heart.* And he mimed an X across his chest.

Floralie smiled. *I should go. It's getting late, and Tom will wonder where I am.*

Nino nodded. *See you tomorrow?*

Yes.

Floralie was about to get up when Nino wrote something else. *And, Floralie—*

Yeah?

Nino's mouth twitched, and he wrote in tiny, barely legible letters, *You fit my ideals.*

Tins of blush and mascara littered Mama's vanity table. As Mama powdered her face, the puff of foundation reminded Floralie of fairy dust. "This is magic stuff," Mama would say. "This is child stuff."

When Floralie asked what that meant, Mama said, "Every child is born flawless. Every human begins as a perfect, unscathed being. But as they grow older . . . regrets collect, mistakes manifest, and fears ignite. That's why us grown-ups need this magic stuff. It makes us feel new again, even if we aren't."

Floralie fingered the tube of scarlet lipstick. She wanted to wear it, but there was something about it that made her feel uneasy. As if putting on that lipstick would change her, somehow, forever. She tucked her fingers back into her palm. Later, she thought. Later.

Mama slipped a sweet alyssum flower inside the vanity drawer and said, "Your worth is greater than your beauty, Flory. Remember that."

10

The next day in the attic, Nino picked up Philomenos, looked to Floralie, and then dropped the mouse into Floralie's hand. Floralie's fingers tensed, but the mouse kept still and quiet, as if he could sense Floralie's fear. His fur felt soft like the skin of a peach, and his whiskers tickled Floralie's palm.

I found him here. He became my first and only friend after I left

The letters stopped mid-sentence, as if the rest of the words had fallen off a broken bridge.

After you left . . . prompted Floralie.

Nino's mouth twitched. *I'll trade you,* he wrote. *Secret for a secret?*

Floralie eyed him carefully.

That way, added Nino, *neither of us will tell.*

Floralie bit her lip and looked to Philomenos, who had curled up in her palm. Something warm pressed against her forearm—Nino's hand.

And then we'll trust each other, added Nino. *With everything, forever and ever. Okay?*

Floralie nodded.

They wrote simultaneously, word after word, unraveling their secrets. The words leached to Floralie's fingernails, holding on with elephant strength. There was something inside the simple letters that wouldn't let go of Floralie. They were unspeakable. Unwritable. She heaved them onto the page.

Finally, the two exchanged their secrets.

Nino's read:

I escaped your grandmother's orphanage. I'm the boy everyone's been talking about, everyone's been looking for. Things were bad before, but they only got worse at the orphanage. People were . . . I felt afraid. Always afraid.

Floralie stared at Nino's words. She felt as if someone had sliced a hole in her stomach. Nino was the kindest person Floralie had ever met. She wanted to tell him, *You didn't deserve that; you deserve marzipan and silk and cuff links and wonderful, beautiful things,* but she seemed only to be able to think in pictures at the moment; any words her brain tried to form came out in hieroglyphics.

Nino waited, and then Floralie handed him her notebook. *We didn't leave my mother; she was taken from us. My father started drinking even more after that. That's how he died.*

It was true, but not the whole truth. The whole truth was far too scary to put into writing, into words. This truth was better hidden in gardens, enveloped in the petals of newly sprung tulips, white, just beginning to bloom. A poem lingered under Floralie's fingers and she was finally able to picture the words in her mind:

Forget-me-not like this
Like this is perfect
Like this you breathe
In and out like morning glories
You hold lifetimes in one bloom

Forget-me-not like this
Like this you know the bluebells
Weep tonight under star shine
You hold oceans in one dewdrop

Forget-me-not like this
Like this is perfect
Like this you live
For one fleeting moment
You are in bloom
You are alive in your universe
So do not forget
So never forget

Like this you live
One petal on the surface
You hold roses in thin-veiled skin
Do not be afraid
Open up your petals, your palms
Your lungs, and breathe me in

Like this, forget-me-not
Forget-me-not
Forget me not.

The words never made it to paper, but Nino smiled. *Good. Now we know each other. For real.* He tore off Floralie's secret, pocketed it, then handed his own to Floralie. An inkling of guilt trickled through her spine as she tucked Nino's secret into her bag, knowing that hers and his were not equal in truth.

And that was that. Not another word was spoken about either secret.

One day Mama pulled Floralie by the hand across a grassy cliff and said, "Hide away with me, my wildflower." In her other hand, Mama carried a parasol flung out behind her. Their steps became cushioned with the wind, feet lighter, breath easier. Nearly flying. When they reached the edge of the cliff, Mama said, "It's too open here. We've got to find a cave. We'll have a picnic of strawberries there. We'll look for

fairies and elves. We'll tell secrets there, just you and I, Floralie. Would you like that?"

"Yes, Mama," said Floralie. She would like that very much.

But they never could find the cave. So they never had a picnic of strawberries, and they never looked for fairies, and they never looked for elves. And never did they tell their secrets that day on the cliff by the sea.

But Mama let a melianthus flower fly away from her fingertips to the grassy hill, saying, "I love you. In time we'll learn each other's secrets."

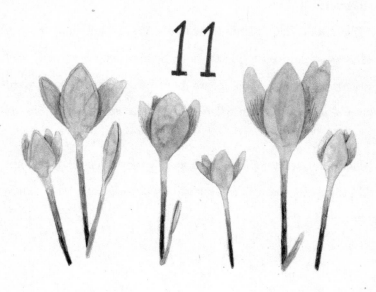

11

That evening, Floralie took the long way home—that is to say, she walked straight past her door, past the cobbler, over the Here and There Bridge, and across the farthest hill of Whitterly End until she met the wrought-iron gate of the Adelaide Laurel Orphanage for Unfortunate Children.

The manor stood tall and stately, hedges pruned and black curtains drawn across every window. Floralie imagined her life behind the gate. Hardly anyone around town ever saw the orphans; they were scarcely allowed outside. She tried to picture what they might look like—but the only images she could summon up were ones of children with heads of beasts, slimy and big toothed, waiting like tigers to gobble her up. And though she had just met him, she imagined her life without Nino. And that felt very empty indeed.

She then imagined what her room would look like: plain, gray, flowerless. Her desk would be spotless, and the sheets of her bed would be either tucked too tightly or too loosely. Tom always tucked Floralie's just right.

She imagined what Tom's life had been like there. The story went that Papa persuaded Mama to let Tom stay with Grandmama during his childhood so he would have a better education than was available in Giverny. But Floralie knew the real reason was that Papa was too busy with his banking career to care for a child, and Mama danced ballet shows every other night. Tom never talked much about his time at Grandmama's orphanage; Floralie wondered how he had kept hope. If he had ever had a wonderland.

And then Floralie made a promise to herself. *Never will I end up behind that gate. Whatever it takes, I will find a way out of this.*

Floralie made her way back to the cottage, and when she crept in through the back door, she found the entire house to be dark—except for the sitting room. As Floralie inched inside, she found Tom sitting at the splintery desk, sorting through bills and bills and bills.

"Tom?" breathed Floralie.

Tom's head snapped up, eyes veined scarlet. The color of poppies, all asleep and dark centered. "Flory. Come in," he said, his voice soft and fatherly. He clasped his hands together, and turned around on his stool.

"What can I do for you?" said Tom.

Floralie's heart pulsated. As she spoke, her voice quaked. "I . . . I just want to ask you something. I had a tiny—minuscule, really—question, maybe about Grandmama and—and what she has planned for me."

"Go on, then," allowed Tom.

"Right, well, I wondered if perhaps I could skip going to Grandmama's and—and find someone else to take me instead. Like, a tutor, or—or perhaps a family member." She felt herself shrinking like a morning glory at twilight.

Tom leaned back in his chair and ran his fingers through his hair. "You know we haven't got any aunts or uncles. So who precisely did you have in mind?"

"Well—well, I don't know, exactly, I've barely even thought about it. It was just an idea, really." Floralie realized her fingers had started to fiddle with the lace on her sleeve, drawing wider an already-present hole. "But—but perhaps Mama."

Tom stopped his hair stroking and turned. "Mama?"

Though his eyes were bloodshot, they pierced through Floralie, and she had to look away.

"Mama is . . . Floralie, Papa and I explained this to you, remember? Mama is not well—"

"She was fine when we left her," whispered Floralie. "Sort of, anyway. I just thought, I always liked Mama. And—and I'll never be happy at Grandmama's, you *know* it, Tom. And Mama was always really good at being ladylike—when she wanted to, anyway—so she could teach me all about that, and I—"

"Floralie—"

"—I'll work really hard. I'll learn multiplication, and I'll play the piano—"

"Flory—"

"—and I promise I won't daydream too much, I swear it. Mama didn't want me to leave her three years ago—I'll make her happy again, and we'll be together. You could come visit; it would be just like before. I just . . . have to *find* her."

Tom sighed. "She's gone, Floralie. She has no connection to us anymore, you know that. She could be anywhere for all I know."

"But maybe if you would just tell me where she went in the first place—the address of her new home, even the color of the walls or the slant of its roof, anything."

"No, Floralie, I can't."

The velvet curtains, still hanging from Grandmama's visit, seemed to close in on Floralie, smothering her vision like fog before a thunderstorm. A flame of anger flickered in Floralie's chest; none of this would have happened if Grandmama hadn't sent Mama away in the first place. "You can't or you won't?"

Tom sighed. "You think I know more than I do."

Floralie was almost certain he knew more than he let on. She also knew he was afraid, not only for Floralie's sake, but for his own. He didn't want to admit what had happened. No one did. No one would. But Floralie had to know one thing: "Is she still alive?"

Tom closed his eyes and took one of Floralie's hands. "I don't know." He squeezed Floralie's hand, then regained his concreteness and said, "Regardless, it matters not. Neither of us can have any contact with her anymore. It's for the best. In four days' time, you are going to go live with Grandmama. That's my final word."

A lump formed at the back of Floralie's throat, and she croaked, "Won't you miss me?"

Tom sighed again. "I think I've indulged you far too much this evening, Flory. It's time for bed."

And so Floralie did as she was told. She crawled into her barren wonderland, stripped of all its magic, and lay upon the sagging cot. And just like that, Floralie's stone wall crumbled down. Ivy bristled her fingers and pulled her away to her beautiful, faraway, magical place. It was raining in Floralie's wonderland, but it was warm rain, hopeful rain. Flowers crouched over like old men with canes, but sparkled with the raindrops like newly crowned queens. Tomorrow, Floralie would fight. Tomorrow, she would make a masterpiece from the pigments of her mind. *Tomorrow, tomorrow, tomorrow.*

When things started going bad, Papa would drive Floralie to the dance studio where Mama practiced to make sure Mama was doing okay. Usually, she was. And usually, Floralie would watch the ballerinas twirl and leap and glide across the wood floor. Everything was beautiful, everything was in bloom—until one day. The rain hammered the roof of the studio, and the air pressed in on Floralie's skin, heavy and damp. She watched from the wood bench at the end of the studio, next to the director, who was shouting counts at the dancers. Mama bourréed to the center of the stage, pirouetted, pirouetted, pirouetted . . . withered. She fell, crumpled like a dying carnation. She screamed. Dancers crowded in, and Papa told Floralie to stay put, but she could still hear this:

"Please, just take me."

Floralie never discovered who Mama was talking to.

Mama left a colchicum flower in her pointe shoe and said she was getting new ones in the morning. "My best days have passed, my wildflower." She sighed, and repeated, "My best days have passed."

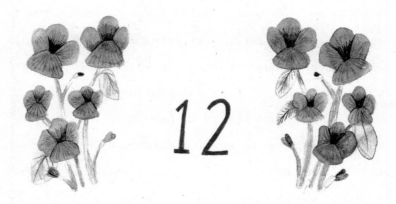

12

Early next morning, before Tom even had time to call Floralie for breakfast, Floralie found Nino not in his attic, but on the doorstep of the Whitterly Library beside the flower shop. Philomenos sat faithfully next to him, and when the little dormouse caught sight of Floralie, he began to squeak excitedly. Nino looked up and at once got to his feet.

Floralie! he scrawled in his notebook in large, curly letters. He leaped over to her, Philomenos skittering along behind him, and linked arms with Floralie. As they ambled toward the library, Nino wrote, *Philomenos and I were thinking this morning about where to start with the flowers. We were sitting on this doorstep, actually, when it occurred to me—the* library *of course! We've got to find Sylvestre Tullier's flower dictionary, so what better place to start than there? And I have something else to show you, too. A surprise.*

Of course, Floralie had visited this library from time to time—mostly just to find Tom, as many nights he studied there as if he were at university. But libraries were not of much interest to Floralie. Museums, though . . . museums were heaven. Perhaps, thought Floralie, libraries were like museums to Nino.

Nino twisted the ivy-laced doorknob, and the two walked in. The familiar, yet ever-so-overwhelming walls of books towered over them. Ladders five times as tall as Floralie clung to bookshelves, and up above was the most marvelous stained-glass window she had ever seen. A golden-rimmed staircase stood at the back, and straight across from it at the front was the librarian's desk, with a green glass lamp and a scattering of notecards atop it. In the center of the desk rested a plaque that read, MISS DELPHINE CLAIROUX. And behind it sat Miss Clairoux.

Floralie thought Miss Clairoux looked a bit like an iris flower—old, wrinkly, but regal. She was tall and thin with a large silver bun piled atop her head. She was holding open a book, but was not reading it. As Floralie and Nino neared her, Floralie saw that Miss Clairoux was *feeling* the book, wrinkly fingers traveling across wrinkly pages . . .

Floralie and Nino now stood barely a foot from Miss Clairoux, and Miss Clairoux turned her head up—but her eyes remained closed. Nino took a funny-looking object—a slate of sorts with holes punched in it—and a stylus from the desk. He then slid a note card beneath the slate and began to punch holes into it with the stylus. He finished in half a second and reached for the woman's hand.

Nino placed the punched paper into Miss Clairoux's hand, and Miss Clairoux's face bloomed to life.

"Monsieur Konstantinos! *Bonjour* to you, too!" Her lips spread wide in a smile so bright and honest it could have belonged to a five-year-old. Her accent was French; Floralie knew it well. "Have you grown taller since I saw you last?" and she opened two milky pale eyes and winked one at Nino, prompting the two to burst into laughter. Floralie breathed a slight laugh, but she really didn't understand what was so funny.

Nino, however, had pulled out his notebook. *Miss Clairoux is blind,* he wrote to Floralie.

You know how to write in braille? wrote Floralie, astounded.

Nino shrugged. *I can write in lots of languages.*

"And who is with you?"

She can hear your breath, explained Nino.

Floralie exchanged a nervous glance with Nino, then cleared her throat. "I—I am, ms."

Miss Clairoux smiled. "And who is 'I'?"

"Floralie," she said. "Floralie Laurel. I sell flowers next door. I'm Nino's friend."

Miss Clairoux clasped her hands together. "Oh, young love! *C'est belle!*"

"No—no, no," said Floralie. "We're friends, just friends."

Nino smiled.

"*Un jour, peut-être,*" muttered Miss Clairoux, which Floralie knew to mean, "Someday, perhaps."

Floralie's cheeks flushed, but thankfully, Miss Clairoux moved the conversation along in a more comfortable direction.

"Now, what can I do for you today, *mademoiselle et monsieur?*" asked Miss Clairoux. "I've got an order of brand-new poetry books coming in for you, Nino, but not until Tuesday."

Nino had already started writing some more braille.

Miss Clairoux's fingers read, and then she tilted her head.

"Floriography, you say?" she said. "Follow me," and Miss Clairoux stepped out from behind her desk. She walked with a cane out in front of her for guidance, but really, she didn't look like she needed it. She zigzagged in and out of the labyrinth of desks and bookshelves as if she had lived in the place for a century. Perhaps she had.

"Now, these books, I will tell you, are a bit hard to come by these days," said Miss Clairoux. "While the flower language was a very popular form of communication in the 1800s, having started in France and spread to England, it did start to fade away around 1900. Which, of course, was nearly three *decades* ago, so we'll be lucky if we can find some."

"It's got to be Sylvestre Tullier's version, Miss Clairoux," said Floralie. "It's important."

"Syl-Sylvestre . . . who?"

"Tullier," repeated Floralie.

A far-off look crossed Miss Clairoux's face. "Tullier," she whispered, then shook her head, wisps of silver hair swirling as she returned to reality. "Well then, we must search our hardest with wit in our heads and gusto in our hearts," declared Miss Clairoux, and a few boys Tom's age scowled up at her from behind their desks.

The three wandered up to the second floor, and finally, Miss Clairoux stopped at a bookshelf in the corner. She ran her fingers along the spines of the books and pressed her ear up against them as if she were *listening.*

Nino pulled his notebook out. *She's feeling the books,* he wrote.

Feeling them? repeated Floralie.

Nino nodded. *Miss Clairoux knows how all her books feel. She knows them by heart.*

After a few minutes, Miss Clairoux had pulled out five flower language books.

"Let's see, I've got Jacqueline Fournier's, Sébastien Laurent's,

Brigitte Leblanc's, Walter Myer's, and Albert Winslow's. But no Sylvestre Tullier. I—I honestly haven't seen his book in years . . . Why don't you two get started with these, and I'll search around to see if Mr. Tullier's book is hiding somewhere?"

And so Floralie and Nino carried the books to a secluded desk between a bookshelf and a window. When they sat, Floralie wrote, *I don't even know where to begin.*

Do you remember any of the flowers in the box? wrote Nino.

Some of them. But I only really know two or three. One was primrose, I remember that. Another was a normal rose—sort of burgundy in color, and . . . oh, I can't remember. I think a lot of them are exotic, or wildflowers, or just really rare.

Well then, let's start with primrose, and the two flipped through pages upon pages of flower meanings. Soon, all five books were opened to their primrose pages:

Jacqueline Fournier's: *Primrose: Youth*

Sébastien Laurent's: *Primrose: Sadness*

Brigitte Leblanc's: *Primrose: Truth*

Walter Myer's: *Primrose: Childhood*

Albert Winslow's: *Primrose: Believe me*

They're all different, scribbled Floralie in frustration. *It's not going to work.*

Let's find Miss Clairoux, suggested Nino. *Maybe she's found something.*

And so Floralie and Nino began to search, but Miss Clairoux was nowhere to be found. However, somewhere along the mystery section, Floralie heard a rustling. She beckoned to Nino, and the two pressed their ears up against the bookshelf—and fell right through.

They hit the floor with a thud, and a pile of books rained down upon them. But when Floralie looked up, she saw that this room was not an ordinary, run-of-the-mill room. It was, indeed, filled with books—thousands of them—just like the library. But these were braille books. Floralie could tell by the small bumps on their spines and their colorless covers. They were not arranged neatly on shelves, however, but stacked in precariously tall piles on the wooden floor. And in the middle stood Miss Clairoux. She spun around so fast a hairpin flew out of her bun. "Who's there?"

"Just us, Miss Clairoux," said Floralie. "Floralie and Nino."

"Oh, gracious dears!" sighed Miss Clairoux, clutching her heart. "You gave me quite a fright."

"Sorry," said Floralie.

"No need for apologies, none at all. Come in, dears."

Nino stood and pulled Floralie to her feet. She brushed off her dress and gazed around at the magnificent sight.

"You're curious about this place," said Miss Clairoux. "I can feel your wonderment, dears." She sighed, slipping into a happy reverie. "Ah yes, this is my dream. Everyone has one, you know.

Mine is to open a braille library. In France, of course; all my braille books are in French. I've been collecting these books for as long as I can remember. And I've read every single one, mind you. Yes, that is my dream. One day, perhaps. *Un jour.*" She shook her head as if shaking off the dreams. "Now, unfortunately, I have not been able to find Mr. Tullier's floriography *anywhere.* Were the others of any use?"

"Not exactly, no," said Floralie, and Miss Clairoux frowned.

"I could have *sworn* I had a copy. I imagine it went out of print ages ago, but I could have *sworn* I had a copy. I am most sorry."

Floralie's heart sank.

Miss Clairoux edged her way to Floralie and Nino and said solemnly, "I'm sorry."

"It's okay," said Floralie. "Really, it is," though she knew it wasn't. She *had* to figure out her mother's message. She had to find her. Whatever it would take, Floralie couldn't end up with Grandmama—not Grandmama with her sharp diamond rings sinking into flesh and lemon-scented hugs suffocating Floralie's lungs. She had to get Tom out of debt, and she had to save Mama from whatever fate she had met. But most of all, they had to be together again, because Mama and Floralie and Tom, they were like mariposa lilies—one petal falls away, the rest fall apart. "Thanks for looking," said Floralie, stringing together new plans in her mind. Perhaps she could catch a train to London—Tom said there was a library there with every book in the world. "I guess we'll go, then."

Miss Clairoux nodded. "Good luck, my dears. *Bonne chance.*"

Floralie and Nino left the braille book room, but as Floralie nodded toward the door, Nino stopped her.

Wait, he wrote. Despite Floralie's own disappointment, Nino was wearing his crooked grin again. *I know you're upset about Sylvestre Tullier. More upset than you'll admit.*

Floralie looked away.

But I want to show you something. He laced his fingers through Floralie's. *Come with me.*

Tom, Floralie, and Mama once took a train to Cappadocia, Turkey, just for two days, but it was enough time to fall in love with the place. They soared off in a hot air balloon together, a bright, pink paint splotch against the big blue sky. And when they landed, Mama left a blue violet in the hot air balloon basket and whispered, "We must take faith, my wildflower. Always."

13

Floralie and Nino snaked through the desks and shelves of the library until at last they came to a small section closed off by bookshelves.

Remember how you told me your room was your wonderland? wrote Nino. *I mean, before Tom tore things down? Well, this is my wonderland. I thought, since yours is destroyed now, maybe we could share it. I know poetry's not your favorite thing in the world, but . . . I don't know. I just wanted you to see it.*

Are these all poetry books? Floralie picked one off the shelf and sat on the floor, flipping through it. Philomenos scuttled over to the book and started to tear at a page, but Nino promptly shooed him off.

That's my favorite, wrote Nino. *It's not all poems. There are some, but mostly, it's simply a collection of thoughts, ideas, and art. Curated dreams.*

Floralie read the title: *A History of Dreamlands.* It had a familiar ring to it, but Floralie could not pinpoint where she had heard it. It was as if the title were a memory within a memory within a dream.

It starts at the beginning, wrote Nino.

The beginning of what?

Time, of course. Well, close enough to the beginning. It starts with Sappho, a most eloquent poet of ancient Greece. She's absolutely fantastic. Someday, I wish to uncover more of her poems.

Floralie smiled. *Is that your dream?*

Nino shrugged.

What is it? wrote Floralie.

What's what?

Something's wrong. You're hiding behind an "I'm fine."

Nino blushed. *I was born in Greece. And when I lived there, before they died, my parents were archaeologists. Every night that they weren't working, they would read me a Sappho poem. Well, one night a tunnel collapsed on them. They were digging for more of her poetry. They were digging for me.*

Floralie squeezed Nino's hand. *I'm sorry.*

Nino shrugged again. *It's okay. I was, maybe, six years old then? Anyway, if I've calculated right, I'm twelve now, so that was a long while ago. Since then I spent my life traveling and scavenging for food. Thieving, mostly. Until one day, a policeman caught me stealing bread at King's Cross Station in London. He took me to Mrs. Laurel's. I won't lie, she could be cruel. The slightest step out of line—resting elbows on the table, or speaking without being spoken to—would get you a week's worth of mopping up the dining hall and eating scraps off the kitchen stove.*

It was hardly any better than the streets. Everyone hurt me there— bullies, but also people I thought were my friends, even the caretakers and tutors. It was because of my voice. I can't talk too well . . . so I just stopped.

But yes. Yes, that is my dream. Someday, I want to finish what they started. He sighed and added, *Anyway. The book. It goes all the way to present day. At the end you've got contemporary surrealist poems, thoughts from philosophers and artists, and a couple essays on modern-day inventors.*

Floralie flipped to the first chapter, which, indeed, read *Sappho* across the top. The first poem read:

Time will pass, but they will remember us . . .

It's short, wrote Floralie.

Nino nodded. *It's a fragment. But you can say a lot in just a few words, no? Try this one.* He turned to page 42.

> *In one breath, night whispers away her flames*
> *And hours entwine in hours*
> *For the moon is slipping to ash*
> *And I am slipping, too.*

The poem beside it caught Floralie's eye.

> *Let me see you, darling . . .*
> *Let me unravel the wonder in your eyes.*

What are the pauses for? The three periods? asked Floralie.

It's broken, wrote Nino, the words small and light as if they were a whisper.

What do you mean?

The ellipses, wrote Nino. *See, when archeologists found Sappho's poems, the papyrus was all crumpled up. Some parts of the papyrus were missing—so, only fragments of the poems could be recovered. The translator uses ellipses to mark the spaces where the papyrus was broken. It's the same with all the short poems that end in ellipses— they're fragments, tiny pieces of poems. That's why they're broken. Isn't that beautiful?*

Floralie didn't exactly understand how brokenness could make something beautiful, but she didn't want to offend Nino. *Yes,* she wrote. *Yes, I suppose.*

Floralie flipped through to the end and was about to close the book when something caught her eye—a photograph of an old, gray-bearded man, a middle-aged man holding a baby in one hand, a book in the other, and a young teenage girl with daisy-blond hair and vivacious eyes. They stood in front of a manor blooming with flowers, a mailbox in the front with the number *84* printed in squiggly script. Floralie had seen that house before, many times, a recurring memory, now turned over to dreamland. Now turned over to wonderland. Floralie read a quote, tiny, whispery print beneath the photograph:

> *I must have flowers, always, and always.*
> —*Claude Monet*

"My mother used to say that," whispered Floralie.

Nino leaned in close to see, but Floralie snapped shut the book. "Never mind."

But the minute she said the words, Floralie's eyes widened as if a match had been lit inside her. She opened the book back up again and read the photograph's caption: *Claude Monet and his gardener, May 21, 1905.*

A swarm of butterflies stirred in Floralie's heart as she stared at the teenage girl. She knew those eyes. *That's my mother,* she thought. *That's my mother. That's my mother, that's my mother, that's my mother.* And then she thought, *And that's Claude Monet. And that gardener is . . .* She squinted closer at the book the man was carrying: *La Floriographie Complète.* Floralie dropped the book. She shook her head, suddenly abuzz, then grabbed Nino's notebook—

I know where to find Sylvestre Tullier.

Mama left a lucerne flower at the circus one day. "For a life on edge," she said. Mama was like a tightrope walker. She liked to walk on the edge of fate. The edge of reality, the edge of dreamlands. She tiptoed along that thin rope of life and death whenever she deepened her backbend, added an extra pirouette. Mama liked forgetting life. Forgetting that death was but one foot out of place, one step too close, one step too far. That, Floralie believed, was what made her seem so alive, the way she tiptoed along death. That was what made her so beautifully, unconsciously, fragile.

14

The flower shop was alit with the bluebell lamp, even though the shop was closed on Mondays. Miss Clairoux insisted on walking Nino and Floralie home from the library as the dusk drew nearer, even though Floralie walked home alone from flower selling nearly every night. But when they neared the flower shop, shouts rattled down the street like tin cans.

"Stay low," said Floralie as they neared the shopwindow. Nino crouched down on all fours as Floralie peered through the window of the Dutch doors.

"That voice . . . ," whispered Miss Clairoux. "I *know* that voice from somewhere."

Grandmama was inside the shop, across from Tom at the front counter. Grandmama was pointing a wrinkly, bejeweled finger at Tom, her mouth taut and nose crinkled. Tom's eyebrows were furrowed and his eyes tired, arms limp. Grandmama waved about a bill, then let it float to the ground.

"She's in there," Floralie whispered to Nino as it dawned on her that Nino's freedom was at risk. If Grandmama caught him, he would surely be sent straight back to her orphanage. And as much as Floralie wanted to burst in and shield Tom from Grandmama, she said to Nino, "You can't be seen."

Tom and Grandmama flourished their hands in anger, and Miss Clairoux's lips pursed, ear pressing against the wood of the door. When the clickity-clackity footsteps of Grandmama drew near, Miss Clairoux took Floralie's and Nino's hands and hurried them into the library.

"What—where are we going?" asked Floralie, panic rising in her chest.

"She mustn't find Nino," explained Miss Clairoux. "No, *mon chér*, I cannot let her snatch you back into that abuse. And, Floralie, I daresay, that woman wouldn't be too tickled to find you sneaking about with a boy at this hour. Come, I know a place where you can hide."

"But—but why are you helping us?" stuttered Floralie as Miss Clairoux hurried them back toward the library, its windows now darkened, as it had closed for the evening just moments earlier.

The flower shop's Dutch doors behind them snapped open. *Click-clickity-clack-clack,* went the dreaded high heels. Floralie's heart jolted as Miss Clairoux fiddled with her ring of keys to the library. "Quick! She's coming!" urged Floralie. "Nino—Miss Clairoux, we've got to hide N—"

But before Floralie could finish, Miss Clairoux had yanked open the library door and scuttled them inside. "Into the braille room. Quick! Quick!"

Miss Clairoux flicked on a few lights and hurried them over to the mystery section and pushed the secret door open. Nino and Floralie tumbled inside, just as the chink of the library's front door could be heard in the distance. But Miss Clairoux was still outside. "*Do not worry,* mes chérs," came Miss Clairoux's whisper from the other side of the braille room.

From inside the dim room, Floralie could hear Grandmama's voice, like the snarl of a coyote hunting its prey: "You said she came here at what time?"

"Early this morning," replied Tom's voice. "She's been here ever since as far as I'm concerned. To be frank, I was rather pleased she was taking interest in literature at all."

There was a pause, and then Grandmama said, "When I came to visit you, the lights in this library were turned off. But now they are on. Curious, don't you think? A library that opens at night."

"As far as I know, it closes at five every evening. Three on Sundays." said Tom.

Footsteps echoed, and then Grandmama screeched, "Who's there? We know you're in here."

Floralie bit her lip, squeezed Nino's hand twice. *"You'll be okay,"* whispered Floralie, but she could feel Nino's pulse pounding in his palm.

And then Grandmama let out an ear-shattering shriek: "If you don't reveal yourself immediately, I am calling the police."

Then came Miss Clairoux's voice. "Hello? Oh, there you are. I'm one of the librarians, just doing a quick cleaning before heading home. Pleasure to meet you. May I help you find—"

"A child, yes," barked Grandmama.

"Ah yes, you're the orphan collector, are you not?" said Miss Clairoux to both Nino's and Floralie's surprise.

Grandmama's lip curled. "Her name is Floralie Laurel," said Grandmama. "Puny little thing, knotted hair, but fair complexion when she bothers to bathe."

Miss Clairoux gave a false cough and said, "And what, exactly, gives you the position to claim her?"

"*I* am her grandmother."

Miss Clairoux's face drained of all color.

"And," continued Grandmama, "I demand you present Floralie to me immediately if you know of her whereabouts, which I have an inkling you do." She paused, then said, arms crossed, "Now, if you do not reveal the child this instant, my grandson here will call the police."

There was a long pause before Miss Clairoux uttered, "So be it. Call. This child is not going home with you."

Floralie squeezed tight her eyes. She couldn't let Miss Clairoux take the fall for her. She burst out from the secret room. Nino scuttled back into the shadows of the braille room, and Tom's eyebrows jumped.

"I'm here. Sorry, I—er—I was reading fairy tales. I've learned my lesson, though, and I vow never again to spear my eyes with such fantastical nonsense." Floralie choked on her own words, but still managed to spit them out.

Grandmama descended on Floralie and tilted Floralie's chin with fingers that smelled like wilting hyacinths. "Floralie, my dear, rebellion does not suit your pretty little face. Just remember, you will be under my supervision within two days. Pack lightly. I'll be keeping my eyes and ears peeled for you, so don't you try any funny business again." Grandmama's attention shifted to the half-opened mystery bookshelf, then flicked her gaze to Miss Clairoux. "I do not trust you," she said, and nothing more was said about the subject. Grandmama yanked

Floralie by the arm and led her home. She tipped her feather hat and bid Tom good night, then left in her shiny black car off to her dreaded orphanage.

"Are you afraid, my wildflower?" Mama asked.

Downstairs, Grandmama could be heard snapping a wooden spoon in half. "Not as if she ever bothers to cook anyway!" she shouted. "Not as if she does anything useful for this family at all."

Floralie turned to Mama and replied, "Yes."

Mama handed Floralie a branch of a French willow and said, "That's what makes you human."

15

After Grandmama left, and Floralie skittered up to her bedroom, stripped of all its magic, a knock came at her door. Floralie gave no reply, but the visitor entered nonetheless. Tom kneeled down to Floralie's bedside, two cups of tea in his hands. One was painted with red roses and rimmed with gold—Mama's—and the other was decorated with blue and turquoise stripes—Papa's. Floralie took Mama's and sipped the honeyed chamomile. Tom stroked Floralie's hair, not bothering to even detangle the knots.

"We'll be okay," he said. "We'll be just fine."

Fine, thought Floralie. She tucked the word into her pocket, and felt the familiar wrinkles, creases, brittle edges of the word upon her skin. She knew that word by touch, by heart, an heirloom from Mama.

Tom went to sleep early that night, and Floralie listened patiently for his breaths to slow so she would know he was asleep. As she waited for her escape, Floralie thought of Mama. She thought about the way she knew her mother by heart the same way Miss Clairoux knew her library books by heart. The day before Mama left, Floralie had made sure to memorize some things. All the things she loved.

Ballet was number one. Mama said it made her feel both young and old, wise and carefree, soft and loud, powerful and small. Floralie had never quite understood that when she said it, but when Mama danced, Floralie understood everything. Or perhaps she understood nothing, but she didn't need to when Mama danced.

Number two was Papa. Every night after supper, Mama would tear him away from his numbers and client letters and teach him how to dance the Charleston while jazz roared from the record player. She retaught him that same dance every night for months, but he never quite got it right.

Number three was country air. Mama never had enough space. She once broke Grandmama's antique grandfather clock while pirouetting through the house. That was why she loved the air—it gave her more space. Floralie wondered if her mother ever got to go outside anymore, if she ever got to breathe the smell of lavender or dance in the wildflowers.

And then she thought of what Mama had hated; they were the same things. Ballet. Waddling around the house like a penguin with her feet turned out 180 degrees, even if her face went red with the pain in her knees. Wrapping an old and fraying measuring tape around her waist each morning. Crying on the floor of the studio, crumpled up like a dying rose; Floralie had never found out why.

Papa. She called him an armadillo because whenever she suggested to go out, have some fun, he would tell her: "Work comes first." But if Floralie were to write those words in a poem, they would look more like *WORK COMES FIRST,* in capital letters, because for Papa, work *always* came first. It came before Tom and before Floralie, and it even came before Mama. Mama didn't like that too much.

Air. Mama's lungs craved it. But there was something in her brain, or her legs, or maybe just her toes that kept her wanting to stay shut up inside. She loved the air when she was outside; she *adored* it. But the thing was, she began not to *want* to go outside. This was one thing that Floralie had never understood about her mother.

And there was one other thing. Flowers. Mama never threw away flowers herself—she always had Tom or Papa do it when they got too wrinkled. But one day, she tossed every flower in the house out the window, left them on the back porch for the crows. She left Floralie that day, too.

Floralie repeated the words over and over and over in her mind. *Ballet. Papa. Air. Flowers. Ballet. Papa. Air. Flowers. Ballet. Papa. Air. Flowers* . . .

When at last Tom's breaths came in long, sleepy heaves, Floralie crept out the barren wonderland, down the rickety staircase, through the back door, and down the cobbled road to the flower shop. Once inside, she scurried up to the attic to find Nino asleep behind an emptied crate labeled, LES TULIPES FOSTERIANAS.

Floralie shook Nino awake by the shoulder, and he jolted upright before sighing back into himself. He grabbed his pen and paper and wrote, *What are you doing?*

This, wrote Floralie, laying a hand on the crate.

Tulips? wrote Nino.

Look at the address. I can't believe I didn't recognize the name when I found the letter. We get all our flower orders from this address. When I saw that Claude Monet photograph, I just . . . remembered. See?

Floralie's fingers traced the address on the wooden crate:

84 Rue Claude Monet
Giverny
France

The flowers are shipped from Monet's manor, wrote Floralie. *And that man in the photograph beside Monet was Mr. Tullier, I know it. Sylvestre Tullier was Monet's gardener. He was holding the floriography.*

And then the word "home" somehow stuck onto the page like residual sap on a maple branch. *I lived around there,* she wrote. *My house was a few roads away from Rue Claude Monet. This is where we have to go.*

Claude Monet? wrote Nino. *The artist? You're joking. You must be joking. Does he really live there?*

Did. Floralie sighed. *He's dead now. Died this past December. He kept to himself mostly, though. Hardly anyone ever saw him leave his garden. Anyway, it's not him we've got to see. It's this Mr. Tullier, whoever he is.*

Do you know how to get there?

I might.

A crooked grin spread across Nino's face. *I feel like a thousand fireflies have gone alight!*

Floralie giggled at Nino's poetics, and her hand shot up to cover her mouth.

Nino looked up, smile fading. He reached out a knobby-fingered hand and gently pulled Floralie's hand away from her mouth. Floralie bit the inside of her lip to keep her mouth closed from the laughter.

Floralie Alice Laurel, the gaps in your teeth are the gaps in Sappho's poems. Your smile is as perfect as one of the greatest works of ancient art. I like your smile, and I like your laugh. You don't have to cover it up.

Floralie thought Nino sounded like Mama. Mama broke a vase once, just for the sake of it being broken. Papa made her glue the pieces back together, but the cracks were still visible, scars in the glass. Mama hadn't called them cracks or scars, though. All she said was, "Floralie, this is Notre Dame stuff," and she had been right. The broken vase did resemble the stained glass of Notre Dame, each shard forming part of the bigger picture. But Floralie was not a vase. She was not a window in Notre Dame. She was not a poem. Those only had pieces of them broken.

Nino, wrote Floralie, but she didn't write anything else for a few minutes. All the while, Nino waited patiently until Floralie was ready. *Nino, it's not just my teeth that are flawed. It's everything. Tom, Grandmama, Mrs. Coffrey . . . I've failed them all.* She bit her lip again, this time, not to hold back laughter, but tears. *Tom—he was supposed to go to university. But he gave it up. He gave it up to look after me and earn enough money for me to go to school. He sacrificed his dream for me to go to Mrs. Coffrey's, and I blew it. I got expelled, and I wasted his dream. I'm ugly in every sense of the word.*

Nino shook his head, but Floralie kept writing, *I am, Nino. Your poetry is lovely, but it's not real. The real world doesn't have time for imperfections. It moves too quickly, and if you're too broken, then you just get left in the dust. Trust me.*

Nino looked down. *I do trust you,* he wrote, and then after a moment, *but I don't agree with you.* Nino stared at Floralie for a long time, but when she did not write anything else, he added, *Well, we've got a firefly to catch, haven't we? When shall we leave for Mr. Tullier's?*

Floralie's eyebrows rose. *My grandmother will be taking me away in two days.*

So tomorrow?

We'd need ferry tickets and taxi money—goodness—we'd need money. How could I ever explain this to Tom?

The edges of Nino's lips curled up. *You have my complete faith, Floralie.*

Floralie made a "tuh" sound, but then sighed. *I'll do my best.*

The vase was not the only thing Mama broke and repaired. When the top button of Mama's favorite coat tore off, she replaced it with another. But this one was not the same round black button that had fallen off. This one was in the shape of a citron flower, white and centered with a shock of yellow. Mama said, "It's pretty, no? It's broken, too."

16

The next evening, after a long day of selling tulips and roses in the village, Floralie returned to the flower shop attic to find Nino giving Philomenos his supper. Floralie knelt beside Nino and dropped her flower basket between them, which was now speckled with silver coins. Nino's eyes lit up, and together they counted. Regrettably, it did not take long.

This'll barely cover the taxi ride, wrote Floralie. She slumped against a crate of crocuses and pulled the flower box from out from her shoulder bag. She opened it up, flicked through the flowers, and then closed it again.

It was completely and utterly inevitable—she was leaving for

Grandmama's tomorrow, and there was nothing she could do about it. *At least we tried.*

Are you honestly giving up? wrote Nino, eyes bulging in astonishment.

Well, what am I supposed to do, steal from Tom?

Nino simply stared, head tilted.

I can't—I could never, wrote Floralie. *I'd get in such tr*

"Floralie?" The voice sounded from far away, but still sent shivers down Floralie's spine.

Tom.

Floralie and Nino exchanged looks of horror.

"Floralie, are you up there?"

Footsteps.

Go—hide! wrote Floralie, and Nino snapped shut his notebook. He scooped up Philomenos and wildly began to search for a hiding place.

Floralie shoved the flower box back into her bag and whispered, "Quick—in here." She heaved open an old tulip crate large enough to hold a small person.

The footsteps grew louder. Nino's eyes flashed toward the door, and he scrambled into the box—

Chink. The doorknob turned.

"Floralie, are you up h—" Tom's jaw dropped.

Nino froze.

"Who are you?" shot Tom.

Nino stared.

"Speak to me, boy, who are you?" Tom clenched his fists and bolted for Nino, grabbing the scruff of his shirt.

"Please—stop! He can't talk," begged Floralie, scrambling over to Nino and Tom.

"You know this urchin?" growled Tom.

"He's not an urchin; he's my friend."

"*Please.*" Tom huffed. "I can tell an orphan a mile away. Tattered shoes, grimy hands—"

Nino shoved his hands in his pockets.

"Tell me his name, Floralie. We must turn him in—what's his name?"

"N—" started Floralie. Nino shot her a look of fear, and suddenly, she understood why Nino had made her promise never to tell his name. "Norman. Norman Clairoux. He's not an orphan. He works—er—at the library. See, the librarian there, Delphine Clairoux, she's his grandmother. That's who he lives with. She'll tell you." Floralie felt as if she were climbing an evergreen tree with no promises of getting down. "Norman thought you knew he was visiting. I told him he was allowed. I'm sorry, I should have asked."

Tom sighed and let Nino go. "Yes, you should have, Floralie. This—" He ran his hands up his face and through his hair. "*This* is why Grandmama wants to take you away, Flory. Don't you see? You just *can't keep out of trouble!*"

Hot tears stung Floralie's eyes. "*I know.*" The words slithered out like garden snakes.

"Well, come on, then. We'll take Norman back to his grandmother. And we'll discuss your behavior *later.*"

Floralie nodded, and the three left for the library.

Some nights, Floralie heard Mama cursing the Lord's name in the kitchen. Floralie would ask her to let her help with the dishes or the laundry. Mama said, "It's not that, my wildflower. Don't you worry about me."

But Papa would come home and hit Mama like a dog.

Floralie would watch, and later that night, she would say, "Mama, I want you to be happy."

Mama handed Floralie a blue bugloss flower. It felt sad. It felt like lies. Then, she said, "I am."

But Floralie cried because Mama believed that was the truth.

17

When Floralie, Tom, and Nino arrived at the library, they found Miss Clairoux in the biography section, reorganizing a shelf.

"M-Miss Clairoux?" said Floralie. She hadn't realized how afraid she felt until she heard the trembling of her own voice. But she shook it off. She *couldn't* ruin Nino's life, not his, too.

Miss Clairoux shelved her last book and turned to Floralie. "Ah! *Ma chérie*, is that you, Floralie?"

"Yes," choked Floralie. She swallowed. "It's me—me and Norman—you know, your grandson who organizes the *Greek poetry* section."

Floralie prayed Miss Clairoux would play along.

Miss Clairoux tipped up her chin. "Ah," she said, crow's feet appearing at the corners of her eyes. "Ah yes. *Norman*, my, my, I wondered where he had wandered off to. Now, is someone *else* with you, Floralie?"

"Oh—yes, how rude of me." Floralie turned to Tom. "Tom, this is Miss Clairoux. Miss Clairoux, this is my brother, Tom Laurel."

"Pleasure," said Tom. "I've come to return Norman. I found him in our attic with Floralie and thought it *most* inappropriate. As such, in the *highly unlikely event* that Floralie and Norman see each other again, I would prefer if such a meeting were arranged and facilitated by either you or myself."

Miss Clairoux bowed her head. "Indeed, Mr. Laurel. I thank you from the depth of my heart for returning—ah—Norman."

"Of course, Miss Clairoux."

"Oh, but before you go," piped up Miss Clairoux before Tom could turn, "I wonder if I might have a chat with Floralie. In private."

Tom eyed Miss Clairoux. "Of what nature?"

Miss Clairoux gave a flourish of her hand and said, "Oh, nothing to fuss over, just a . . . a little girly chat." She held a hand to her mouth, blocking Floralie from the conversation the way so many had done at Mrs. Coffrey's school, then whispered to Tom, "Poor thing hasn't got a mother to explain it all to her."

Tom's cheeks flushed, and he agreed, "Ten minutes, precisely."

"But of course," said Miss Clairoux, and Tom sent a stern gaze down to Floralie before turning and leaving the library.

After the door slammed shut, the three were left in silence. Miss Clairoux stood, arms crossed and smiling wryly. "So," she said. "Which one of you is going to tell me what this is all about? Shall it be you, Floralie? Or perhaps *Norman?*"

"We're sorry," started Floralie. "It's just—it's just—" Her throat tightened; she couldn't hold it in anymore. "I've got to go to Giverny."

Miss Clairoux's eyes widened. "Giverny?"

Floralie burst into tears, and it all came tumbling out. Everything. Grandmama, the dried flowers, Mama, and, finally, her and Nino's plans of traveling to France. And Miss Clairoux listened the entire time, nodding here and there, saying nothing but an occasional "mmm" and "uh-huh."

When she finished, Floralie looked to Miss Clairoux in fear that she might say something pitiful, but she did not. She simply stood, head tilted up and her expression unreadable. When she finally spoke, she said, "I'm very sorry to tell you, *ma chérie*, but I think your ten minutes are just about up."

"I should go, then," whispered Floralie. "Thanks for not turning us in," and she swiveled for the door.

But Miss Clairoux spoke promptly. "My dear," was what she said, as if catching Floralie with a fishhook.

Floralie turned. Miss Clairoux had a most determined expression on her face. "Stories are skittish things, you know. A bit like—*comment dit-on?*—ah, fireflies. Yes. They dance through your hair and flit through your fingers, but when one lands in the palm of your hand, you've got to catch it."

"What do you mean?" said Floralie. Miss Clairoux was beginning to sound like Nino.

"I *mean*, there's a story flitting about your very palm, young lady, and you'd best be off catching it now." A smile played at the corners of her wizened mouth, and she swept over to a section labeled TRAVEL and began pulling books. "You will need adult supervision of course, me"—she tossed two books to the floor—"food, we can buy along the way, a slate and stylus for Nino to write to me—would you mind grabbing that, dear? We'll bring the rat, of course—*mouse*, sorry, Philomenos—and what else . . . oh. And a note ensuring your safety for Mr. Laurel."

"Tom," breathed Floralie. Her stomach squirmed as if someone had let loose a jar of—*ah,* thought Floralie—that would be the fireflies. "But, Miss Clairoux, I don't understand. Why are you helping us? You have a life here, a job, a whole *library*. Why run off to France with us?"

A twinkle caught Miss Clairoux's eye. "Indulge an old maid's wanderlust, *ma chérie*. Give me one last adventure."

Floralie half smiled, and Miss Clairoux strained her neck

toward the door as if listening. "Now," she whispered, "if my ears aren't failing me yet, I'd say Mr. Laurel has made his way back home, up the stairs—rather loudly—and into his room for a calming spot of tea—chamomile, with"—she tilted her head—"ah-ha! Two spoons of honey."

Floralie and Nino exchanged glances of astonishment. Miss Clairoux stopped her frantic book-pulling, in her right hand, *Treasures of Italy*, and in her left, *Switzerland's Best Cheeses*. She lowered her voice and said, "And now he's watching that grandfather clock of his. Waiting."

Floralie looked down to her hands. The ink of the poems there had gone faint. Nino caught Floralie's gaze and took her hand in his. He examined the poems, eyes narrowed, then took a pen from his pocket. He traced three words with his forefinger, then underlined them: *Be a wildflower.* The words had been Floralie's mother's favorites. Mama had spun them into poems, into lullabies, into dances, and oh, had they danced like wildflowers to Mama's out-of-tune humming . . .

Floralie took a breath. "Okay. Okay, let's go."

Miss Clairoux clasped together her hands. "Excellent."

The seventh night in a row that Papa came home the same way, stumbling, slurring, shouting, Floralie found a full-bloomed rose atop two buds on her pillow. When it was time for bed and Papa's shouts could be heard from downstairs, Tom whispered to Floralie, "Tell no one."

Secrets grew like wildflowers in the back of her throat.

18

Tom—

Gone to France for a few days. Don't worry, be back soon.

—Floralie

P.S. I'm sorry.

Floralie quick-kissed the note, then slid it under the door before turning her back to the cottage. She felt afraid. She hardly had a clue where she was going, and she didn't even know whether Mama was still alive.

Miss Clairoux stood under a streetlamp across the road. She was dressed in a long emerald coat and cloche hat, and she held her cane out in front of her. Nino stood beside her, Philomenos peeping out from his hole-speckled pocket.

You've got the flower box? wrote Nino as Floralie neared them.

Floralie nodded and patted her bag.

A smile spread over Miss Clairoux's lips and wind swept through her silver hair. "Ah yes," she whispered. "There are stories in the air tonight."

The moon rose like a buoy at the edge of the sea. Following in its path of silver light drifted a ferryboat carrying Floralie, Nino, and Miss Clairoux all the way from England to France. Miss Clairoux had dozed off a few seats away from Floralie, hat flopped over her eyes. Floralie and Nino had claimed a row of seats and were lying head-to-head along the row.

A note landed on Floralie's nose. *You awake?*

Yeah, wrote Floralie, tossing the note back over her head to Nino.

Can't sleep.

Me neither. I keep thinking about Tom.

There was a long pause until Nino wrote back. *I keep thinking about your hands.*

My hands? Floralie almost laughed.

Yes, your hands. Remember the first day I met you, and there were words all over them? Like today? The words keep appearing. And then fading. Like heartbeats, pulsing in and out, in and out.

Oh. Floralie didn't laugh at Nino's poetics this time, for she felt far too fearful of what he was going to ask next.

I don't think I know much about you, Floralie, wrote Nino. *You keep things inside. But no matter how much you may disagree, your words matter. Will you write me a poem? About the letters on your hands?*

*I—*Floralie took a breath. *I already wrote one. A bunch, actually. Only one was any good. It was a while ago, I couldn't sleep, but . . . you'll look at me differently.*

Yes. I probably will.

Floralie didn't write back for quite some time, simply let the boat rock her in gentle rhythms, gentle heartbeats. Nino was right about one thing, and that was that words were like heartbeats. And so was water. And all three had this in common: Each could grant you breath, but could suffocate you just as well.

The words that slipped out of Floralie's fingers were these: *I'm afraid.*

What felt like hours later, Nino tossed back the paper. *You don't have to be,* he wrote. *I want to look at you like I know you.*

Like you're not a stranger. I want to meet you.

Floralie traced the words on her hand, blood pulsing in her ears. When Floralie and Nino had first exchanged secrets, Floralie had told him the truth about her mother, but not the whole truth. The whole truth was that Mama had, indeed, been taken, but not by bandits or pirates like in fairy tales. She had been sent to an asylum by Grandmama. Floralie knew Mama wasn't insane, though—how could she be? Not Mama with a laugh like bells, not Mama with eyes green enough for gardens to grow; no, Mama was not insane. They had stolen her. Locked her away for no good reason.

The ink on Floralie's skin was faded, but Floralie had memorized the poem.

Okay, she wrote, and then she began:

> *Dollhouse*
> *By Floralie Alice Laurel*
>
> *When I was small,*
> *We lived in a dollhouse.*
> *Six windows wide and two windows tall,*
> *Our doorway painted poppy red*
> *My brother said to complement the flower beds,*
>
> *But I know now those poppy pigments were to grant us*
> *Sleep in sleepless nights,*
> *And still the neighbors would laugh*
> *And say again,*
> *We must be made of porcelain.*

But as my rose-painted smile grew
Tired like my father's wine cabinet hinges,
I watched my mother wither
To a paper doll
Every tear melting her paper skin
She became azalea petal thin

Until she disappeared into air
Leaving nothing but a long-forgotten trail,
Perfume and lullabies, pointe shoes and memories,
Because regrets and nostalgia
Fog the windows all around,
But I remember clearly now:

When I was small,
We lived in a dollhouse.
Six windows wide and two windows tall,
Our doorway painted poppy flower red.
Three porcelain dolls collecting dust on a shelf,
We turned to ghosts in that haunted dollhouse.

Nino didn't write back. Floralie liked that about him. The way he didn't want to know her to pity her or judge her. He just wanted to know her.

19

The ferry arrived in Calais, France, early next morning. Workmen clattered around the port, golden dawn spattering the deck. Floralie sucked in the salty air, remembering the last time she had been in Calais, the day she had believed she would never breathe French air again. She was wrong.

Miss Clairoux ushered Floralie and Nino through the bustle, and when they reached the street, Nino waved down a taxi.

"To the train station, please," trilled Miss Clairoux in French, and the three hopped into the cab.

The entire taxi ride, not once did Floralie's eyes leave the window. She felt as if she had yearned so ardently for France for so long that she had gone numb to the hunger for it . . . until now. Until now that she was home, until now that she could taste, swallow the milk-and-honey sweetness of it all.

When the taxi pulled up to the train station, Floralie hopped out and breathed in the scene. French flooded her ears—mothers babbling to children, newspaper boys calling out to train riders, taxi drivers chattering with passengers. Though both her parents had originated from England, Floralie had learned French before English, and the language still sounded like music to her.

Miss Clairoux handed the taxi driver a few coins, and then shut the door. As the taxi rattled off, however, something across the street caught Floralie's eye. It was a large banner draped over a building with a heading that read: LE BALLET ROYALE DE PARIS PRESÉNTE GISELLE, and below that were the dates and place: JUILLET 3–16, PALAIS GARNIER, PARIS. The banner featured a ballerina with her leg in arabesque. She wore the exact same costume Floralie's mother had worn when she had played the role of Giselle nearly four years ago.

That had been her last principal part, her last role before she got sick. Though it wasn't an ordinary sort of sick . . . she didn't cough or sneeze or itch. But she did stop dancing around the house. She stopped lilting her off-key ballet songs. She stopped laughing for the most part, and when she did laugh, it didn't sound like bells anymore; it sounded cracked like an old, decaying redwood tree. Except she wasn't old. She was young, especially for a mother. When the ballet kicked her out, she stopped wearing her wedding ring. She stopped calling Tom her *petit étudiant*, and she stopped calling Floralie her wildflower. In fact, most days, she just stayed in her bed. And one day, she wouldn't come out.

"Ready?" said Miss Clairoux, turning to Floralie and Nino.

Floralie shook herself back to reality. "Yes."

Floralie gripped Nino's and Miss Clairoux's hands as they boarded a train that looked exactly the same as the one Floralie had boarded for England three years ago just after Papa's death— same hibiscus-red passenger cars, same gold-framed windows— and she could have sworn the blue-coated steward ushering them aboard was the same as well.

When they settled into their seats, Miss Clairoux pulled out a braille book.

Philomenos crawled out of Nino's pocket and took a nibble at the book. Miss Clairoux yanked the book away and yelped, "Argh! That *mouse*"—but she caught herself short and gave a quick huff— "deserves a story just as much as any other."

After the ticket master punched their tickets, the train engine roared to life, and Miss Clairoux read aloud from her braille book of the magnificent adventures of *Alice in Wonderland*. When she came to the part with the Cheshire Cat (at which Philomenos wrinkled his nose), however, Miss Clairoux's breath grew heavy, and her voice drifted away, slowly, softly, until she was fast asleep.

Floralie was drifting, too, but not into dreamland, not even into her own garden wonderland. Her thoughts were leeched on to one thing only—Mama's ballet.

Nino? wrote Floralie, as the train chugged past a field of sunflowers.

Yeah?

Did you see the banner? Before we left?

Nino shook his head no.

It was for Giselle.

Giselle? Isn't that one of those African animals? Kind of like a moose-zebra?

That's "gazelle," silly. Floralie giggled. *"Giselle" is a name. But it's also a ballet about a peasant girl—that's Giselle—who marries a man who was already betrothed to another girl. When Giselle finds out, she goes mad and dies. And then the wilis come, which are these ghostlike women, and Giselle becomes one of them. They haunt some men, and it all ends with Giselle's former fiancé crying over Giselle at her grave.*

Nino whisper-laughed. *Sounds cheerful.*

My mother played Giselle. It was her last starring role. And I just thought that maybe . . . Floralie scratched out the words and wrote instead, *I just thought it was interesting.* What she had wanted to write was, *We should see it, since we're so close to Paris anyway*, but she held the words back. They had come to France for one reason, and one reason only: to find Mama, not some ghost of her.

Mama and Floralie watched the family cat give birth to seven kittens. Their bodies were slimy, but small and fragile, like snowballs. Mama gave the kittens away to various neighbors, all except one, who had died within twenty minutes.

They buried her in the garden and named her Renée. Mama laid a pile of autumn leaves and a sprig of oregano over the patch of dirt.

That night, as Mama tucked Floralie into bed, Floralie asked Mama if she thought the surviving kittens would be okay. Mama said, "I don't know. But I do know they're home. And I do know you're home."

"Oh," said Floralie.

"Home is wherever, in the morning, you are new again. And you are loved because of it."

20

Four hours and another taxi ride later, Floralie, Nino, and Miss Clairoux rolled down a cobbled road walled by shops and houses more ivy than stone. At last, they pulled up to a long stretch of tulips with a narrow dirt path cut through it, leading to a house. But not just *any* house. This was Monet's manor. Miss Clairoux paid the driver, and the three stepped out of the taxi and into the tulips. Floralie squinted through the sunlight to the house at the end of the field.

She took a breath. "This is it," she said. Her heart was racing, her ears were buzzing, and her fingers were tingling. Tom would figure out where she had gone soon enough, and Grandmama could arrive within hours. And Mama wasn't getting any younger in that asylum of hers; Floralie imagined the room, dark, dank, small. Mama was a wildflower. Mama was a viscaria flower. She needed space, and she needed freedom; she needed room to dance, and she needed Floralie. They had to find her fast.

Floralie led the way down the path. Pebbles crunched below her feet and the sunshine sunk into her skin as she made her way through the tulip field. Mama used to say that Giverny was so quiet you could hear the sky move, the clouds shift, and the stars shiver like wind chimes. "They're still there, you know," Mama would say. "The stars. Even in daytime. Even when you can't see them." And then they would listen, and Mama would say, "Hear that? It's raining in Singapore."

Floralie listened to the clouds as hard as she could. The closer she came to the house, the louder the clouds pulsed—or perhaps that was her heart.

The house was even larger than Floralie remembered, and she recalled neighborhood children calling it the *Château de Giverny*—Castle of Giverny. The front was rather unkempt, overgrown bushes and trees and vines swallowing the house, as if into another world—a wonderland, perhaps. One thing, however, was different from how Floralie remembered, and that was the bright green shutters. They had always been kept open when Floralie had lived in Giverny, but now, all were closed.

As they climbed the seven green steps to the door, Miss Clairoux whispered, "*Es-tu prêt?*" She flicked a bead of sweat from her forehead and smoothed back her hair, which was significantly more frizzed than when they had begun their journey.

"*Oui*, Miss Clairoux," said Floralie, "I'm ready."

Floralie clutched her bag to her chest. Her heart beat against the box inside. She knocked. The door creaked.

"*Qui est là?*" came a grunt from the other side.

Floralie grabbed Nino's arm.

The door chinked open, and a man appeared. He smelled of stale coffee and mothballs. He was tall, thin—skeletal almost—and he wore a faded brown bathrobe with tattered pockets and drooping, too-long sleeves. His back was hunched and his lips chapped. But though his eyes were sunken behind a pair of silver-rimmed spectacles, they held the blue of a hundred forget-me-nots; they were the only things alive about him.

Nevertheless, excitement bubbled up inside Floralie, and she spluttered, "It's—it's you—you're *here*!"

Sylvestre Tullier gave a short *hmph* and then grunted in French, "Where else would I be? Live here, don't I?" He scanned Floralie, Nino, and Miss Clairoux up and down, then narrowed his eyebrows at Miss Clairoux. "You?"

Floralie looked up to Miss Clairoux. "You know him?"

"I—I—of course I don't *know* him. Don't be silly, *ma chérie!*"

"Hmph," said Mr. Tullier.

"Oh. Er—all right." Floralie cleared her throat. "Well, then, Mr. Tullier, *je m'appelle Floralie Laurel. Et c'est mon ami—ah—Norman—*" said Floralie, remembering again her promise with Nino. "*Et mon autre amie, Madame Delphine Clairoux.*"

Mr. Tullier's eyes widened, but for only a moment. "Floralie and Delphine. Such . . . *intéressant* names."

Floralie wasn't quite sure what Mr. Tullier was on about, but she took a breath before continuing. "I sell your flowers. In England—Whitterly End, to be precise. My brother, Tom, sells them in the shop, and I sell in the street, and I just—"

"Spit it out, mademoiselle," said Mr. Tullier, rolling his eyes.

"Okay, I know you're busy, but I just had a question for you. It's about this box I found, filled with dried flowers—I want to know their meanings. But I can't find your floriography any—"

"*Get out.*" Mr. Tullier's voice froze to ice.

"What?" said Floralie.

"I said get out! Now! Go! *Allez!*" and he jerked to slam the door, but Floralie grabbed the edge.

"No, *please*," begged Floralie, but Mr. Tullier was too strong, and the door slammed shut. The clink of a lock twisting sent invisible spiders down Floralie's spine.

Now what do we do? wrote Nino.

Floralie bit the inside of her lip, but wrote back, *I'm going to stay here, in Giverny. I'm going to find her. You both can go home. I'm sorry I wasted your time.* Nino translated the words into braille for Miss Clairoux.

"Nonsense!" exclaimed Miss Clairoux. "I will have none of that, *ma chérie*. We'll stay the night here, somewhere. Our Monsieur Tullier"—her voice swung up to a peculiarly melodic lilt when she said the name—"he will come around. Trust me." But then her voice wavered on the words. "Let's find a place to stay. Come."

The three came upon an inn, roof sloping and red paint chipping. Shutters hung at odd angles, and window cracks were patched with sheets of gray fabric. An off-kilter sign above the door read: L'OASIS DE VIEIL HOMME, or, in English, "Old Man's Oasis."

"It's not ideal. But it's warm and it's cheap," said Floralie.

The innkeeper grunted something about "keeping the children under control," then handed Miss Clairoux the room key, and the three trundled up the winding staircase to their room. It was a dank space, three skinny beds taking up the majority of the room. The walls were bare except for the lace-curtained windows that looked over to the street below.

Nino collapsed onto one of the beds immediately, and Miss

Clairoux fell into the bed beside him. Floralie, however exhausted she felt, did not want to sleep. Guilt slithered through Floralie's curls and into her ears. She felt positively *stupid*. She had put her friends at risk for what? A mother she didn't even know what had happened to? And even if she knew what happened to Mama, would that truly change anything? Would Mama take her back? *Of course she would,* Floralie thought, trying to soothe herself, but her hands jittered with the possibility that she would never be home again. Because home was wherever Mama was.

Within minutes of leaning against the gray wall, Floralie began to feel ghosts all around her, and she wanted to learn their names . . . They were names she knew long ago, had once memorized just as well as Mama's letter, but now were forgotten. Confused and lost and spirited away, to gardens far, far away.

Mama's eyes were bloodshot. The footsteps pounded. Tom squeezed Floralie's hand as they watched from the crack in the kitchen door. Mama stood from her seat at the dining table and went to open the front door. The minute she unlatched the lock, a body fell into her. It was a man, horribly, terribly familiar, yet his face ten times as red.

"Getoffome," shouted Papa, his words slurring together. "Get off! I hate you!"

"I know, John-Paul. I know. Come lie down. Come to your bed."

"How could I ever've loved you? You're ugly." And he spat in Mama's face.

Tom covered Floralie's eyes, but she heard Mama say simply, "I know, John-Paul. I know. Come lie down. Come to your bed."

That was how it always went at the beginning, before Papa's shouts became contagious, and before everything began to fall apart. But Mama never did cry. No, Mama never cried.

Instead, she put a basket of spruce pine needles on the windowsill and said, "These will give us hope. These will give us light."

21

Later that afternoon, the ghosts tugged at Floralie's hair, yanking her outside to the streets of Giverny, alone. She wandered down Rue Claude Monet and into the village. The roads wound like Viscaria's favorite pearl necklace. The buildings played a dress-up game: shopwindows draped in scarves of vines and flowers, and doors painted so bright the people paled. With each footstep Floralie took, a memory leaped into her mind as if it had just won a game of hide-and-go-seek.

The peculiarly raised cobblestone at the edge of Monsieur Géroux's bakery: Eight years ago, Floralie had tripped over it on her way into the bakery to buy bread with Tom. She had made quite the fuss, so Tom assuaged her with a butterscotch teacake from Monsieur Géroux.

Madame Lévêque's yellow rose garden: Floralie had passed that every day on her way to school, and each time she passed, she had wondered what made the roses yellow instead of red. Mama used to say that Madame Lévêque must have watered them with lemon juice; it was only now that Floralie realized she had been joking.

And then there was Madame "Elephant Ears" Elliard's scarlet-shuttered window: Whenever Floralie bicycled by when she was little, Madame Elliard would poke out her head and screech at Floralie for her bicycle making too much a clatter, even though all the children rode bicycles through the village. The person Madame Elliard *really* didn't like was Viscaria, who Madame Elliard saw as irresponsible, newfangled, and ridiculously untamable. Floralie supposed Mama was indeed all of those things—but those attributes were what made Mama, Mama.

It was then, as she was remembering Madame Elliard, that Miss Clairoux appeared as if out of nowhere. Earlier, both she and Nino had settled in for a nap.

"*Ma chérie*, it's getting late," she said.

"I know," said Floralie. She wanted to say, *I miss this place. I miss it even while I'm here, standing within it, I miss it.* But the words caught in her throat. Instead, she said, "What do you think of Mr. Tullier?"

Miss Clairoux looped her arm through Floralie's as Floralie led her through an archway. "What do I think of him?" said Miss Clairoux. "Well, I think he is rather disagreeable—before you get to know him."

"But . . . you don't know him."

Miss Clairoux's cheeks flushed. "I . . . I think he has the potential to be a gentleman. He has the talent for it, but uses it sparingly."

"Doesn't that bother you?"

Miss Clairoux fumbled with her hat, then turned to Floralie. "So many *questions*, my dear. But no, I wouldn't say it bothers me. It's just a skin; everyone's got one in some way or another. We'll peel back his, *ma chérie*. I promise you that."

"Miss Clairoux?" said Floralie.

"Mmm?"

"Do you think it's possible to like someone because of the things that are wrong with them?"

With agile fingers, Miss Clairoux plucked a lemony rose from Madame Lévêque's garden. She ran her fingers along the petals in a spiral motion, taking in all the twists and turns of the rose from the inside out.

"People are like roses, *ma chérie*. They've got lots of layers. I think Mr. Tullier's a bit like a rose, don't you think?"

Miss Clairoux handed Floralie the rose, and she took it with gentle hands. She peeled off a few petals, and they fluttered to the ground. Mama was like a rose. In every way, she was like a rose—beautiful, vivacious, lovely. "D'you think Nino's got layers?"

Miss Clairoux closed tight her eyes and nodded deeply. "Mmm, yes, I do, very much so."

"And Tom?"

Miss Clairoux nodded again.

Floralie bit her lip. "And . . . and me? Am I like a rose?"

Miss Clairoux stopped her nodding. "Why ever would you ask that?" Her voice was incredulous.

"Just . . . do you think I am?"

"I do think so," said Miss Clairoux. "I think people live as the outmost layer of their rose. And that outmost layer can't see all that it's protecting inside. It may see itself as nothing more than a shell, simply because it doesn't have the proper angle of view. That's why you can't use your eyes all the time. You've got to feel those layers instead."

Floralie didn't like that answer much. Because if layers were made up of *feelings*, well, then certainly Floralie was nothing but hollow. That was how she felt. Hollow. Hollow as the gap in her teeth. Mama wasn't around to fill that gap anymore, and Nino . . . Floralie just wished he would *speak* to her. He knew everything about her, and she wanted to know him. But he wouldn't let her. Floralie plucked off the last petal, then dropped the stem as well.

As Floralie and Miss Clairoux passed a crumbly-stone shop, Miss Clairoux stopped short. "*Ma chérie*, does it smell like books to you?"

Floralie looked up to the shop sign—but it wasn't a shop at all. Floralie's heart pounded. In spidery script, the sign above the door read, LA BIBLIOTHÈQUE DE CLAIROUX.

"Miss Clairoux . . . is there something you haven't told me?"

"Whatever could you—" but Miss Clairoux did not finish. Her face grew ashen, and her mouth, limp. "My father's library."

"What do you mean—you've *lived* here?"

Miss Clairoux half smiled.

Floralie was flabbergasted. "What—how—when were you going to tell me this? Is this why you came here?"

But Miss Clairoux was not paying attention. She slowly approached the building and ran her fingers along the stone, whispering, "I can't believe it's still *here*."

"Miss Clairoux—answer me!" insisted Floralie, hurrying to Miss Clairoux's side. "This is why you came here, isn't it? To find the library. You knew it was here."

Miss Clairoux turned to Floralie. "Yes," she said, sighing. "Yes, in part, I came for a library. I never in a thousand dreams would have imagined my *father's* would somehow still be standing, still bear our name. But in part, I came for something lost. Someone . . ."

"But who—" Floralie stopped short. She knew. "You came to see Mr. Tullier, too, didn't you?"

Miss Clairoux closed tight her eyes and said, "I think we'd better take this inside."

Mama filled the windows with juniper flowers "for protection." The tiny petals became perfect shells to guard the house's sacred insides. Those messy insides. Ugly insides that Mama came to love.

22

Miss Clairoux pushed open the library door, a tiny bell tinkling from above. Dimness enclosed Floralie in a hug that reminded her of one of Tom's: familiar, comforting, yet distant. Perhaps, as Nino would have put it, *melancholic.* She had been to this library before—simply hadn't realized it had a name. It had always been simply, *"la bibliothèque."* Many a time as a toddler, she had sat on the threadbare rug, flipping through books she knew not how to read, but all the same pretended to. Mama would call her ever so smart, and Tom would scoff and say she was simply *theatrical.*

Now three boxes were stacked on the rug, the topmost one overfilled with books. In fact, the entire library was filled with boxes upon boxes of books. The shelves were half naked, stripped of everything but a few dozen faded, stained, and tattered books, and a small collection of lion-faced bookends.

"Looks like they're closing down," muttered Floralie.

"We are."

Floralie spun around twice before she caught sight of the woman. Tiny, chestnut-haired, and pale-lipped, she blended in perfectly with the books and the boxes and the dimness.

Miss Clairoux's mouth did jumping jacks. "But—but where shall the books live?"

The woman shrugged. "Zey will get thrown away, I suppose. Ze place is running out of money. Ze family who owned it years ago—ah, *comment dit-on?*—vanquished?"

"Vanished," corrected Floralie.

"*Oui*, zey vanished. We 'aven't a choice now. Ze parents are dead, and zeir little girl, well, we 'aven't any idea where she's gone. She must be very old, though—zis was all many years ago, before I was even born."

"And you, Madame—ah—"

"Favreau. Édith Favreau."

"Yes, Madame Favreau. Your family has been keeping up the library?"

Madame Favreau nodded. "Ze least we could do. Henri Clairoux was my *grandmère*'s best friend. 'E once paid for my father's fever treatment, so after Henri died, we decided to keep up 'is beloved *bibliothèque*. I will be sad to see it go. But please, look around. We're not closing until next week."

"*Merci*, Madame Favreau," said Miss Clairoux, and she turned to Floralie and whispered, "There should be a nook in the back for us to chat, how about that?"

Floralie nodded and followed Miss Clairoux to the back of the library, where indeed, a tiny reading space was nestled between three bookshelves. In the corner was an overstuffed armchair, big enough for the both of them (and probably a spare), and Miss Clairoux sat, patting the velvet cushion for Floralie.

Miss Clairoux let loose a hum. "When I was young, I had a boy very close to my heart, much like Nino is to yours. We grew up together. He was born blind, like me. But something changed for him. He would tell me he could see things—things that felt like joy, and things that felt like sadness. Just outlines, faint colors. I thought he was going mad, but really, he was getting better. By the time we were seventeen, his blindness had disappeared entirely. Also by then, we were in love and engaged."

"How was he cured, though? There's no cure for blindness . . . is there?"

Miss Clairoux cracked a smile. "He said luck. I say angels. We never brought him to a doctor about it—didn't want him reduced to experiments, et cetera. Now, where was I? Ah yes. As a child,

I rarely took much curiosity in how things looked, for sight is such a strange concept to me—how can I imagine something I have never experienced? Color, such a perplexing idea. When I was little, I thought it just as unreal as magic. But as I grew older, and I gathered my braille books and read the most beautiful descriptions of colors—sunsets and moonrises, forests and villages—I began to feel a longing to *know*. I needed someone who understood what it was to both be able to see and not see."

"And your fiancé . . ."

Miss Clairoux nodded. "Yes. I asked him what the world looked like. But he would not describe anything to me. He simply refused, saying the world was too monstrous for fragile things like me to imagine how it looked. Me? Fragile? Ha! He said I was better off blind, which I gave him a nice smack across the cheek for—that, I do regret, of course, but can you *imagine*? Your greatest love telling you you're better off blind?" Miss Clairoux clucked and shook her head. "Of course, it was more complicated than that, but those are stories for some other days. I suppose, as they say, that was the straw that broke the camel's back."

"But what happened to him? After . . ."

Miss Clairoux swallowed audibly. "He married."

"Oh," said Floralie. "I'm sorr—"

"Don't be. Not for me. I am happy, and I like to believe he was, too. Today, though, I've been . . . second-guessing that." Miss

Clairoux sighed and patted Floralie's knee. "All the same, I left him and never fell in love again. And that's that."

"That's so sad."

Miss Clairoux shrugged. *"C'est la vie, ma chérie, c'est la vie."*

They sat in silence for much time before Floralie finally said, "It was Mr. Tullier, wasn't it?"

Miss Clairoux squeezed Floralie's hand. *"Oui, ma chérie."*

"So why would you want to see him again?"

"I . . . he might not realize just yet, but . . . we have a similarity."

"And what might that be?"

Miss Clairoux's forehead wrinkled, silver eyes receded. "I lost a child. And he lost two."

"Oh," said Floralie. "I'm sorry."

"Me too," said Miss Clairoux, and they sat in silence for some time.

But Floralie had another question. "I thought you said you never married. The only man you ever loved was . . ." And then it dawned on her. "It was the same child—one of them, anyway."

"Yes."

"He died?"

"No. And 'she.'"

Floralie's heart rattled against her rib cage. "So what happened to her?"

"I don't know. I've been told she . . . she had some trouble. I've been told she went mad."

A drop of sweat slid down Floralie's forehead. "That's impossible—how—*Miss Clairoux*—does this mean . . . ? The letters . . . *V.A.C.*"

Miss Clairoux nodded. "Viscaria Alice Clairoux."

"Why didn't you tell me?"

When she spoke, Miss Clairoux's voice quaked. "Because I thought you would hate me. And you have every right to."

"Why—why on earth would I hate you?"

"Viscaria was not born with that name, you know—I had named her Alice, after *Alice in Wonderland*. That was Mr. Tullier and my favorite book as children. Well, Viscaria took on this new name of hers when she ran away from home. From me. I was the exact way to Viscaria as your grandmama Laurel is to you. I wouldn't let Viscaria do what she loved most—dance. I was more afraid for her future than for her happiness.

"And so she left me, forever. She was only a little girl, your age perhaps. Ran away to her father—Mr. Tullier—believing he was simply a family friend. After Mr. Tullier's wife died in childbirth, he employed Viscaria to take care of his other daughter. A newborn. The baby died soon after. But that's all I know of that story." Miss Clairoux's other hand found Floralie's, and she squeezed both of Floralie's tight. "Floralie, I didn't just come here to find the library, nor did I just come to find Mr. Tullier, not even Viscaria. I came here to meet my granddaughter."

Floralie couldn't help but beam. She threw her arms around Miss Clairoux, breathing in the smell of ancient books and old lady soap and maybe even a hint of viscaria flowers. Miss Clairoux gave a laugh, running her hands through Floralie's hair. Floralie's eyes ached with tears, not of sadness, not of anger, but happiness. That had never happened before. "*I'm happy I found you*," she whispered, pulling back from Miss Clairoux.

"Me too, *ma chérie*."

The two left the library, grandmother and granddaughter, hand in hand, *happy, happy, happy*.

Floralie and Miss Clairoux returned to the inn and woke a rather sleepy Nino to tell him all they had shared at the library. After the shock of it all passed, Floralie and Nino watched the colors spew out from the horizon at the dusty window back at the inn. People bustled below, not like the bustle of Whitterly End, though. Here, people stopped and said hello, chitter-chattered, and kept their shops open for an extra ten minutes if someone was in need. They exchanged hugs and kisses, and my-oh-my, was Giverny lovely. Floralie had forgotten how lovely Giverny was.

But then came the feather hat. The feather hat and the smell of prunes and sour lemons, wafting even upthrough the closed window. Floralie's heart thundered and dread seeped down her body like sap, clinging to every rib. *No.*

"She's here," she whispered. "Grandmama's here."

Mama kept but one photograph of her wedding day. In it, she wore a floor-length veil and a lace dress amidst a garden of half-wilted dogwood flowers. Papa was dressed up in black beside her, and Grandmama stood beside him. Mama smiled with thin lips, but her eyes were scared. Grandmama scowled, and Papa eyed Mama cautiously.

Whenever Mama told about the wedding, she said, "It was the best day of my life, second to your and Tom's births." But she said it with a clenched jaw and tight fists. Whenever Grandmama talked about it, she sneered, "That mother of yours was simply the beginning of the end. Of your father's end. Of my end. Our whole family's end." She would cluck her tongue and shake her head, and Papa would mutter, "It's best not to hold regrets." But Floralie knew too well that he did.

On the back of the photograph, Mama had written:

There is nothing comparable to fear.

It wraps itself around you, sinks into your

skin, makes a house in your lungs, sprouts butterfly

weeds around your heart. Every once in a while it will go out for groceries. You will believe you are free. You will get used to your lungs, soft breath; you will be okay.

But then you will feel a tap on your shoulder, a whisper in your ear: "I'm home."

23

Grandmama glided down the street, peacock feather bouncing up and down atop her head, then stopped at the sight of the inn. Floralie and Miss Clairoux snuck back into the inn, and once inside, Floralie swished back her curtain and slid down the wall, concealed from the outside world. *Please don't come in, please don't come in, please don't come in . . .*

She came in.

Nino and Miss Clairoux crouched over to Floralie. *It's going to be okay,* wrote Nino.

"We've got to get out of here," said Floralie as Miss Clairoux wrapped an arm around her and held her close. "I want to try Mr. Tullier again."

The doorknob jiggled. And then came the voice. "I *know* you're in there. They've told me where you are, and *I*"—she banged the door—"*intend*"—she kicked it—"*to find you!*" The wood creaked with one final tug, but stayed closed.

Floralie first considered jumping out the window, but it was a three-story drop. She heaved up the window anyway and poked her head out. Something was rusted—a glorious, rusted pipe, traveling from head to toe of the inn, just in arm's reach.

"The drainpipe," she said. "We can climb down the drainpipe."

Miss Clairoux's mouth went slack, and Nino eyed Floralie.

"It's our only choice."

All was silent as the jiggling grew fiercer, but at last, Miss Clairoux said, "*Oui, ma chérie.* I trust you."

And so out the window they crawled, Miss Clairoux first, then Nino, then Floralie, swinging onto the drainpipe. Their fingers built calluses as they descended, flakes of rust jabbing into Floralie's palms like thorns. Her arms quivered with the strength, and she pressed her heels into the pipe to stay balanced. When at last Floralie neared the ground, Miss Clairoux reached up and caught Floralie by the waist, pulling her to the cobbles.

"Down you go," said Miss Clairoux.

"We'd better go," said Floralie, "before Grandmama realizes we're gone."

And so Floralie, Nino, and Miss Clairoux scurried down the lavender-scented, lamp-lit street to the flower house of Claude Monet. When they arrived at Mr. Tullier's door again, he opened it, still wearing his tattered bathrobe and stony gaze.

"You again," he grunted. "I told you to scram."

"Please," begged Floralie. "Someone is following us."

"Not my problem," said Mr. Tullier.

"Please just give us a chance. We need a place to hide. We won't be a bother, we swear."

"No. *Au revoir, petite fille*," and Mr. Tullier made to slam the door again, but before he could, Floralie grabbed on to it, holding it open with all her strength.

And then Floralie remembered something from Viscaria's letter. Something marvelous. *You should know that Sylvestre was a great friend to me.* So Floralie pleaded as quick as her breath would allow, *"It's about finding Viscaria!"*

Mr. Tullier let go of the door. He stumbled back, shoulders hunched and eyes glossy, filled with nothing but forget-me-nots and ghosts. *"Viscaria,"* he whispered, as if making a wish on a dandelion clock. Then his jaw hardened, and the ghosts in his eyes ebbed into the corners. "How do you know her?"

Floralie crossed her arms, held up her chin. "She's my mother."

Mr. Tullier's lips parted, but no words came.

"I need your help," continued Floralie. "I've got to find her. She left me some flowers, and I've got to know what they mean. They're in your flower language, and you're my only hope. *Please.* I'm your granddaughter." The last word hung in the air like perfume, wafting around them and putting all four of them in a daze.

Mr. Tullier turned, slow as a rusted wheelbarrow, and muttered, "Well, come in if you're going to. No reason to let the draft in."

Floralie's heart fluttered, and she stepped into the house, followed by Nino and Miss Clairoux. The foyer was small and sickly yellow—the same color, Floralie thought, as Mr. Tullier's teeth. She supposed the yellow would be pretty, if only the windows were not shuttered. At the end of the foyer hung a painting composed of wild strokes and dancing colors—Monet's.

As Mr. Tullier led them through a yellow corridor, Miss Clairoux walked between Floralie and Nino and took both their hands. Floralie had a feeling it wasn't so much to steady herself, but to keep them safe, just in case. But Floralie was not afraid. Admittedly, Mr. Tullier could have given a warmer welcome, but she was *here*. She had found him, she was safe from Grandmama, and Mr. Tullier could find Mama. And then Mama could be free, and she could be with Floralie, together at last.

Something was not quite right about the walls, though, and it wasn't the yellow paint. Every now and then, something would brush up against Floralie's ankle or shoulder—vines. They grew from tiny cracks in the walls, between the floorboards, from under the shutters. The hallways twisted and sloped like tree roots, and how curious it was that the farther they ventured into the house, the more vines appeared. A few flowers bloomed in the dull light, appearing more frequently until the corridors became an aurora borealis of colors—zinnias, roses, tulips, azaleas, lilies, morning glories, violets . . . It was as if the place had been abandoned for years, left to nature's devices.

At last, they arrived at a door made of glass. Floralie knew this not because she could *see* the glass—it was covered in flowers—but because of the golden light blazing through from between the cracks in the petals and the vines.

However, just when Floralie thought Mr. Tullier was going to open the door, he strode right on past it. As they passed, Floralie dared ask, "What's that room?"

Mr. Tullier grunted, "That's off limits, is what that room is. No one goes in there, understand?"

Floralie and Nino nodded vigorously, but curiosity tugged at Floralie's mind. She felt close to something . . . She felt close to her wonderland, and she wanted to find out what was behind that door. *No,* she thought, *I am not a child anymore. Grown-ups do not give in to their wonderlands. Grown-ups don't even* have *wonderlands.*

Floralie's eyes stayed fixated on the door until Mr. Tullier turned a corner, and the door went out of view. Finally, he stopped at another door—though this one was rather ordinary compared to the last.

He pulled it open, a rack of pots rattling from inside. It was a small sitting room, painted entirely blue—walls, counters, tables. Mr. Tullier crossed through it, pulled open a second door, and led them into another dim, yellow-walled room. A lemony table set with fourteen chairs stood in the center of a red-and-white-tiled floor. Mr. Tullier gestured for them to sit.

"You must have a large family," said Floralie.

Mr. Tullier glared at her. "*Non,*" he spat. "It's just me."

Floralie wanted to say, *Well, you have me,* but she thought that would be rather forward. So she bit her lip and skipped across the tile floor, avoiding the white tiles like always.

Mr. Tullier narrowed his eyebrows. "*Mon Dieu,* you're just like her."

"Sorry—" started Floralie, confused. "Who?"

"Your mother. She used to do that skipping thing, too. Drove the cat mad staying out of her way."

Nino led Miss Clairoux over to the table, and they took their seats. Floralie sat beside Nino as Mr. Tullier grabbed an iron pot from the stovetop and poured a watery black liquid from it into four mugs.

"Here," he said, sloshing them around the table. Floralie took a sip from hers, and then stifled a cough as the lukewarm, bitter coffee slithered down her throat. She placed the mug back on the table.

Mr. Tullier lit a candle in the center of the table, and its glow beat gently like an unsteady heart against his wizened face. He and Floralie stared at each other for a moment before Mr. Tullier blurted, "*Well?*"

Floralie gripped the side of her chair and cleared her throat. "Well—we—I mean, I just need to know about your floriography. That's all, then I'll leave, honest. I found this box of flowers from my mother, and I've got to decode them to find her. That way, I can live with her instead of my nasty grandmother, and I can set her free. Here, see?" and Floralie pulled the box of flowers from her bag. She opened it and handed Mr. Tullier the letter.

Mr. Tullier adjusted his spectacles and read. When he finished, he stretched out a hand and slid the box closer to him. Carefully, he inspected the flowers before saying: "Tell me, now. Whatever happened to her? Viscaria?"

"I—I'd rather not tell, actually," said Floralie.

Mr. Tullier's lip curled. "Well, how about this: I don't tell you about my floriography until you tell me about Viscaria."

Floralie took a breath. "Okay. Okay, fine. But you should know that I don't really know. Not everything, anyway. I mean . . . What I know is—" She bit her lip and glanced to Nino. "She was a ballerina. And the year before she left, she started getting sad, and sometimes angry and forgetful. She broke down onstage one performance, and that's all I really know, because my father made me leave the theater. I only saw her once after that, and she wouldn't even talk, she just let me hold her hand." Floralie remember how fragile her mother's hand felt, like the bones were made of paper.

"And you have no idea where she went after that?" pushed Mr. Tullier, taking a swig of coffee.

"That's why I'm here, remember? All I know is—well, all I *think* is that she's in an asylum somewhere, but I don't know where or which one. She's not sick, though, or mad, I swear it. She was just different. And maybe she was sad, but she would never hurt someone, cross my heart," and Floralie crossed her heart. She squeezed shut her eyes, and then added ever so quietly, "But maybe if I *found* her, maybe I'd be able to get her out of there. And maybe we could be together again. Just the two of us. Maybe she'd start a new ballet company, and maybe she'd help me sell some art, and maybe we could send Tom to university and have a nice house in the country like we used to, except it wouldn't have to be as big; it could be really, really small, and that would be okay, if only she was . . ." *Here.* The word stuck to the back of her throat like molasses.

Mr. Tullier's forget-me-not eyes clouded over. He lowered his coffee mug and said, "So, essentially, what you're telling me is my daughter ended up in a nuthouse?"

"*No*—" shot Floralie, but then she lowered her eyes, a curl slipping out from behind her ear, across her vision. She had her father's curls, but her mother's color. And as she stared intently at the daisy-blond strand, she whispered, "Kind of . . . yes."

"Hmph," said Mr. Tullier. He wrapped his bathrobe tighter as if the words gave him a chill. "And your father?"

"What about him?"

"Don't be smart with me, girl; what happened to him?"

"He—" Floralie paused. She didn't want to tell about the alcohol. She didn't want to tell about the funeral. "I don't have contact with him anymore."

Nino narrowed his eyes at her.

"He worked as a banker for as long as I knew him," said Floralie. "My brother and I moved away from him, and that's all I know."

Mr. Tullier muttered, "Hmph," again.

Floralie huffed away the curl, and said, "Your turn."

"Hmm?" said Mr. Tullier.

"Your turn," repeated Floralie. "That was my half of the bargain; now it's yours. I'd like to see your floriography, please."

Mr. Tullier shifted uncomfortably in his chair. He downed the rest of his coffee, then said, "Tomorrow."

"What?" breathed Floralie.

"Tomorrow I'll tell you about the flower dictionaries." He dropped the letter back into the box and slid it back to Floralie.

"No—no, it's got to be today—you *promised*."

"I did no such thing." Mr. Tullier guffawed. "I said I'd tell you after you told me about your mother. Tomorrow is after."

The sound of pen scratching against paper caught Floralie's ears, and she turned to Nino. *You want to find her, too, though, don't you?* he wrote, but not to Floralie. He handed the notebook to Mr. Tullier, who narrowed his eyes at Nino, then turned to Floralie again. "What's wrong with him?" he said, nodding to Nino.

Floralie huffed. "Nothing's *wrong* with him. What's it to you if he doesn't like to talk?"

Mr. Tullier's lip curled. "Odd bunch, you are," he muttered, and then he read Nino's note. He seemed to read it five more times before sighing. "I'll tell you in the morning. If I am in a better mood. And if *you*, mademoiselle"—he glared at Floralie—"manage to hold your tongue while I am speaking."

"But, Mr. Tullier," said Floralie, "we've nowhere to sleep."

"Is that *my* problem?" said Mr. Tullier.

Floralie sighed. "It's just, your house is so large . . ."

Mr. Tullier rolled his eyes. "There are three spare rooms in the west wing, past the *Gare Saint-Lazare* painting. You shall sleep there. Now go." Mr. Tullier grunted as he pulled himself out of his chair and shuffled toward the door. "And you two"—he gazed down at Floralie and Nino—"*enfants*, I will not insult you so much as to tell you not to go exploring my property." And then he left the kitchen.

Floralie looked up at Miss Clairoux. Her jaw was clenched. Nino scrawled something into his notebook and handed it to Floralie. *Are you sure this is a good idea?*

Floralie nodded. *We'll be fine. He's creepy, but harmless. And he's my grandfather, after all. We've just got to give him time, I'm sure of it.* But really, she wasn't sure. She wasn't sure why Mr. Tullier wouldn't help her right then and there, and she wasn't sure why he seemed so hostile to his newfound granddaughter. But most of all, she was beginning to feel unsure about Mama. Why had Mama never told Floralie about Mr. Tullier, if she really had known him? And why would she, Viscaria, vivacious eyes and laugh like bells, have been friends with someone as stony-hearted as Mr. Tullier?

"She's my wife, Ma," said Papa, gathering his briefcase for work.

Grandmama stopped him at the door and looked him in the eye. "She's a wretch with a pretty face. Your biggest mistake."

"I'm sorry," said Papa. "I'm sorry she took me from you."

24

It was as if Mr. Tullier had vanished. Floralie, Nino, and Miss Clairoux could not find him anywhere in the corridors, so they snaked their way through the maze of flowers and vines to the west wing, where, indeed, they found three vacant rooms by Monet's painting of the famous railway station.

"This house is *huge*," marveled Floralie. "How d'you think he ended up getting it from Monet? And what d'you think he uses it all for, anyway?"

"I haven't the foggiest, my dear," said Miss Clairoux. "Now, if either of you two need *anything*, come straight to my room. Understand?"

"Yes, Miss Clairoux," said Floralie, and Miss Clairoux disappeared into her room.

The sparrows in the rafters of Floralie's room fell asleep before she did that night. The walls, covered in Monet's paintings, kept Floralie's eyes locked open. There was something familiar about the paintings, something that gnawed at Floralie's heart. Each one portrayed a girl wandering through a garden. She had daisy-blond hair and looked perhaps two, three years older than Floralie, but otherwise, her features were blurred in the sweeps of paint. It wasn't really the *features* that were familiar, but rather the way the figure seemed to move—as if she were made of feathers and silk and air.

Floralie squeezed shut her eyes. Heat weighed upon her chest as she lay on the hay-stuffed mattress, waiting for sleep. *Waiting, waiting, waiting.* She traced the words onto the back of her hand, and then those words melted into the words that so often dissolved into Floralie's mind: *Ballet. Papa. Air. Flowers. Ballet. Papa. Air. Flowers. Ballet. Papa. Air. Flowers. Ballet. Papa. Air—*

Air. Floralie needed air. She felt as if a ghost were strangling her throat. She pushed back the flannel sheets. *Flannel, why do they have to be flannel?* Then she tiptoed over to the window, yanked up the glass, and pushed as hard as she could on the shutters.

"*Come on*," she muttered.

Floralie leaned a shoulder against the window, gave a great *push*, and the shutters snapped open. Dust erupted in her face, settled into the crooks of her eyes, but a moment later she was breathing in the tulip-scented air.

A breeze swept through the room, shaking the bedpost and the wardrobe doors. In the corner, a rocking chair cloaked in a pink crochet blanket swayed back and forth. Floralie wondered what use Mr. Tullier had for such a blanket; it would hardly be big enough to cover Floralie, no less a full-grown man. And for some reason, the creaking of the wardrobe reminded Floralie vaguely of the sound of a baby rattle. Floralie remembered Miss Clairoux saying Mr. Tullier had had two children, one being Viscaria. But what had happened to the second child? How old was he or she now? Where had they gone?

A gust of wind whipped through the room, and one of the wardrobe doors swished open. Floralie tore herself away from the window and went to close it. As her fingers met the rough oak, however, something silky brushed against her hand. It was seeping out from inside the wardrobe.

Floralie narrowed her eyes and opened the wardrobe door wider.

"No . . . ," whispered Floralie. As she gazed into the wardrobe, Floralie felt very much like she was four years old again and seeing a sunflower for the first time. How small she felt against the grandness before her.

Inside the wardrobe hung ballet costume after ballet costume. Puffs of tulle skirts covered in lace and feathers and silken flowers. Gossamer sashes fluttered in the breeze and gemstones twinkled in the moonlight. Five pairs of threadbare pointe shoes huddled together in the corner like desolate schoolgirls. As the wind rattled the wardrobe once more, one of the shoes toppled out to Floralie's feet. She picked it up, the weight of it taking her by surprise.

And when Floralie peered inside the shoe, she almost dropped it, for etched in black ink on the grayed-away sole were three initials: *V.A.C.* The very same as those engraved on Mama's box of flowers—*Viscaria Alice Clairoux.*

Floralie stumbled back, gripping tight the shoe, and then raced out her room. She flung open Nino's door, and whispered, "*Nino?*"

There was a rustling of sheets, and Nino sat up, rubbing his eyes. Upon glimpsing Floralie, he leaped back and gathered up his sheets to his neck.

"*Shh!* It's all right, it's just me," said Floralie, and Nino relaxed. He pushed back his sheets, then lit a candle on his bedside table as Floralie sat down beside him.

Nino took his pen and notebook from the table and scrawled, *What are you doing here? Are you okay?*

Yes, wrote Floralie. *Yes, I'm fine, but look at this,* and she held up the shoe for him.

A pointe shoe? Where'd you get it?

The wardrobe, and look! Floralie held the shoe up to the candle and pointed to the initials. *I think these shoes belonged to my mother.*

Nino took the shoe and rubbed the toe box. *She must have lived in your room when she lived here.*

Floralie remembered now the photograph in *A History of Dreamlands*, the girl with vivacious eyes and daisy-blond hair standing beside the young Mr. Tullier and Claude Monet . . . Floralie took the pointe shoe from Nino and ran her fingers along the splitting seams, across the tattered block, over the smooth, smooth sole, molded by her mother's foot. Floralie felt as if she were holding a piece of Viscaria in her own two hands. A ghost of her, perhaps. She felt close. *Nino?*

Yeah?

There was a room that I want to see. I know Mr. Tullier told us not to go looking, but I've just got to see it.

It was the door. The door with the flowers, wasn't it?

Floralie nodded. *That's the one. I've got to know what's inside. I have this feeling about it.*

Just then, Philomenos leaped out from beneath Nino's sheets. Floralie smiled and patted the mouse as it began to squeak. Nino smiled crookedly at Floralie. *Mice and feelings,* he wrote, *are never to be ignored.*

Down the corridor, they crept, footsteps soft as maple seeds spinning to a pine-needled floor.

"This is it," said Floralie when they reached the aurora borealis door.

Thorns prickled her fingers as she twisted open the doorknob . . . They stepped inside.

The lady sold dance shoes in the parking lot of the village church. Floralie watched her mother try on twenty-seven pairs before she chose her pointe shoes. When paying the lady, along with the money, Mama gave her a dog rose. "They will hurt for a while, my dear," the lady said. And indeed they made Mama's feet bleed. She wore them to bed each night to break them in, and when Floralie asked if the shoes hurt, Mama always said, "They make me happy."

25

Floralie's bare feet sunk into cool, moist dirt. Soft air tickled her eyelashes, waltzed with the pointe shoe ribbons. The crickets sang a lullaby, and frogs croaked a drumbeat. Gnarled trees arched over Floralie and Nino, and as they made their way through them, a pale light filtered down from above. Floralie looked up to the full moon, hung like a silver coin in the sky. This was not a room. This was a garden. A bizarre indoor garden, glass-dome ceiling, and earthen floor.

It was as if her wallpaper had bloomed to life, as if her enchanted forest had taken root. Flowers bloomed low and high of every variety Floralie could imagine. A stream gurgled in the distance, and cicadas chirped in the hedges. In the center of it all grew a willow tree barely any smaller than Floralie's cottage at the end of Whitterly End. Its leaves rustled as if whispering lullabies in an intangible, yet ever so present, wind.

Nino trailed his fingers along a tiger lily. Floralie knelt down to a patch of tiny purple flowers. They danced in her fingers like miniature ballerinas, and Floralie knew.

"These are viscarias," she muttered.

Nino tilted his head.

"The flowers—they're viscarias." She hadn't a clue how she knew it, but she did. She felt it in her bones.

Something sparked in the corner of Floralie's eye, and she squinted up at the great willow tree. "Fireflies!" she yelped, looking to Nino.

Nino glanced up, and the two sprinted toward the tree. Floralie swished under the waterfall of leaves and pulled Nino along with her. The willow's trunk was wide and knobby, as if it had been growing there for hundreds of years.

"Look!" exclaimed Floralie. She dropped Mama's ballet shoe and pointed up to the fireflies, flickering like candle flames in the twisted branches. "Try and catch one."

It was then, as Floralie and Nino grabbed for the air, that Floralie realized she had not painted since Tom tore down her wallpaper. As a firefly lit up at the base of the tree, she scurried over and cupped her hands around it.

"Come look, Nino! Look, I've got one." The firefly stumbled along the ridges of Floralie's palm, lighting up her skin so it glowed a rosy pink. And as she held the firefly, Floralie thought about how catching fireflies was a little like painting. How she could hold freedom in her palms, how paintbrushes were like fireflies, and how wallpaper was like hands. Wallpaper caught colors, just like hands caught fireflies. And Floralie thought about how impossible—contradictory, really—it seemed to catch *freedom*, yet how simple it really was. All you had to do was open a palm. All you had to do was speak.

"Nino?" whispered Floralie.

Yeah? wrote Nino in his notebook.

Floralie held the firefly in her left hand and took the pen in her right, trembling. *Why won't you speak to me?*

I am speaking to you.

No. I mean, really speak to me. I want to hear your voice.

I can't.

Why not?

Because you might leave, or turn on me, or laugh. You'd probably laugh. Like all my friends at the orphanage.

But I'm not like that. Don't you know me at all? Remember how you told me that the gaps in my teeth were like the gaps in Sappho's poems? That that's what made them beautiful?

Nino paused, and then etched, faint as mist, *Yeah.*

Well, if beauty isn't perfection, then what is it? What is beauty?

Nino's mouth twitched, and he buried himself in his notebook. Floralie let the firefly crawl over her thumb and back into her palm until finally, Nino held up his notebook.

> *Firefly*
> *By Konstantinos*
>
> *Poetry is a firefly*
> *Caught in your night-struck hands.*
> *And you contain chaos*
> *Under thumb, between palms.*
>
> *Chaos is a firefly*
> *Caught in your night-struck hands,*
> *And you contain freedom*
> *Under thumb, between palms.*
>
> *Wonder is a firefly*
> *Caught in your night-struck hands,*
> *And you contain vulnerability*
> *Under thumb, between palms.*
>
> *And beauty is chaos*
> *Caught in wonderstruck poems*
> *Already etched in our hearts,*
> *But when it came to speaking out loud*
>
> *We just didn't know how.*

Floralie read it five times. She thought of painting, the way there were a trillion emotions and shapes and colors of paint—chaos—but only once they were organized onto wallpaper would they be beautiful. Only then would they tell the story once trapped inside the artist.

She thought of ballet, Viscaria contained on the stage, steps locked into place, her movements sculpted of freedom, but her body caught inside the choreography. Somewhere between that freedom and captivity lurked beauty.

So, then, wrote Floralie, *why won't you speak to me?*

Nino's honey eyes grew hollow. *Why should I?*

Floralie felt ridiculous—poetics were for Nino, not her. *Because . . . ,* started Floralie, *because maybe your voice isn't perfect, but it's your contained chaos. It's your beauty. Everyone's voice is. Everyone's voice is a firefly in a hand, forming ideas out of images out of sentences out of words out of letters out of dots and lines out of sounds. If our vulnerability makes us beautiful, and if voices are our greatest vulnerabilities, why hide yours?*

Nino dropped his pen and shook his head. His hair flopped over his eyes, and there was just something about them that drew Floralie in. *You know everything about me, Nino, but you won't even speak to me.* Floralie realized she had drifted closer, an inch from his ear, and she breathed, "You don't have to be afraid." She let her mouth go slack, let the night fill the gap in her teeth. She clutched the firefly tight.

Nino shook his head again and stood. Floralie stood, too, a branch snapping beneath her foot. Nino began to back away like a feral cat.

"You're a coward." Floralie couldn't stop the words from falling out.

You don't know anything.

"But I'm trying to, and you won't *let me.* I've put my trust in you, and all you do is take. You take all my sadness and turn it into poetry, and fine, I don't care, but you never share anything with me. You barely let anyone even know your *name. Konstantinos.* Ha! *Konstantinos, Konstantinos, Konstantinos;* I never even get to *say* it. You're my best friend, and you won't even talk to me." Anger flooded Floralie's face, seeped down her spine. "Why can't you trust me?"

Nino said nothing, but backed away, and then broke into a run all the way to the edge of the garden until he disappeared through the door.

Floralie fell to her knees, dress covered in dirt. She pounded her fists on the ground and squeezed her eyes shut. Her breath came in jagged bouts, but as her breathing slowed, she realized she was still holding the firefly. Slowly, she uncurled her palm, and out fell the bug, limp, lightless, lifeless. Suffocated.

"*No.*" Floralie wanted to scream. She wanted the whole world to know how mad she was and how sad she was, but at the same time, she found herself once again scared of opening her mouth and revealing the gap in her teeth, even if no one was there to see it. Because *she* was there, and always, she would be aware of that gap in her teeth, and always, she would be aware of the gap in every single thing she did. *Everything,* thought Floralie, *everything I do will be ugly. Ugly, ugly, ugly.* She traced the word over and over again in the dirt until the letters ran together like sidewalk chalk after a rainstorm.

And somewhere between the time she was crying beneath the willow and the time she was sleeping beneath the willow, a thought drifted through Floralie's mind similar to the one she had had when Tom tore down her wallpaper, a thought that went something like this: Everything disappears. Nino, Mama, flowers, wallpaper. It simply wasn't worth the trouble, caring about things that disappear.

When Floralie remembered this day, she called it the Last Day of Everything. Floralie followed the taxi to the edge of the village. The sunflowers swallowed Mama up.

26

Sleep swept over Floralie, and it wasn't until the moon had nearly sunk to the edge of the garden that Floralie heard it. The creak of a door. Floralie sat up and rubbed her eyes, confused for only a moment as to where she was. *The garden,* she remembered. *The beautiful, terrible garden.* She held her breath, praying it was Nino, come to write poems and make everything better. But the footsteps were slow, heavy . . . not the mouse-quick steps Floralie knew so well. As they grew louder, Floralie scrambled to her feet and slipped behind the trunk of the willow.

"Now, let's see," came the low grunt of an old man. He said the words in French as he swished under the willow's veil.

Floralie squeezed her eyes shut as Mr. Tullier's footsteps came closer, closer. Branches snapped, and Floralie knew the only thing separating her from Mr. Tullier—and his wrath—was the willow's trunk.

"I wanted to tell you about her, darling," whispered Mr. Tullier. At first Floralie was confused; was Mr. Tullier talking to *her*? But as he kept speaking, she realized he wasn't talking to her at all . . . It was as if Mr. Tullier were having a conversation with the tree. "About the little girl who came to see me today," continued Mr. Tullier, a trace of laughter in his voice. He sounded younger somehow. "She had her mother's eyes, my God, I couldn't believe she had her mother's eyes."

Floralie peeked around the tree ever so slightly. Mr. Tullier was kneeling at the foot of the willow where a patch of pale pink flowers grew. He patted the dirt around them, stroked their petals. "I don't know if you remember her or not—Viscaria," he went on. He looked up, and Floralie snapped her head back around the tree.

"She would have wanted you to remember her," continued Mr. Tullier to the flowers. "Anyway, the girl—Floralie—she's her *daughter*. Imagine that. She's my . . . never mind. Well, this Floralie—she wants me to help find her. Viscaria, I mean. I've wondered about Viscaria for a long time . . . And I—" His voice snagged. "I *regret* everything I said to her that last day. I suppose

I'm just an old man now," he chuckled. "You're lucky you don't have to take care of me . . . You wouldn't like me now, darling."

Mr. Tullier sighed and blew his nose into a handkerchief.

"I've grown fearful over the years. I don't know if I could stomach to see Viscaria in whatever state she's become. The memories—" His voice broke off to a sob. "The memories are lovely. I don't—I don't want them to become tainted."

Floralie listened as Mr. Tullier wept. There was just something about the willow tree—perhaps the way its leaves swayed the same way Miss Clairoux nodded when Floralie spoke to her, or the way its branches twisted up to the night sky, crooked—like the way Nino smiled when Floralie wrote to him—that made Floralie feel as if the tree were listening.

As Mr. Tullier's breathing calmed, so did the wind that had crept through the cracks in the dome above. Floralie competed with the silence, holding her breath. But Mr. Tullier stood. "How . . . ," he whispered, and then louder, colder, "Who's there? I know you're there."

Floralie held her breath tighter. Surely, *surely*, Mr. Tullier could hear her heart, *thump, thump, thump* . . .

Something squeaked. *No, please, no*, thought Floralie, as she spotted Philomenos scurrying around her foot. She scooped up the mouse and whispered, "*Shh*," but he just kept squeaking.

"*You!*" Mr. Tullier whipped around the tree.

Floralie stumbled back, holding Philomenos in one hand. Her foot caught on a root, and she fell to the ground. She gazed up into Mr. Tullier's forget-me-not eyes; they were sparked with rage. Against his heart, he clutched Viscaria's pointe shoe, flecked with dirt.

"I told you not to come in here!" His face went poppy red, out of anger or embarrassment, Floralie wasn't sure. The wrinkles on his face seemed even more pronounced, and his mouth was twisted into a grimace.

"I—I just—"

"I have shown you nothing but kindness, and this is how you repay me? *Je déteste les enfants!*"

"But, Mr. Tullier, who were you—"

"Get out! Now! *SORTEZ*, EGLANTINE!"

The name hung in the air, ringing like one of Mama's laughs. *Eglantine.* Mr. Tullier's anger wilted away. His face grew ashen, and his eyes lost their fire. He staggered back, as if slipping into memory.

Time stopped; the moon stood still.

"Eglantine?" said Floralie. "Who's Eglantine?"

Mr. Tullier slackened his grip on the pointe shoe, and it fell to the ground. A cloud of dirt puffed around it, settled into the scuffed peach silk.

And then Mr. Tullier hissed, *"You are no longer welcome in this house."*

"No, please—I was just—I came all this way—I—I'll pay you. Until we can find Viscaria, I'll pay you to be here. It's only right, anyway. I should have offered before."

"I don't need money," grunted Mr. Tullier.

"Then I'll work—I'll help you," offered Floralie.

"I don't need help."

"I could water the plants."

"Plants are sensitive."

"Or—or organize your things, clean up around the place, cook for you, wash the dishes—you must need help washing the dishes—no offense. I'll run errands; You'll barely notice me, promise. I'll do anything."

"You can stay the night," said Mr. Tullier. "But then you're gone."

Floralie's stomach twisted in knots. She had to stay, simply *had* to. What could she offer Mr. Tullier? She had failed her French and grammar classes at Mrs. Coffrey's, had always forgotten an ingredient or two in her cooking classes, and had twisted up numbers in arithmetic. She could do nothing but paint flowers. Oh yes, she knew how to paint flowers. But that was just about all. So, simply, she said, "I'll paint for you."

"What?" breathed Mr. Tullier.

"I'll paint your flowers. Like Monet did. I can paint. Honest, I can."

Mr. Tullier stared at her for what felt like hours, and then, to Floralie's utter surprise, he grunted, "You start in the morning. Now away with you."

Floralie couldn't believe it! She scuttled all the way through the garden, down the winding corridors and past the *Gare Saint-Lazare* painting until she reached her room, mind racing.

When the dusty morning light filtered in through the window and the sparrows began to sing, Floralie sat up in her bed, head aching and eyelids heavy. One word reverberated around her brain: *Nino. Nino, Nino, Nino* . . . She had to find *Nino*. Floralie crawled out of bed and skittered through the ivy-walled corridors until she reached Nino's door. She paused, heart pulsing in her ears. Her fingers trembled. Then, slowly, she cracked open the door. "Nino?" she whispered.

Silence.

Floralie neared the bed and pulled back Nino's sheets; the bed was empty. "Nino?" Floralie shouted this time. Blood rushed through her ears, across her cheeks. She placed Philomenos on the bed and darted to the wardrobe. She threw open the doors, but Nino was not inside. She checked under the bed, in the corners, behind the curtains, but Nino was nowhere to be found. Floralie felt her heart plummet into her stomach.

"Nino?" she called, even louder now. "Nino, it's *not* funny. Come out!" But Nino would not come out. Nino had disappeared.

Floralie was three the first time she picked up a paintbrush. Her first painting was a blob of red and a line of green that she called a rose. Mama framed it on her vanity table and said, "Come with me, my wildflower. This rose will need water soon."

And the whole day long, Floralie and Mama painted blobs and lines. Together in the garden, just them two, they were happy, hands painting more colors than Floralie could name.

27

Nino's bed smelled like him. Old books, mouse droppings, Indian ink, and the faintest aroma of honey. Floralie lay swathed in the sheets, trying to fall asleep in those early morning hours. She felt tangled up in despair and euphoria—despair for Nino's disappearance, euphoria for Mr. Tullier's willingness to let Floralie stay. The possibility of finding Mama sent lightning down her spine, and her heart chanted, *Mama, Mama, Mama*, but then lamented, *Nino, Nino, Nino*.

Floralie simply could not sleep. So instead, she flew to her forest. It was as if it were the first time flying to her wonderland. Just like that first time, that lovely, awful first time. It had been the day Mama left. And now Nino . . . the sorrow carried her away.

It was nighttime in her wonderland, and Floralie watched the beautiful things bloom around her. Beautiful trees, beautiful animals, beautiful flowers. She lay in a patch of green, green grass, running her hands and feet along each and every silken blade as if she were making snow angels without the snow. Circles of mushrooms popped up around her; they belonged to the fairies.

A hawk cawed from above and swooped down beside her. Floralie climbed upon its back and up she soared, over treetops, among the stars. She gazed down upon the beautiful things, how happy they all looked. Happy trees, happy animals, happy flowers. But she wasn't happy. For the first time ever in her forest, Floralie felt sad. Because now it dawned on her that among all the pretty things in her forest, she was the only ugly thing there. Perhaps she had always felt this, but before had lived with hope that some of the beauty would rub off on her; perhaps some of it even had . . . but tonight all that beauty got whisked away by the wind tearing at her skin.

As the hawk plunged, Floralie held tight to the feathers, and when it grazed the ground, Floralie slid off onto the grass with a thud. The hawk soared off, and Floralie was alone.

She had to find the gardener. Through trees she searched, over hills and across streams, but the gardener was nowhere to be found. Floralie lay in the grass, waiting for her breath to catch up to her. As she gazed up to the trees, however, she spotted the figure. It sat alone, the same fuzzy, ethereal shadow, perched atop the tallest oak tree in the forest, chin on fist, elbow on knee.

But where was its watering can? Out of the corner of her eye, Floralie spotted it—at the bottom of the oak tree. The gardener *needed* it. Floralie raced over to the watering can, but as soon as she got close enough to see it properly, it disappeared, and so Floralie called up to the gardener. "Hey," she shouted. "Hey, come down! You've forgotten your watering can!" But the gardener could not hear her. Floralie called and called, but still, the gardener simply sat atop the oak tree, surveying the forest. Floralie hollered until her throat grew scratchy and her voice went hoarse.

As she turned around, however, something had changed. A hint of orange tinted the trees; by her foot, a rose withered before her eyes. She knelt down in the grass, and the patch shriveled to coarse, brown blades. *No,* she wanted to scream, but found she could no longer speak. *No, no, no.* And she wept for the grass, and she wept for the trees, and she wept for the rose, and all the while, the gardener stayed atop her tree, stoic as ever.

And then Floralie was asleep.

Floralie awoke to a squeaking.

"Who is it?" she murmured, and then her eyes flickered open.

A pale shaft of light filtered in from the window, illuminating the dust. Floralie squinted in the brightness. A grandfather clock by the wardrobe read eight o'clock. "Philomenos!" she exclaimed upon spotting the mouse. "But you should be in Nino's room!" and then her stomach dropped. "Nino . . ."

For one glorious, fleeting moment, Floralie believed it had all been a dream, but no. He was gone. Floralie shoved back the covers and hopped out of the bed. She scooped up Philomenos and hurried out the door and into the hall. Once there, she began to bang on Miss Clairoux's door.

"Miss Clairoux," she called. "Miss Clairoux!" *Please be awake. Please, please, please.*

Not a moment later, Miss Clairoux appeared at the door, hair frizzed and fear etched in her face.

"What—what is it, *ma chérie*? Are you hurt? Where's Nino?" She felt Floralie's face and hair. "*Ma chérie*, you're crying. Oh, *mon Dieu*, I should not have brought you here!"

"Miss Clairoux, I'm fine, really—but Nino—Nino's gone."

Miss Clairoux's face blanched two shades paler, and for a moment, Floralie feared she might faint. She gritted her teeth, then lowered herself onto the bed.

"I knew this would happen," Miss Clairoux muttered. "I just *knew* it. What was it about?"

Floralie narrowed her eyes. "What was *what* about?"

"The fight, of course, the fight! What did you two fight about last night?"

How Miss Clairoux knew about Floralie's fight with Nino, Floralie could not fathom. Spooky—witchy, even—as it was, there were just certain things that Miss Clairoux seemed to *know*.

"It—" started Floralie, but then she wondered, *What* had *it been about?* "It was complicated."

"I'm listening," said Miss Clairoux.

Floralie sighed, and she told all of what had happened the previous night. And Miss Clairoux nodded the whole time, listening with her entire heart. And when she finished telling about Nino, she told about Mr. Tullier, how he had called her *Eglantine*, and how strange indeed that was. And she finished with, "And he said we can stay here. All I have to do is paint for him."

Miss Clairoux shuddered. "Like a ghost."

Floralie looked up at Miss Clairoux. "Sorry . . . What's like a ghost?"

"Remember how I told you about the roses?" Miss Clairoux asked. "And how it's possible to love someone even with their flaws. Not in spite of the flaws . . . just *with* them."

Floralie nodded.

"It's strange, fate. Things disappear one day, and the next, they're back. The last thing Mr. Tullier told me before he left me was, 'It's better this way.' I didn't believe it for one second."

"I will find him," breathed Floralie. "Nino."

Miss Clairoux kissed the top of Floralie's head. "We will." She sighed and then said, "You focus on your job with Mr. Tullier, and I'll focus on finding Nino. We've got information to get from our Mr. Tullier. And how, of course, will we get that?"

"My job," said Floralie. "It's going to give me time. All I need is time."

When Floralie arrived at the kitchen, Mr. Tullier was already slumped over at the end of the long table sipping black coffee.

"You're up," he said.

"Yeah," said Floralie.

No one said anything for a long while, until Mr. Tullier grunted, "Well, don't just stand there. Sit." And Floralie sat.

Her thoughts seemed to flow so fast she couldn't catch their current, not even a word. "Why are you allowing me to stay?"

"You're painting my flowers, are you not?"

Floralie nodded vigorously. "Of course, I just meant—"

"I know what you meant." He paused, then softly replied, "I want to find out about my family just as much as you want to. So, you start at nine."

The first day Floralie ever sold flowers at the bridge, a beggar came to her and told her how pretty the orange blossoms were. Floralie said, "Yes. Yes, they are pretty," and she gave one to the beggar.

Tom was not too pleased when he found out, but later that night he said, "I look up to you sometimes, Flory."

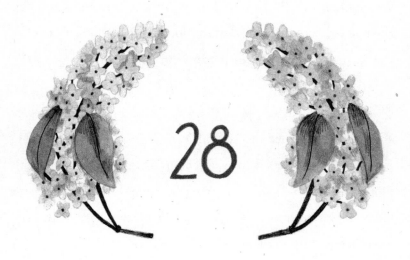

28

Later that morning, as Floralie approached the aurora borealis door, she heard laughter. The flowers brushed against her fingers as she pushed open the glass. At the edge of the willow, Mr. Tullier and Miss Clairoux sat atop a small boulder, backs to Floralie. They were talking, and though Floralie couldn't hear the words, she could hear the happiness. Floralie felt as if she were intruding on something private, so she coughed slightly as to announce herself.

Mr. Tullier snapped his head around and barked, "What?"

"Er—you told me to come here for work," said Floralie.

"Oh." Mr. Tullier's shoulders lowered. "So I did."

Mr. Tullier hopped off the boulder, knees cracking like twigs. His hand found Miss Clairoux's, and he guided her off the boulder, too. He muttered something in French to her, and she nodded and strode toward the door. Floralie noticed that her cheeks had turned rosy and her lips quivered as if trying to stifle a smile.

"G'morning again, Miss Clairoux," said Floralie coyly, eyes shifting between her and Mr. Tullier.

Miss Clairoux blushed even redder. "Oh—yes, morning, dear. Floralie, I've decided to go looking for Nino. I will be back later today. If you need me, I won't be far from the house, " and she hurried out of the garden.

Mr. Tullier bent down behind the boulder, then stood and turned to Floralie. When he emerged, he was carrying a large, dark-wood box. "Here," he said as he approached Floralie, and he shoved the box into Floralie's arms.

The weight of it made her knees buckle, but she held on tight and said, "What's all this?"

"Paint."

"Paint?" Floralie looked from the box to Mr. Tullier.

"Paint. Now come," and he beckoned for Floralie to follow. Mr. Tullier led Floralie to a bush of peonies and said, "Paint them."

Floralie bit the inside of her lip. Paint had never made her nervous before, not once. Mr. Tullier stood there waiting, arms crossed and chin tilted. Floralie sat in the dirt before the box. It smelled horrible, as paint did—like gasoline, or vinegar that's been left in the cupboard for too long. But it was a familiar smell. A smell that felt, in some bizarre way, comforting.

As she opened the latch, a small "whoa" escaped Floralie's mouth, for Mr. Tullier's box was filled to the brim with oil paints. There were also a few small canvases, a palette, a bottle of turpentine, and a dozen brushes. Floralie had painted on a real canvas only two, perhaps three, times before. And she had used the same brushes since she was six, even though the bristles had gone prickly years ago. These brushes, though, these felt like silk.

"A little something from Monsieur Monet's collection," said Mr. Tullier.

Floralie's jaw dropped as she pulled a canvas from the box and dug through the paints, curating colors with utmost heed as if they were to be displayed in a museum alongside Monet's *Water Lilies*. With so many colors, she could be choosy about them. *Alizarin, cadmium orange, crimson, raw sienna, Vandyke brown, viridian green* . . . The colors piled up beside Floralie until she was satisfied with the collection.

Floralie then chose a brush, opened the jar of turpentine, and began to build up layer upon layer of color. The paint spread more smoothly on the canvas than on wallpaper. She could not recall ever painting peonies before, which made her feel as if she were wandering through a dark corridor, searching for chaos, searching for fireflies.

When at last she finished, Mr. Tullier pulled out his glasses and examined the canvas first an inch from his eye, and then at arm's length.

"Who taught you to paint?" he grunted, squinting at the canvas.

"Taught myself," Floralie said shyly.

Mr. Tullier sighed like he was resigning himself to some inevitable truth. "You've got some talent."

"Thank you," said Floralie. There was a pause, and then Floralie looked up and said, "You will help me find my mother, won't you? You will help decode the flowers?"

Mr. Tullier's mouth twitched. "In time."

When Floralie was little, she had a baby doll that Mama named Lilac. Floralie took Lilac everywhere, and every once in a while, she would stand her up on the floor and say, "Look! Look at her taking her

first steps!" Firsts. Mothers get to see firsts. First word, first steps, first haircut, first recital, first day of school, first love, first good-bye. First time one holds a pencil. First time one opens a box of paints. First time one sits to create. Mothers see firsts. Mothers see firsts.

29

By the day's end, Floralie had painted a dozen flowers. She had also discovered some miscellaneous objects in the paint box. Within it, Floralie found that Mr. Tullier knew a lot of dead people. The box was haunted by obituary clippings and funeral service booklets. Floralie remembered her father's obituary. She had cried so much over it that the ink ran together, words colliding with one another like armies on a battlefield. The newspaper had nearly disintegrated from all the tears. Floralie had kept it anyway, even though it looked like it was a hundred-year-old handkerchief. But the curious thing about Mr. Tullier's obituaries was that all of them were in perfect condition. Even the funeral booklets had nothing more than a hint of a thumb indention at the bottom. Floralie took this to mean one of two things: either Mr. Tullier didn't feel sadness, or he didn't like to show it.

One paper, Philomenos found. Or rather, attempted to steal. It was a scrap of paper littered with words at odd angles, sloping up and down like dandelions growing on a hill that doesn't know where it's going. They were names. *Eglantine Victoire, Eglantine Adèle, Eglantine Clothilde, Eglantine Marie, Eglantine Lisette.* And then in the corner, one name was circled and flecked with lines like sunrays. This one read: *Eglantine Floralie. How strange*, Floralie thought. She gently slipped the piece of paper in her bag.

Among the stranger things Floralie found in the bottom of the paint box were an ivory baby rattle, a tube of scarlet lipstick, and a tin of gray ashes. Dropped in the middle of them was a smooth white stone engraved with the words, JE T'AIME, MA FLEUR. 1902–1903. Floralie's spine shivered, for she knew she held in her hands not only a tiny tin, not only a tiny tombstone, but tiny ashes. Human ashes.

Floralie ran down the corridor in hopes of finding Miss Clairoux, and more in hopes of Miss Clairoux having found some information about Nino's whereabouts. Halfway down the corridor, she nearly rammed right into her.

"Have you found him yet? Anything, any clues?" exclaimed Floralie, skidding to a stop.

Miss Clairoux shook her head. "I'm sorry, *ma chérie*. Nothing."

Floralie looked down to her shoes and bit her lip.

"Take heart, *ma chérie*, we will find him yet! Now, how did things go for you today?" said Miss Clairoux.

Floralie perked up a bit. "Mr. Tullier likes my flower paintings, and I get to paint with *Claude Monet's* paint! It's a lot of work, but I'm getting paid to paint. And the more I get to know him, the more I can find out about my mother."

It occurred to her then that Floralie had nearly forgotten about Mama in the excitement of painting Mr. Tullier's flowers. She had just about forgotten Tom, too, and Grandmama, and even Nino. It was as if the house had some enchantment over it that made time slip away. Sappho's poem rang in Floralie's mind:

> And hours entwine in hours.
> For the moon is slipping to ash
> And I am slipping, too.

Floralie wondered if her mother's hours were entwining in hours. If this very moment, Viscaria was slipping to ash. She wondered if time moved faster or slower in the hospital, and she wondered which was worse.

"That's splendid you have a new job," said Miss Clairoux. "But do press him . . . He is not easily persuaded."

"He will be," said Floralie. "I've got a good feeling about this. Once he gets to know me, he'll come around."

All week, Floralie worked in the garden. All week Miss Clairoux searched Giverny and the surrounding villages, always coming back with nothing but a bouquet of adonis flowers. All week Floralie probed Mr. Tullier about Mama and the floriography, but all week, he simply replied, "In time." Most days, Mr. Tullier sat in silence beside her, furiously scrawling notes into a leather book or making his rounds of watering the plants. Friday, Mr. Tullier was rather late, and when he did finally show up, his eyebrows were furrowed and his teeth clenched. He caught Floralie on her shoulder, causing Floralie to spill her turpentine all over a patch of violets.

"Who—oh, it's you, Mr. Tu—"

"Thief!" hissed Mr. Tullier. "You've stolen it, haven't you, girl! Where've you taken it? Go on, spit it out."

"Taken? I haven't taken *anything*." But as Mr. Tullier yanked up Floralie's bag, the braille book clunked against the flower box.

"Oh yes, you did! You were the only one using Monet's box of paints, and now it's gone. My paper is *gone!*"

So this wasn't about the braille book. "Don't be ridiculous!" she shouted, snatching back her bag and taking a breath to calm herself. "And if you would be so kind, please take your hand off my shoulder *this instant*. Why would *I* even want one of your papers?"

And then she remembered—the list of names. But what would be so important about that?

"I keep track of this paper, girl, and if you lost it, you'd better—"

But Floralie never did find out what she had better do, because just then, Philomenos went skittering across the puddle of turpentine, crumpled paper between his teeth.

Mr. Tullier's eyes widened. He let Floralie's shoulder loose, glanced from the mouse to Floralie, then back to the mouse. And then he lunged.

"Wait!" called Floralie, leaping to her feet and speeding after Mr. Tullier. "Don't hurt him; he's Nino's!"

"Don't care *who* he belongs to," and Mr. Tullier chased after Philomenos as Floralie chased after Mr. Tullier. The two tumbled over boulders and ducked under branches. They ran in circles until Floralie's foot caught on a tree root, and she stumbled headfirst into the violet patch. When she looked up, she saw

Mr. Tullier sprawled on the dirt, too, arm outstretched, and something wriggling at the end of his fingertips.

Mr. Tullier straightened up, holding the mouse by the tail at arm's length. Floralie brushed the dirt off her hands and stood. She felt a bruise forming on her chin, and her left knee throbbed. Mr. Tullier glared so intently at Floralie, she thought for a moment he might strangle her.

But no. Instead, he approached Floralie, took the paper from the mouse's mouth, and then dropped Philomenos into Floralie's palms.

Philomenos squeaked, and Floralie smiled weakly. Mr. Tullier and Floralie knelt down, both panting, and Mr. Tullier's knees creaking.

"S-sorry about Philomenos," said Floralie, placing the mouse in the violet patch beside her.

Mr. Tullier cleared his throat and then murmured, "Sorry for—er—accusing you of—you know—thievery. Et cetera."

"I'm scared of you sometimes," said Floralie. "Why are you so angry?"

Mr. Tullier's face twisted into a scowl.

"I just want to understand," said Floralie. "But for now, we'll call it all even. No hard feelings," and she held out her hand for Mr. Tullier.

Mr. Tullier eyed it carefully.

"I won't start calling you 'Grandpa' or anything," said Floralie. "I just want to be friends."

Slowly, Mr. Tullier shook Floralie's hand. His hand was more callused than Floralie had expected, as if the wrinkles were set in stone from all his years of gardening.

"You're not so bad, kid," said Mr. Tullier, sighing.

"Thanks," said Floralie.

He leaned in close and added to Floralie's immense surprise, "I promise to keep you safe. You haven't got much, but you've got me. I promise you've got me."

And after that exchange, somewhere between the mouse and the paints and the flowers, Floralie Laurel and Sylvestre Tullier became the oddest of friends. There was something enchanting about living with flowers that made it impossible not to bloom or wither along with them. Indeed, if there was one thing Floralie had come to understand, it was that nothing stayed the same in gardens. Not flowers, not trees, not soil. Not even people.

The fireflies were alight. The twilight seeped into Floralie's palms, soft, like crushed velvet.

"Come look, Flory. I've found a fairy," said Mama from across the garden.

Floralie came running, but as soon as she got close, Mama snapped her fingers and said, "It got away."

Floralie sighed in disappointment, but Mama brushed a buttercup under Floralie's chin. "Don't be glum," she said. "There are wings on all our backs. We just can't look back enough to see them."

30

The next day, Mr. Tullier asked Floralie to send a letter for him. Strangely enough, a thick ribbon covered the address, but Floralie thought little of it and exchanged Philomenos for the letter. He was looking a bit ill, and Floralie thought he should be watched by someone.

Floralie took the letter into the village, breathing in the roses and tulips and lavender. When she passed the library, Madame Favreau was setting up a FOR SALE sign in front and piling books outside. Floralie approached slowly, sadness dropping into her stomach.

"You're selling it?" said Floralie to the little librarian.

"*Oui*," said Madame Favreau. "We just cannot keep up with ze money."

"Oh," said Floralie, "I'm sorry."

She picked up the nearest book from a precariously high-piled stack. It was *Peter Pan*, and Floralie flipped through the pages until she reached the end, where she read the words, "Never say good-bye, because saying good-bye means going away, and going away means forgetting."

Floralie hoped she was not forgotten. She hoped Mama had not forgotten her, and perhaps even more so she hoped Nino wouldn't forget her. But Nino hadn't said good-bye, and neither had Mama, and that let the hope hang, if only by a thread, to Floralie's fraying heart.

"Are you selling all your books?" asked Floralie.

"*Non*, just giving zem away. No space for zem anymore," replied Miss Favreau, unpacking a new box of books.

"Is it possible for . . . Could I take *A History of Dreamlands*?"

"Is zat ze odd book? Ze collection of thoughts book?" said Madame Favreau.

Floralie nodded.

"How funny—a boy was looking at zat exact book not a day ago. Raggedy thing, 'e was."

Floralie dropped the *Peter Pan* book. "A boy? Raggedy? Did he say anything—I mean—not *say* anything—did he write to you?"

"Write to me? Why of course not! 'E was standing not two paces off from where you are right now. But, now zat I think of it, 'e didn't say a word ze entire time. 'E spent a good 'alf hour pouring over zat book zere." She gestured to a pile a few paces away, on top of which was, indeed, *A History of Dreamlands*.

Floralie picked up the book and let her fingers curl over the spine and ruffle through the pages. There was something about the tattered pages that reminded Floralie of Nino's shirtsleeves, and the grimy cover that reminded her of his fingernails. It was like holding his hand.

It all seemed so impossible. Finding Nino's book like that. It all seemed too *unlikely*, too tangled, too messy, too . . . perfect. But a voice rang in Floralie's mind, and strangely enough, the thought had the lilt of Miss Clairoux's voice, dreamlike. It said, *"Perhaps that would be the angels."*

"I felt sorry for 'im, really, 'ow skinny 'e looked," piped Madame Favreau. "Told 'im 'e could take ze book if 'e liked, but 'e didn't."

"He didn't? Why not?"

Madame Favreau shrugged. *"Pas d'idée.* 'E carried it all ze way to ze archway over zere, but just as 'e was about to leave, 'e spotted a different book—something about botany and drawing, if I remember quite right. 'E took zat one instead, and zen 'e left. Peculiar *garçon.*"

As Madame Favreau was speaking, something caught Floralie's eye: a bright purple feather. It bobbed over the bustle of people striding by. Floralie's heart thundered and her hands quaked.

"*Merci*, Madame Favreau," said Floralie hurriedly. "Er—would you mind terribly if *I* took that book?"

"I don't see why not; ze rubbish bin is not going to find more use for it zan you, now is it?"

"Right—thanks," said Floralie, and she dashed down the street, book in hand.

"Floralie!"

No, pleaded Floralie in her mind. She ran.

And then Grandmama screeched, "Police!" again and again, running after Floralie. Grandmama's high heels click-clacked on the cobblestones, drawing ever nearer.

Floralie slipped into an alleyway, then zigzagged down a series of back roads until she was thoroughly lost. Grandmama's footsteps faded in the distance.

"She was just here!" came a wisp of Grandmama's voice.

The voices filtered away after that, as Floralie's heart pounded in her ears. *She saw me,* thought Floralie. *Grandmama saw me.*

Grandmama came for a visit to France at Christmastime, bringing copious amounts of gifts and chocolates and marzipan with her. Mama would dance as the sugar plum fairy in The Nutcracker *at that time, and gather scarlet geraniums from the audience every night.*

Grandmama would scoff at the theatrics of it all. "Such whimsy, it makes my stomach turn." She whispered it to Papa, but was loud enough for everyone around her to hear. But the word "whimsy" sounded beautiful to Floralie. "Whimsy, whimsy, whimsy." Floralie wanted to melt into that word. Crawl inside it and make a home with soft walls and magic stairs and Mama's geraniums scattered everywhere.

31

Floralie sat crouched against the back side of a small café, breathing in the smell of coffee and croissants for at least half an hour until she was positive Grandmama had given up. When at last Floralie returned to Rue Claude Monet, she slunk toward the letterbox, which was but one hyacinth archway and two storybook houses away from the library. A rusted, vandalized thing it was, nailed to a crumbling brick post office. Floralie felt wary the letter would arrive safely, if at all. It would seem a miracle if it even left the letterbox.

Floralie turned from the letterbox and pushed open the front door. A bell tinkled above her as she slunk inside. Well, she supposed, at least they were *open*. The only light inside came from a green glass lamp atop a wooden counter. Behind the counter sat a large, whiskery man inscribing numbers into a thick logbook. Paranoia flittered in Floralie's chest—what if the whole town was searching for her?

But Floralie was lucky. The man dropped his pen, let loose a long sigh, and grunted in French, "The letterbox is *outside*, young lady."

Floralie fingered the lace at her sleeve. "Oh," she said. "Right, yes, I know. I just wasn't sure if it was still operating, that's all."

"Course it is," said the man. "I run the best post office in all of Giverny."

By that, Floralie supposed he meant the *only* post office.

"Everybody comes here," added the man. "Where're you sending to?"

Floralie nudged Mr. Tullier's ribbon off the envelope, then squinted down to the letter's address:

Monsieur John-Paul Laurel
22 Rue Lachance
Giverny
France

Floralie's heart stuttered. She heard her own voice as if from the other side of a mountain: "Actually—actually, never mind.

Have to go—bye," and she was halfway down the street at the jingle of the bell.

Floralie whizzed down Rue Lachance and, sweating and panting, arrived at a house with a mailbox labeled 22. Poetry itched at Floralie's fingers.

> The door was painted poppy red,
> Flower beds like library books left unread.
> Six windows wide and two windows tall,
> No one dared live in a dollhouse so dead.

No one had bought the house. "Haunted," the entire village had called it. They would, Floralie supposed, be right to some extent.

Floralie unlatched the iron lock of the weathered picket fence and crept into the skeleton of a garden. Weeds strangled the stone pathway and ivy gobbled up the front steps. Scabs of rust coated the doorknob. Surely, it would be locked, but—

Floralie caught her breath.

The key was already in the lock.

Every once in a while, when he was least expecting it, Mama would take Papa by surprise, and swing him into a dance. She would hand Papa a red rose and tell Tom to put the song "I Found a Rose in the

Devil's Garden" by William Raskin and Fred Fisher on the record player, and, oh, how Mama and Papa would dance. So often this happened that the song carved its words into Floralie's heart. It went like this:

Lost in a city that has no pity I found a rose,
Little lonesome rose;
Where smiling faces, hide broken hearts,
In happy places, where sorrow starts:

Some body's sister, whose folks have missed her,
A mother dear,
She's a lonesome tear;
For little baby, who went away,
She's kneeling maybe, just now to pray:

I found a rose, in the devil's garden,
Wandering alone, little lonesome rose,
For her the sun is never shining,
For her the clouds have, no silver lining
I found a rose, in the devil's garden,
Playing the game, of the Moth and Flame,
Beneath the powder and paint,
Maybe the heart of a saint,
Where sorrow grows, I found a rose.

I found a rose, in the devil's garden,
Wandring alone, little lonesome rose,
For her the sun is never shining,
For her the clouds have, no silver lining
I found a rose, in the devil's garden,
Playing the game, of the Moth and Flame,
But maybe deep in her heart,
She's thinking of a new start,
Where sorrow grows, I found a rose.

32

Inside, the house was like a poem fragment—only half there. Except that poems were beautiful, and this house was barren, dirty, and desolate. Naked walls and dust-carpeted floors, it was no-man's-land. Nearly everything Floralie and Tom hadn't brought with them to Whitterly End, they had sold or thrown away.

Floralie dared not take more than two steps in. She closed the door behind her and dropped *A History of Dreamlands*, a volcano of dust erupting from beneath it. Then, she slid down against the door and tore open Mr. Tullier's letter. She read:

Dear Mr. Laurel,

   You may remember me from your and Viscaria's wedding. I believe we met briefly over drinks—I am still scrubbing the champagne stain from my good tie. I do not know how you Englishmen handle your children, but to abandon them to fend for themselves seems to me the utmost of shameful acts for any parent. As I assume you are oblivious, I wanted to inform you that your daughter has arrived at my home requesting assistance in finding Viscaria.

   I admit, many years have slipped by, and I, too, have grown curious about the Viscaria I knew long ago. Floralie has brought with her something most curious indeed—a box of dried flowers with a letter from Viscaria. Viscaria writes in her letter that the flowers must be decoded in my flower language. Alas, all three copies of my floriographies were destroyed long ago.

   If you care at all for your daughter, I suggest you pluck up some courage and assist Floralie in reuniting with her mother, no matter Viscaria's state of well-being. I do wish you all the best in your remaining years and would most appreciate a prompt response.

> Fondly,
>
> Sylvestre Tullier

Floralie dropped the letter. So Mr. Tullier had lied—his flower dictionaries were destroyed. Gone. Questions whipped so fast through Floralie's mind, she felt the way an umbrella might feel in a hurricane, but one question was clear: *What now?*

If Mr. Tullier's floriographies were destroyed, how would she ever find Mama? Why had Mr. Tullier lied to her? Was Papa truly the only one who knew where Mama was sent? If so, then it was finished. Everything. The secret had died two deaths: once with the floriographies, and again with Papa.

Grandmama's awful perfume wafted under Floralie's nose at the thought. Grandmama once watched Floralie paint irises, and when Floralie finished, Grandmama said that the flowers were not botanically correct. Floralie's brush strokes were too sweeping, too impressionistic for Grandmama. She tore up the painting and made Floralie repaint the flowers her way. And then Floralie remembered spending one Easter holiday at Grandmama's with Tom. Grandmama kissed Floralie on the cheek, then told her that if she didn't fix the gap in her teeth, she would yank it shut herself, as if Floralie had any control over it. And when night rolled in, the orphans' weeping could be heard even from Grandmama's manor, and Tom whispered to Floralie, *"It's okay to be afraid."*

Floralie stood. She should have felt useless, hopeless. She had come all the way to France for *nothing.* No answers were to be found here. But she didn't feel hopeless. There was something in the air of this long-forgotten, dead, and dusty dollhouse that breathed fervor into Floralie's lungs. She was a wildflower; that was what Mama always said, and wildflowers grew within the weeds. They pushed through the cracks in cathedral walls, and just there—if Floralie squinted—she could see them creeping through the windowsills of this skeleton house. She was a wildflower, and wildflowers bloomed in hopeless places.

There had to be *something* she could do, some way "in." Some mouse hole to crawl through. And Floralie just so happened to know that this house was full of mouse holes. Two rooms away and one staircase up was Mama and Papa's room. Surely, Floralie thought, one of them must have left something—some clue, some memory, anything.

Floralie's footsteps echoed throughout the hollow house as she skittered up the stairs. Perhaps it was simply the look of the place that brought about the smell, but Floralie could swear Mama's bedroom still smelled of the wildflowers Mama kept in her windows and the incense she once tried to burn to "ignite her creativity," but only ended up igniting the curtains.

The only furniture that remained was the four-poster bed frame and mattress that had been too large to fit through the door. As Floralie neared the bed frame, out of the corner of her eye, Papa's big blue chair and Mama's ornately carved vanity table flickered. But each time she looked again, all she saw were shadows.

The mattress was sunken and marred with dirt. How dirt had found its way to the mattress was a mystery to Floralie, but as she looked closer, her breath quickened. The dirt was not dirt—it was charcoal. Someone had drawn in charcoal all over the mattress. Childish, clumsy, and disproportionate, but drawings they were—or *were* they?

Pins and needles prickled up Floralie's spine. She stepped back and examined the mattress drawing as a whole; it was a map. Or, at least, something similar to a map. The image was made up of a series of arrows connecting five pictures.

The first picture, Floralie took to be a tree (though it could have more easily passed as a broccoli floret), and beneath it sat two stick figures, one boy, one girl. An arrow pointed from that picture to one of the boy walking down a winding road. At the end of the road stood a dollhouse, six windows wide and two windows tall. Another arrow pointed to two male stick figures, one twice as tall as the other. The second-to-last picture was a triangle divided by horizontal lines into thirds. It looked to Floralie like an obelisk.

The final one was so poorly drawn that Floralie could not make out exactly what it was. The drawing depicted two slender triangles lazily crossed over each other to form a lopsided X. It could have been a million things—a crossroads sign, a pair of swords, perhaps even a feeble attempt at a four-leaf clover.

Floralie returned her gaze to the first picture—the boy and girl under the tree. Looking at it again, Floralie realized it wasn't just any old tree, and the children weren't just any old children. The tree was a willow, the children were Floralie and Nino, and one thing was certain: The drawings were Nino's. He had been here, and these drawings were his story since the night he left Monet's house.

Floralie tore through the streets to Monet's manor. She had memorized the drawings by heart, repeated them over and over again in her mind: willow and stick figures, road and house, tall and short figures, obelisk, mystery triangles.

She found Miss Clairoux outside the manor carrying a stack of books up to her eyes.

"What've you got there, Miss Clairoux?" said Floralie, forcing a laugh. She tried to act as normally as possible, even though her heart was still stuttering over the run-in with Grandmama. There was no need to worry Miss Clairoux.

The books leaned precariously, and Miss Clairoux swayed to balance them. "I had to rescue them, *ma chérie.* Had absolutely no choice when I heard that Madame Favreau was tossing them out of her library. Now, never mind me. What's got you in such a dreadful state? You smell of dirt and dust, and . . . is that charcoal?"

"Miss Clairoux—" but Floralie stopped, for she simply did not know where to begin.

"Yes," prodded Miss Clairoux. "Go on."

"I've found Nino—I mean—no, I haven't found *him*. But a piece of him."

And as they ambled back to Monet's house, Floralie told Miss Clairoux about the drawings.

"I didn't know Nino could draw," said Miss Clairoux as they reached the end of Monet's tulip path.

"He can't," said Floralie, pushing open the front door. "Not well, anyway. I couldn't figure out what the last drawing was. But you know what I'm sure of, Miss Clairoux?"

"What's that, dear?"

"I'm sure that was Nino at the library. He took that drawing book, and he's learning to draw—however horribly. Somewhere out there, he's drawing." *He's learning my language. He's trying,* was what Floralie wanted to say, but she kept that to herself.

As they reached the door, Floralie turned to Miss Clairoux again. "I don't think he left those drawings in my old house for his own amusement," she said. "He's guiding me someplace . . . I've just got to figure out where."

Floralie was about to take the doorknob when she remembered the crumpled letter growing hot in her palm. Floralie clenched it harder, listening to it crackle in her fist.

"And, Miss Clairoux, there's something else." She gritted her teeth. "It's about Mr. Tullier. He's been lying to us. This whole time, he's been nothing but a wrinkly old liar."

Miss Clairoux tilted her chin. "My—*ma chérie*, that is no way to talk of Mr. Tullier. You must be mistaken. Let's get you inside; surely, you've just had a spot too much sun."

"I'm not mistaken, Miss Clairoux. Mr. Tullier's flower dictionaries are destroyed. Every last one."

"Art is believing in the possibilities of things you cannot see," said *Mama, leaving a squiggly purple passionflower behind La Musée du Louvre. But Floralie knew that time is built on belief, too. And she knew*

that belief can change memories, and she knew that memories change people, and people change their minds. People change their minds.

Yet still, Floralie couldn't flick away her belief in Mama, no matter how impossible. No matter how improbable.

33

"You two are late. Did everything go smoothly in the village?" said Mr. Tullier when Floralie and Miss Clairoux marched through the yellow kitchen. He leaned against the counter, sipping a mug of coffee. Philomenos lay curled in a napkin on the table. "What've you got there?" he added, gesturing to Floralie's dreamland book and Miss Clairoux's teetering stack. His subtle smirk made Floralie's stomach twist with anger.

Floralie did not answer. Instead, she demanded, "When were you planning on telling me? When were you planning on telling us your floriographies were destroyed?"

Mr. Tullier set his mug on the counter. "You read the letter. You had no right to read it."

"It was addressed to my father. My *dead* father. I had every right to read it, and now I know the truth—you've been lying to us all along."

Mr. Tullier waggled a finger at Floralie. "You said your father left you—nothing about him snuffing it. I think that makes *you* the liar here."

"*Me?* You've been the one playing games—getting me to work for you for free! You never had any plans of finding her. It was just a game to you. I've been so *stupid.* My mother never meant anything to you."

"Don't you dare—"

Miss Clairoux cut in: "Let's all just calm—"

But Floralie fired, "I *do* dare—"

"VISCARIA—" Mr. Tullier whirled around and banged his fists on the counter.

Philomenos jolted awake.

Wrinkles branched like tree twigs along Mr. Tullier's eyes. "Viscaria"—he choked on the word—"meant *everything to me.*" There was something about the stops and the sighs and the sadness in his voice that sounded like a broken poem. "All I needed," breathed Mr. Tullier, "was time."

"You've had your time," shot Floralie.

"I HAVE—" Mr. Tullier yanked a chair from the table and slouched into it. "I have *something*."

He reached into his pocket and pulled from it a wrinkly, yellowed paper. There were mouse bites in the corner; it was the same paper Philomenos had attempted to steal in the garden. "My last page," he said, handing it to Floralie.

Floralie and Miss Clairoux both sat down across Mr. Tullier. Floralie took the page and read,

EGLANTINE: Poetry; I wound to heal

Eglantine (*Rosa rubiginosa*), also known as "sweet briar" and "wild rose," is a flower from the Rosaceae family native to Europe. Eglantines are characterized by five pink petals surrounding a cluster of yellow stamens.

The eglantine's meaning is one of confusion for some, but of truth for others. While its two meanings, "poetry" and "I wound to heal," may appear separate, I argue they are tied as one. It is more often the poetry that aches with longing, sorrow, and brokenness that heals those with despairing hearts, rather than the poetry that is complete in happiness. Indeed, poetry wounds to heal. Therefore, the eglantine is a powerful flower, as, much like poetry, it encompasses not only joy and sorrow, but also healing.

A watercolor of the pink flower dotted the edge of the page. Floralie recognized it immediately as one of the box's flowers.

"Reminds me of Nino," muttered Floralie. The anger yanking at her stomach eased its grip. She looked to Mr. Tullier and added, "He left me some drawings—more of a map, really. I think he wants me to follow it."

"Well, go on—draw them out," said Mr. Tullier, heaving himself out of his chair. "There are newspapers on the sitting-room love seat—use one of those. I'll get a pen."

Floralie nodded and crossed the kitchen to the blue-walled sitting room. Atop the love seat was, indeed, a stack of newspapers. Floralie grabbed the topmost paper, and was about to dash back to the kitchen when a headline at the bottom right of the page jolted her heart. She dropped into the love seat and peered closer . . .

MISSING PERSON ALERT!
Floralie Laurel, 11, of Whitterly End, Kent, England, reportedly vanished the evening of

July 5 with Delphine Clairoux, 68, and her alleged grandson, Norman, whose surname and age are unknown. They were last seen inside the Whitterly Public Library by Laurel's brother and legal guardian, Thomas Laurel, 20. Said Thomas in an interview to the Whitterly Times, "I will go to the ends of the earth to bring back my sister. She will be found, and she will return home." The only evidence left was a letter from Laurel to her brother stating she would be traveling to France. Authorities have begun searching both England and France to bring Laurel home.

This is the second report of missing children in the area after orphan Konstantinos Leventis, 12, disappeared from the Adelaide Laurel Orphanage for Unfortunate Children, also of Whitterly End, only two months prior. It is uncertain whether the incidents are related, as well as whether either case is one of kidnapping or runaways.

Laurel is a petite child with curly blond hair, green eyes, and fair skin. Clairoux is tall, gray-haired, and blind. If spotted, do not approach Clairoux, as she could react with violence. If you have any information regarding the whereabouts of Floralie Laurel, please contact the British Association of Missing Persons at the address below.

"Floralie? Floralie, are you quite all right?" Miss Clairoux's voice drifted through the hall, and she and Mr. Tullier appeared in the doorway.

Mr. Tullier narrowed his eyes. "You look like you've seen a ghost."

"The paper, it . . ." Blood rushed from Floralie's head and pounded in her ears.

"Yes?" breathed Miss Clairoux. "Yes, what is it, dear? Tell me what the paper says."

"They're looking for us. And I don't think it'll be long now till they figure out where we are."

Floralie read the article for Miss Clairoux, then added, "I saw her. Grandmama. I saw her today in the village."

Mr. Tullier crouched down on his knees, creaking and crackling with the floorboards. He handed Floralie a pen and whispered, "*Draw them now*. Draw what Nino drew."

Floralie took the pen, and in the newspaper's margins, she sketched Nino's symbols, explaining each as she went.

"These figures under the tree are me and Nino," she said,

pointing to the first image. "And this one here is my old house—that's where he left the drawings. And this one, with the tall and short figures, I'd assume one figure is Nino, but I'm not sure of the other. This one, I think is an obelisk, and the last"—she drew in the two crossed triangles—"I haven't a clue."

Miss Clairoux trailed her fingers along the bumps in the page. Mr. Tullier studied the drawings carefully, then, after a moment, he said, "The fourth one—that's not an obelisk. That's the Eiffel Tower."

Floralie looked to the fourth image again. "Y-you're right." How could she have missed it? The triangle, the three lines separating each level . . . It was obvious.

Floralie looked up. "D'you think Nino's gone to Paris?"

"Yes," said Mr. Tullier. "And those crossed triangles—could they be pointe shoes?"

Something stirred in Floralie's stomach. Butterflies, perhaps—no—*fireflies*.

"I think that boy is on to something," muttered Mr. Tullier. "Don't know *how* he's onto it, but he knows."

"Knows what?" said Floralie.

"About the last floriography."

"The last floriography?" chirped Miss Clairoux. "I thought you said they were destroyed?"

"Mine were. But . . . there was one other. One that escaped."

"Well—where'd it go? Who took it?" asked Floralie.

"Viscaria," said Mr. Tullier. "It had belonged to her, after all—well, sort of. Some might argue she stole it from me."

"Well, that doesn't help us much, now does it?" Floralie said with a sigh. "If I could find Viscaria without the floriography, I would."

"*Listen*, Floralie," pressed Mr. Tullier. "Viscaria kept the book in Paris. In Paris, in the same place she kept her pointe shoes—at least, that was the last place I remember her keeping it."

Floralie held her breath. "And where was that, Mr. Tullier?"

"Palais Garnier, where she used to perform with Le Ballet Royale, even before she was a principal dancer. She kept it in a secret compartment beneath a drawer in the vanity of her dressing room. She kept it there to hide it."

"From who?"

"Me. Viscaria thought if I ever found it, I would burn it. But you know what's funny? I did find it. Viscaria began performing with the ballet when she was a teenager, still working for me. She kept a copy backstage at the theater in Paris. After we lost touch, I gave up on getting it back. Even living in the same village, we never really saw each other. I kept to myself. Seeing her, I knew, would hurt more than most anything.

"Besides, I just couldn't . . . I couldn't bring myself to hurt it. Not even to touch it. That one last book. I can hardly imagine it's still there now, though. That was years ago . . . She must have been no older than fifteen when I found that book. She danced in many theaters after all; it wasn't as if she *owned* that dressing room. But my, was it her favorite."

"So there's a chance," said Floralie. "There's a chance the book is still there."

"Yes," said Mr. Tullier. "There is a chance."

"Then I'm taking it. When do we leave for Paris?"

"Now."

"Now?" Floralie's head was spinning.

"Yes, Mr. Tullier's right," Miss Clairoux replied. "The sooner we find Viscaria, the better."

And so Floralie and Miss Clairoux readied themselves to leave. Floralie packed in her bag the flower box, the dreamland book, and the Eglantine page. Miss Clairoux tucked a sleepy Philomenos into her coat pocket. When they returned to the kitchen, they found Mr. Tullier surprisingly dressed in slacks and a button-up vest rather than his usual bathrobe, sipping another mug of coffee.

"You've got your things, then?" he said.

Floralie nodded.

"You and Miss Clairoux will need disguises. We'll stop by the village, then leave from there." He placed his mug in the sink, licked his lips, and said, *"Allons-y."*

And off they went.

The first time Papa took Floralie to watch one of Mama's ballet shows, Floralie thought the dancers looked like cotton seeds in the wind. They danced with great elegance, but when Mama came onstage, all eyes turned to her. The audience leaned in so close, so quietly, one could almost hear Mama's breath, soft and gentle. She was grand, she was roses and marigolds and poppies, blooming with every step.

And Papa would lean in close and whisper, "Isn't she something, Flory?"

After the performance, Papa gave Mama a bouquet of carnations, all different colors. Mama kissed Papa's forehead, and then kissed Tom's forehead, and then kissed Floralie's. They were happy.

34

As Floralie, Miss Clairoux, and Mr. Tullier sat on the train from Giverny to Paris, Floralie gazed out her window, watching the tulip fields disappear. The green, green grass melded into Mama's eyes, so bright, so full of life. Excitement and nervousness fluttered in Floralie's stomach at the thought of maybe finding Mama. She held Philomenos up to the window so he could see the fields disappearing, too. Mr. Tullier sat with a newspaper covering all but his legs, and Miss Clairoux slept, hat over her face.

Floralie pulled the dreamland book from her suitcase and leafed through to the last pages—a section devoted to impressionist artists. Degas's ballerinas danced across the pages, Van Gogh's skies swirled and twinkled, even in black and white. And then Monet. The same quote Floralie had read the day Nino first showed her the book stared back at her. The same quote Mama would hum on summer days, sigh on winter ones. *I must have flowers, always and always.* But what was most peculiar was what was beside it.

Floralie's own flower drawings bloomed in the margins of Monet's page. Floralie knew that when she was younger, she drew on just about every surface she could find, but how strange it was that she would draw in this particular book. Someone—Tom, Papa, or Mama—must have checked out the book from the library.

Beside the drawings, a photograph of a Monet painting was circled. Within the frame, a girl, daisy-blond hair and faraway eyes, wandered down a garden path, carrying an armful of flowers. Floralie recognized the path from Monet's garden. The caption read, *Young Girl in the Garden at Giverny*, by Claude Monet, at La Musée de l'Orangerie, Paris. Floralie vaguely recalled seeing the painting once when she was younger—she had, after all, visited La Musée de l'Orangerie many times with Mama and Tom. Beneath the caption was a quote:

Everyone discusses my art and pretends to understand, as if it were necessary to understand, when it is simply necessary to love.
—Claude Monet

It was a lovely painting and all, and a lovely quote, too, but Floralie wondered why it was circled. And perhaps more important, who had circled it, and why were Floralie's own drawings beside it?

Floralie closed the book and then her eyes. And though she knew there wouldn't be flowers, and she knew the grass would be golden, the trees barren, she tried to fly to her enchanted forest. But something held her back, as if simply *knowing* winter had fallen in the forest anchored her to the ground. So instead, she wrote a poem on her hand.

> *Flowers*
> *By Floralie Alice Laurel*
>
> *Preserve my flowers in oil and pigment*
> *And memories in long-winded letters never sent.*
> *I know that fears grow in gardens*
> *And my heart will harden*
> *Yet still, I never want to leave*
> *I am naïve*
> *Because of the wretched season's turn*
> *I never learn.*
>
> *And I am to blame*
> *For letting my heart play the garden's game*
> *Of this cruel vulnerability,*
> *Watching my flowers wilt in the cold reality.*
> *Come back the next day,*
> *And the next day, and the next day*
> *To the frostbitten wasteland of rainbows turned gray.*

But despite constant persistence,
All my forget-me-nots keep their distance.
I know that regrets grow in barren land,
And until the day I understand
The importance of caring about things that disappear,
I swallow the fear
And know that there is a reason
For the changing of the season.

Floralie wondered what Nino would think of it. She held *A History of Dreamlands* to her heart and wondered about Sappho, the great poet catching fireflies and words thousands of years ago. She wondered what her life was like. If she had ever felt vulnerable and alone and scared. If she ever felt like she had a gap in her heart. Certainly, Floralie couldn't be the only one; but at that moment, she felt like it.

Mama's measuring tape lay tangled on the living room floor. Its ends were frayed and numbers blurred, but still, it made its daily route around Mama's waist. Mama sat with Floralie perched on her bony knee, reading aloud Alice in Wonderland, *and giving all the characters different voices—some serious, but mostly silly.*

"You're not a paper doll, Floralie," said Mama when they came to a chapter break. "You're made of porcelain, glass eyes, hand-painted lips. Never let anyone press you into paper." She shut her the book on a wild

tansy between pages 68 and 69.

Floralie nodded her head, but that was where Mama and Floralie differed. Because Floralie believed she was flesh and bone, not porcelain, not glass, not paper. And that one belief made all the difference.

35

"Ah, Paris!" swooned Miss Clairoux, taking a gulp of air as they stepped onto the station platform. Floralie gulped in some air, too; it smelled of thick smoke and metallic train engines, but tasted like freshly baking bread and marmalade. It tasted like Mama's perfume, too; it tasted the way wildflowers smell.

Mr. Tullier strode ahead, and Miss Clairoux and Floralie followed. When they emerged into the streets of Paris, Floralie soaked in the scene of bustling men and women. Black cars rattled by, voices leaped to and fro, and the buoyant jazz of a street musician's saxophone galloped down the pavement. The sky was bleak and drizzle spattered her dress, but Floralie was still in awe. She remembered Paris, of course, from years ago when her mother had taken her and Tom to see the shows. Mama had even shown Floralie her dressing room and let Floralie play with the tins of makeup. And when it was time for the show, Tom and Floralie would sit in the far back with Papa and watch Mama fly.

As they strode through the streets, coal-faced boys skittered by, and every time Floralie glimpsed one, for a fleeting moment, she would swear it was Nino. But no, they were just thieves and chimney sweeps, crooked grins and grimy hands . . .

They turned corner after corner, and soon, lights began to ease the evening darkness. One more corner, and the streets swarmed with women in silken dresses and bejeweled cloche hats, draped over the arms of their black-suited escorts. A gigantic banner hung across a tall building. Floralie's heart fluttered; she had seen a banner like it before. LE BALLET ROYALE DE PARIS, it read, PRÉSENTE LA BELLE COLETTE BEAUCHENE DANS GISELLE.

Floralie tore her eyes from the banner and hurried to keep up with Mr. Tullier and Miss Clairoux. "Mr. Tullier, is that it?" she said, unable to mask the excitement from her voice. "That's Palais Garnier, isn't it?"

Mr. Tullier glanced down to her. "Yes. Don't get too excited, though. You won't be in the audience."

"Oh." Floralie's shoulders slumped. "Then where will I be?"

"Come with me." Mr. Tullier led Floralie and Miss Clairoux

into a hat shop beside the theater and asked the shopkeeper for the restrooms. The shopkeeper led them to the back and left them be.

"Delphine, you change into the dress from Madame Bonnet's Boutique," said Mr. Tullier. "And, Floralie—for now, you'll need something a little different." Mr. Tullier unzipped his suitcase, and when he opened the lid, Floralie's hand shot for her mouth. She stared in awe. The suitcase was stuffed with lace and silk; Floralie *knew* that silk. Mr. Tullier pulled out the dress and handed it to Floralie, before pulling out a black suit for himself.

The skirt of the dress was made of white tulle dotted with pearls, and it had a veil to match. It was the very same dress Mama had worn in her earlier performances with Le Ballet Royale, only this one was a few years older, as it appeared it might suit a girl hardly older than Floralie.

"This was my mother's ballet costume," said Floralie.

Mr. Tullier nodded. "Yes. She left it with me when . . . when she left me. It was for one of her first bigger roles. She was a wili."

Floralie knew the wilis to be the ghostlike figures that used to haunt Floralie's dreams after every performance of *Giselle*, not because she feared them, but because they entranced her. She ran her fingers along the puffy fabric, Philomenos crawling over its ridges as if riding ocean waves. "But I'm not—I'm not a *ballerina*, Mr. Tullier, what—"

"You have one job, Floralie, one job only, and that is to sneak into the dressing rooms and find the book. The only way in is to be a part of the cast."

"But all the dancers are older than me, surely—"

"Wear the veil, and no one will notice," said Mr. Tullier, but then he muttered, "*J'espère.*"

I hope so too, Mr. Tullier, thought Floralie, for she was starting to feel rather uncertain about Mr. Tullier's plan.

"Leave your dress in my suitcase by the stairwell to the dressing rooms. When you've got the book, change into that dress *immediately*, so no one sees what you're up to."

"Okay," said Floralie, though warily. "Okay, I'll try," and she changed into the costume, Miss Clairoux into her gown, and Mr. Tullier into his suit. On their way out, Floralie draped Miss Clairoux's emerald coat over herself to hide the costume, trying not to trip on the over-long fabric.

As they entered the theater, Floralie felt as if she were spiraling back in time to when she was small, to when the gold-encrusted ceiling looked farther away than the sky and the chandeliers looked brighter than stars.

"Do you remember the way to the dressing rooms?" whispered Mr. Tullier.

"I think so," said Floralie.

"Then go now. We will meet you outside at intermission." He

handed Floralie the suitcase with Madame Bonnet's dress.

Floralie slipped Philomenos into her bag, then handed the bag to Miss Clairoux along with the coat.

"*Bonne chance*, Floralie," whispered Miss Clairoux, and Floralie began to weave through the crowd, wili veil crumpled in her free hand like paper stolen by mice.

When the dance master threw Mama out of the theater, Mama simply stood, staring at her name lit up on the banner.

"I danced there first," said Mama, coltsfoot flower drooping out from her low-slung ballet bag. "It just isn't fair. I danced there first."

36

Floralie had never entered the dressing room alone before; it felt strange, not to have her mother's fragile hand to hold on to. As she neared the narrow side-staircase leading down to the dressing rooms, Floralie tucked the suitcase behind a banister. She fastened the veil to her hair and draped it over her face, then descended the stairs. The chattering above disintegrated, and Floralie was plunged into memory. She slipped off her shoes and held them in her hands like one might at the beach. *Shoes,* Mama once told her, *are the enemies of dancers.*

Floralie counted off the doors: *One, two, three, four.* Mama's dressing room had been the fifth, which she shared with seven other ballerinas. Floralie's fingers met the brass doorknob, and she twisted . . .

Four dancers were there, three of them at their mirrors and one stretched out on the floor in a split. Floralie avoided eye contact with them as she made a beeline for Mama's corner vanity table, praying the new owner of the vanity was not the dancer on the floor.

Floralie took a breath, pulled back the chair, and sat before the mirror. A small plaque above the mirror read in curly gold letters *Colette*. Atop the vanity table, among the tins of blush and tubes of lipstick, was a small childish drawing, tiny potatolike figures hugging with stick-arms bigger potato figures. At the top of the page, in wobbly script read, *"Ma Tante Colette et Moi."* "My Aunt Colette and Me," Floralie translated. And she smiled because she remembered leaving drawings like that on this very vanity table for her mother as well, scribbles that evolved into stick figures that evolved into paintings. But oddly, she didn't feel *happy*, precisely, at the memory . . . It was strange the way it made her both sad and happy at the same time.

Floralie brushed away the memories. She had to find the book; that was what she came here for. Find the book, decode the flowers, save Mama. Floralie remembered Mr. Tullier's words: *"She kept it in Paris, in the same place she kept her pointe shoes . . . a secret compartment beneath a drawer in the vanity of her dressing room."*

There were two drawers beneath the table. Floralie reached for the topmost one and slid it open carefully, quietly. Inside were two pairs of ratty ballet slippers, a hairbrush, and a sewing kit. She slid the drawer shut, then pulled open the second and peeked inside. There were at least a hundred hairpins, a pair of pearl earrings, a silk flower, and copious amounts of gauze.

The compartment, thought Floralie. *It's got to be here somewhere.* As she sifted through the drawer, however, someone shouted, "Colette!" A wili at a vanity table a ways off sprang out of her chair and clasped her hands together.

A tall, slender woman glided in, pointe shoes in hand. She wore the same blue tulle skirt and velvet bodice that Floralie's mother had worn for the first act of *Giselle* when she had played the starring role.

"You're beautiful!" bubbled a wili in French, and the other wilis gathered around Colette as well, saying, "You make a perfect Giselle!" and "Are you nervous? *Don't* be nervous."

Floralie's heart beat three times faster. She slid shut the drawer and slunk back from the vanity table as Colette brushed off her fellow dancers and ambled over to it. Floralie stood in the corner, waiting for one of the dancers to realize she wasn't one of them, but they were all too preoccupied with Colette.

Colette laced up her pointe shoes, poked a few more hairpins into her bun, and said, "How do I look, my loves?"

The wilis chorused back: "Gorgeous!" "Fantastic!" "Stunning!"

Someone knocked at the door. "Yes, it's open," said Colette, and an older man with slicked-back gray hair and a black suit and bow tie stepped in. Floralie recognized him as the ballet master, Edgard Bertrand, from when her mother had danced for him. "Audience is settled, ladies. Are you just about ready?"

Colette and the other dancers nodded, and the man said, "Good, follow me backstage please."

Floralie froze; she clutched the rim of a vanity table behind her as the dancers filtered out of the dressing room. Mr. Bertrand was about to leave when he caught sight of Floralie. "You too! Come, this is no time for nerves."

Floralie couldn't speak. She simply nodded and followed the dancers into the corridor. She watched them from the back as they floated down the hall like snowdrops in a breeze. Floralie tried to match their elegance—their soft footsteps, perfectly turned-out feet—but simply felt like a waddling penguin.

When they arrived backstage, Floralie found herself amidst a crowd of at least fifty dancers, all in dazzling costumes. She sidled to the corner as Mr. Bertrand ushered the first group of dancers into the stage's wings.

The first scenes dragged on and on. Floralie half wished she could watch in the wings, and half wished she could disappear altogether. She watched the other dancers backstage and tried to mimic some of their stretching as she waited, and with each minute that passed, she felt as if something yanked her stomach even tighter—not to mention her hamstrings. When at last, act 1 neared its end, Mr. Bertrand hurried all the wilis—including Floralie—into the wings.

Floralie knew she should leave, sneak away and find the drawer, but her feet would not listen to her head, and they carried her to the front of the crowd of ballerinas. And as she peeked out to the stage, she felt as if her heart would burst, for it was as if she were five years old again, watching her mother glide across the stage. But though Colette danced with much grace, she could not even come close to Viscaria's vivacity.

As the music slowed and the curtains closed, Floralie snaked back through the crowd. *Focus*, she thought. *The drawer, the compartment, the book*. She repeated the words over and over again as she flew down the corridor until at last she reached the dressing room.

She cracked open the door; it was empty. She crept inside, tiptoed over to Colette's vanity table, and pulled open the second drawer, as quiet as possible. The pounding of her heart, she thought, could very well have been an elephant stampede. She brushed aside the hairpins, pearl earrings, silk flowers, and gauze . . . nothing. No secret compartment, no floriography.

Floralie slammed the drawer (immediately regretting it as

the sound reverberated around the room) and sat on the wood floor, arms crossed. And then something squeaked. Floralie narrowed her eyes, for the sound had not come from the room, but rather, within the drawer. Floralie pulled it open, and the squeaking grew louder. She knew that sound well . . . It sounded like Philomenos.

Floralie pulled the drawer all the way out from the vanity table and placed it beside her. When she looked inside, she found a mouse hole chewed inside a tiny door at the back of the drawer. *This must be it.* Floralie unlatched the door . . .

Her fingers trailed along the wood, gathering cobwebs and dust under her nails. She twisted her elbow to reach farther into the compartment. Still, no book. And then Floralie's pinky finger brushed against something that made her arm shoot out of the compartment. Something dead; something *spidery.* But as her hand came whizzing out, so did the spider—or, at least, what Floralie had *thought* was a spider. Indeed, it was dead, but it was not an insect. It was a flower.

A bony hand grabbed Floralie's shoulder; she whirled around. Colette towered over her, wide eyes blazing. "Imposter!" she screeched. "Imposter in the dressing room!" Her voice bounced off the line of mirrors, and footsteps pounded from the hallway. "What are you doing in my things? Little thief, are you? Stealing my pearls, no doubt? Hand them over."

"I—no—I'm not—I haven't taken anything, honest!" Floralie curled her fingers around the flower.

Mr. Bertrand burst into the dressing room. "What's going on?" he bellowed.

"This girl is an imposter!" declared Colette, digging her fingernails into Floralie's shoulder.

"No—well, yes, just listen!" pleaded Floralie.

But Mr. Bertrand would not listen. He seized Floralie's arm and dragged her into the corridor. He slammed her against the wall, his nose an inch from hers. His breath smelled like onions and burnt cabbage. "What are you doing in Mademoiselle Beauchene's vanity? Is that one of our costumes?" he snarled.

"No—no, it's my mother's! Please, Mr. Bertrand, please! I'm Floralie, Viscaria's daughter, Viscaria Laurel, don't you remember? She danced for you up until a few years ago. I used to come here all the time . . ."

Mr. Bertrand's grip slackened, but his eyes grew hard. "*Viscaria*," he spat. "So *you* are the spawn of the dancer who nearly single-handedly demolished my career?"

The memory of Mama crumpling onto the Palais stage crashed through Floralie's brain. And though Floralie had watched from a balcony seat, the jagged breaths of Mama still beat in her ears.

"I just need to know what happened to her," said Floralie. "All

I was doing was looking for something she may have left behind—something important."

But Mr. Bertrand would not listen. He clutched her forearm and dragged Floralie down the hall, up the staircase, and toward the wide doors. And then he hissed, "I shall let you go now, but only because I take pity on your pathetic life."

Mr. Bertrand threw Floralie out into the street, and she landed with a splat in a puddle. The doors swung shut, and Floralie dragged herself up, brushing mud off the wili costume. Two figures appeared from the fog and rushed over to her—Mr. Tullier and Miss Clairoux.

"What are you doing here?" said Floralie.

"It's intermission, of course," said Miss Clairoux. "Like we said, we'd meet you here. Goodness, why are you all wet?" she added, stroking Floralie's hair.

"No time for chitchat," cut in Mr. Tullier, scanning Floralie up and down. "Where's the book? Did you find the book?"

"No," breathed Floralie. "I didn't find a single—" but Floralie stopped short.

She uncurled her palm . . . The petals of the cobwebbed flower hung by threads to the stem. And then the flower disintegrated in her hand, slipped through her fingers . . .

Memory was tricky that way. How it played hide-and-seek,

cat and mouse. How it turned over itself like a shaken hourglass. Floralie remembered. She remembered everything now. Mama left flowers. Like this one behind her vanity, she left them in places that meant something to her; always, they were different. A celandine behind a gargoyle on their family trip to Switzerland, a butterfly weed in Papa's sock drawer, a lupine in Mama's windowsill, a laurestine beneath her bed.

"The *musée*. We've got to go to La Musée de l'Orangerie," said Floralie, for Mama had left her last flower there, behind a very particular painting that Floralie had come to know well. After all, the museum was the last place Floralie and Mama had visited before things changed. And now, things were about to change. Everything was going to change.

After the ballet master officially kicked Mama out of the company, she wore her pointe shoes for an entire week, and though her feet bubbled with blisters, not once did she take them off. It was not until Sunday that she yanked her feet out. She buried the shoes in the garden, muttering prayers all the while. She came back into the house weeping over a mourning bride flower. But she said to Floralie, "I have you, and my love for you dances with far more grace than any ballerina. That is all that matters."

37

La Musée de l'Orangerie was hardly a ten-minute walk away. The rain swept through Paris as Floralie, Miss Clairoux, and Mr. Tullier swept through the streets. While Floralie raced through the puddles, passersby looked on in a mixture of amusement and disdain at the girl in the mud-spattered ballet costume.

Floralie had no time—or breath—to explain to Miss Clairoux or Mr. Tullier. They simply had to trust her. "This way," said Floralie, beckoning to Mr. Tullier and Miss Clairoux.

The Tuileries Garden, large enough to fit a small village, blossomed with street performers and tourists, families and newlyweds. Floralie raced through the rows lined with tulips and daffodils, colors blurring in the corners of her eyes. The rush of the River Seine filled Floralie's ears; they were close. In no time, a grand building complete with pillars and sparkling windows towered over them. The front doors barely kept shut as visitors filtered out in a constant stream—it was nearly closing time.

Floralie, Miss Clairoux, and Mr. Tullier squeezed inside and waited in line for barely three minutes, record time for Floralie. When they stepped up to the ticket counter, the teller scanned Floralie's outfit and raised his eyebrows.

"And . . . how may I help you?" he asked.

"Three tickets, please," said Floralie.

The teller glanced down to his watch and frowned. "We close in a half hour."

"Perfect!" spat Floralie. "I mean—yes, that will do fine."

Miss Clairoux exchanged a pocketful of francs for three tickets and maps, and Floralie whizzed down the hall.

"*Ma chérie*, wait!" called Miss Clairoux from behind. "What exactly are we here for?"

Floralie skidded to a stop and turned back.

"A painting," breathed Floralie. "Mr. Tullier—you were Monet's gardener; you must've known his paintings better than anyone. You've got to help me look." Floralie recalled the image from *A History of Dreamlands*. "This one is of a girl with a flower basket. She's walking through Monet's garden at Giverny, and she . . . she looks like me," Floralie suddenly realized. She felt the way one feels upon remembering a dream months, years even, after having dreamed it. "It's called *Young Girl in the Garden at Giverny*. Please, you must know—"

Mr. Tullier nodded. "I know the one. Of course I'll help." Floralie thought that may have been the most agreeable thing Mr. Tullier had ever said.

The three zigzagged through long corridors and zoomed up grand stairwells. Each painting Floralie passed was a new wonderland, someone else's garden. The paintings tugged at her fingertips, inviting her into their gardens. Each one was like a mother telling her child a bedtime story. She could have stared at every painting for hours, got lost in them . . . but no. She had to focus. *The painting, the painting, the painting.*

When they came to Monet's department, Floralie stopped short.

"It should be here . . . somewhere," she muttered.

"She left flowers in places that were important to her," Floralie explained to Miss Clairoux and Mr. Tullier. "And the last one she left was here."

Floralie strode into the room full of Monet paintings, and Mr. Tullier and Miss Clairoux hurried to keep up.

"So . . . ," said Miss Clairoux, huffing, "what you're saying is that your mother left a flower here—by a painting?"

"Yes. I found the painting in Nino's book—*A History of Dreamlands*. I thought I remembered the title from somewhere, and it was my mother. Every time we visited the library, she pored over that book. That's why my own drawings were in the book, and that's why the painting was circled. My mother circled it. That girl in painting, that's not just any girl. That's *Viscaria*."

The black-and-white photograph from *A History of Dreamlands* did not do the painting justice. Mama gazed somewhere over Floralie's head, just beyond the painting's edge, eyes lost in wonderland. Her white dress was not white, but fashioned of the most delicately curated colors—the palest of pinks, hints of cerulean blue, tints of viridian green. Her back was turned to darkness, and she carried her poppies and daffodils into bright light, a place of windswept flowers almost as radiant as her. Nearly as vivacious.

Miss Clairoux gaped at Floralie, then at Mr. Tullier. "Is that *true*? Our daughter? The subject of one of Claude Monet's paintings?"

Mr. Tullier smiled wider than Floralie had ever seen him smile. "Clever girl," he muttered, patting Floralie's shoulder.

Floralie clutched Miss Clairoux's hand as they treaded closer to the painting until they were inches from it. "We left the flower together," said Floralie, "when I knew she would be leaving soon. The day we left it, Mama told me the flower was the 'gap' in her.

And in the letter in the flower box, she said I would find her in the gap between petals and leaves . . . *This* is the flower. This is the flower that will lead me to her. And we left it right . . . *here.*"

Floralie recalled Mama tucking the flower behind the frame at the edge of the painting's left-hand corner.

"*There. That little girl will keep her safe for me,*" Mama had said. She was talking about the flower between her skeleton-thin fingers, but still called it *her.* She hadn't always spoken about flowers in that way; it was one of the reasons Papa had her sent off.

"*Will you be kept safe, Mama?*" Floralie had asked.

Mama's fingers went limp as she tucked the flower behind the painting. "*I will be. But, my wildflower, some flowers are not meant to be kept safe. Some flowers are meant to grow by train tracks and on mountaintops.*"

The words had sounded like poetry, and now, they rang in Floralie's ears as she stood on tiptoes, reached for the top of the painting. Her fingers traced the edge of the frame . . .

"*Tu! Arrêtez!*"

Floralie whipped around.

A guard hurtled toward Floralie, arms outstretched, navy coat flapping. "*Oui, tu! Petite fille!*"

Floralie scrambled back as the guard lunged. Two more guards caught notice and rushed to the scene, shoving tourists and art students out of their way. As Floralie struggled to her feet, a hand gripped her ankle and she fell back. Another hand grabbed the neck of her dress and yanked her to her feet. Floralie's vision muddied, and people swirled around her, paintings spun, corridors melted. She felt like a bug lost in a labyrinth of carnation petals, too small to tell what exactly was happening.

"*Non, monsieur,* she's with me!" shouted Mr. Tullier.

A flock of tourists gathered near to watch the spectacle.

"*S'il vous plait!*" cried Miss Clairoux. "She's just a child."

The guard's grip on Floralie slackened for but only a moment as he glanced from Miss Clairoux to Floralie, and back to Miss Clairoux again. Floralie seized her chance to break free, but the guard only grabbed her shoulder, sinking his fingernails into her skin.

"Stop it! That hurts!" Floralie shouted, once in English and once in French.

"*Saisissez-les, aussi!*" the guard instructed, and the two other guards grabbed Miss Clairoux and Mr. Tullier.

"FLORALIE!" The voice echoed from the tourists. It was a boy's voice—strange accent, crackly, unfamiliar. It sounded like one of Sappho's poems; there were gaps in every consonant, mouse holes in every vowel.

Floralie strained her neck to see around the guard, who only yanked harder at her shoulder. A boy in rags stumbled through the tourists toward Floralie.

"Nino?" gasped Floralie.

The guard whirled around, twisting Floralie's arm. "*Et lui!*" he spat.

The guard clutching Miss Clairoux's wrist stretched out his free arm and seized Nino by his hair. Nino squirmed, but the guard would not let loose.

Floralie's guard turned to the tourists and barked, "*Sortez! Maintenant!* Zis *musée* is closing!"

The guards dragged Floralie, Miss Clairoux, Mr. Tullier, and Nino down six hallways and four flights of stairs until they came to the very last door of a long and narrow corridor, surely underground. Floralie's daydreams overtook her, and she was plunged into visions of prisoners hanging by their thumbs in decrepit stone dungeons. Floralie crouched in the corner, scrabbling for food in the cracks of the floor, the stench of unwashed feet filling her nostrils, as a big-bellied guard stood watch above her . . .

Floralie's guard kicked open the door, launching Floralie back into reality. He threw in Floralie, Miss Clairoux, Mr. Tullier, and Nino, then slammed it shut. A fourth guard sat behind a desk cluttered with papers and empty coffee mugs. He was older than the others, a ring of gray hair circling a large bald patch. The moment he set eyes on his surprise visitors, he fumbled for his hat and stuffed it over the patch. He spoke in lightning-fast French that even Floralie had trouble keeping up with, but she had no trouble understanding that he was angry with the guards.

"She was tampering with a Monet," explained Floralie's guard in French. "Found her with these two"—he gestured to Miss Clairoux and Mr. Tullier—"and then this one showed up." He jabbed a finger in Nino's side. "But that's not all."

Floralie's guard sifted through a pile of newspapers in the corner of the desk and pulled up yesterday's. "*C'est elle*," he whispered. "*C'est Floralie Laurel.*"

He flipped around the paper to reveal a photograph of Floralie on the front page.

The guard knelt down to Floralie's eye level. Three inches from her nose, he breathed, "Is zis you, *petite fille*?"

Floralie's mouth twitched, but no words came out. *No, no, no,* her mind screamed, but her lips spat, "Yes." He hardly even needed to ask. The portrait was a mirror image of Floralie.

The four guards exchanged glances. Finally, the bald guard sprang from his chair, pulled a key from his pocket and jammed it into the door's keyhole. Nino's guard let go of his hair, and Nino crumpled to the ground. The guard babbled in French to Floralie's guard, "Just look at that reward, Benoît! We'll be *rich*!"

"*Non*," said the bald guard. "*I* am head of security here, and *I* will be rich."

"But I caught *two* of them!" barked Miss Clairoux and Nino's guard.

"But I caught the girl!" shouted Floralie's guard.

"*Silence!*" fumed the bald one. "We'll figure out the money later! I'm calling this number," and he snatched the paper from Floralie's guard and picked up the telephone.

Nino and Floralie exchanged glances as the guard dialed. Nino's hand enclosed in Floralie's, and he squeezed tight, as if no time had passed since he left. As if the argument in the garden hadn't even happened. As if nothing had changed, nothing at all.

The guard cleared his throat at the telephone and babbled to someone on the other end. "*Oui*, yes, we 'ave found 'er . . . La Musée de l'Orangerie . . . *Non* . . . Yes, I believe so. *Merci beaucoup*," and he hung up.

Floralie's stomach dropped as the guard turned to her. "You wait here," he hissed. "And *silence*."

Floralie's hair clung with sweat to her forehead. "*Allons-y*," said the head guard to the others, and they marched out of the office, bolting the door behind them.

Floralie looked from Nino to Miss Clairoux, and then to Mr. Tullier. "*Shh*," she hushed. She crept over to the door, pressed her ear against it, and listened to the shuffling of feet, a cough, and a breath. "They're guarding the door," she whispered. "We've no way of getting out."

Miss Clairoux closed her eyes. "This is my fault," she muttered. "I should never have brought you here."

"It's okay, our plan could still work," said Floralie. "We're all in this together."

"F-Floralie's r-right." Through his stutters, Floralie recognized Nino's accent as Greek.

"*Mes chéries*, as much as I love you, we've got ourselves into deep troub—" Miss Clairoux stopped short. She covered her heart, cheeks paling. "Who was that?" she breathed. "Was that you, Floralie? I could have sworn that sounded like a boy . . ."

"No, it was m-me." His voice had the same brokenness as before.

"Nino? Our Nino? You—you talk?" gasped Miss Clairoux. "I *knew* it. I just knew you could do it!"

Floralie grasped Miss Clairoux's arm. "Shh! The guards will hear!" But even so, Floralie had to restrain herself from whooping with joy. The wind in her lungs swelled with pride, her bones shuddered—but she knew she could not express the happiness, not here, not now.

"Right, sorry," whispered Miss Clairoux.

"I t-talk a l-l-little bit," stuttered Nino.

"Street rat boy's learned to talk, what a miracle," grunted Mr. Tullier. "But that doesn't solve our problem."

"You're right," sighed Floralie. She slumped into the head guard's chair. "We didn't even find the flower. How're we supposed to find Mama now?"

"Flower?" piped up Nino.

Floralie nodded, and scooted over so Nino could share the chair. "We came here to find a flower behind Monet's *Young Girl in the Garden at Giverny* painting. How did you know I'd be here anyway?"

"I didn't," Nino muttered. He plunged his hand into his pocket and withdrew, among a handful of lint, a small pink flower. "Is this what you're l-looking for? F-found it behind the p-painting. I escaped f-from Tom—"

"Tom? You were with Tom?"

Nino nodded. "He found me outside your old h-house. He was looking for you, and I stayed there with him before leaving for Paris. You g-got my drawings, didn't you?"

Floralie nodded. "But why did you leave me drawings instead of just writing to me in plain English where you'd be going?"

Nino's mouth twitched. "I w-wanted to tell you in *your* language—art. And b-besides that, I didn't want Tom to f-figure out I was writing secret messages to you. Anyway, Tom said if I c-c-came with him, he would bring me to Viscaria, as long as I brought him to you after. B-but he tricked me. It t-turns out he's no idea where Viscaria lives. I found Tom at your house in Giverny, searching for you. Then he brought me here and th-threatened to have police force me to tell where you were unless I told *him*. So I ran for it. I escaped to the Musée de l'Orangerie and f-found the *Young Girl* painting. The little girl reminded me of you, so I've been t-talking with her—the girl. Practicing."

"Practicing what?" said Floralie.

Nino blushed. "The th-things I wanted to say to you if I e-ever saw you again"

"Then," continued Nino, "the other d-d-day, I found the flower while talking with the little girl." He handed the flower to Floralie.

Floralie pinched the flower between her fingers the way a crow might pluck a piece of gold off the ground. She dug into her bag and pulled out the crumpled eglantine page from the floriography.

Mr. Tullier and Nino leaned in close. Floralie smoothed out the page on her lap and placed the eglantine on the page beside the painted one.

"*Mon Dieu*," muttered Mr. Tullier, lowering his glasses. "They're a perfect match."

"It's a code," said Floralie. "I think I *know—*"

The door burst open.

Floralie crinkled the eglantine page and held it tight in her fist with the flower as the guards marched in. Three men followed them, and so tight they had to cram inside that Floralie could see but only the tips of their hats.

The guards locked the door and shuffled sideways so the men could squeeze through. Two policemen slithered through the crowd and immediately yanked back Mr. Tullier's and Miss Clairoux's arms, holding them tight. The head guard locked eyes with Floralie, stretched out a sunflower-huge hand and pulled Floralie out of the chair. "Is zis 'er?"

A skinny hand weaseled through the crowd, followed by a fancy leather shoe beneath fraying trousers, a combination Floralie knew only too well. A pair of quicksand-colored eyes edged with worry wrinkles. And then—tears. Umbrella-weather-wet, dandelion-wild, Whitterly-End-in-April tears, all splashing down on Floralie as Tom swept her up in his arms.

Floralie stumbled back before wrapping her arms around Tom as well. Not once had she seen her brother cry like that. Not even when Mama left, and not even when Papa died. But strangest of all, was what Tom kept whispering in Floralie's ear: "*You're home, you're home, you're home,*" because Paris, as both Floralie and Tom knew, was not home and had never been home. But arms were a home. And Tom's, Floralie believed, made quite a home. Quite a proper home indeed.

There was a day in May when Tom and Floralie blew soap bubbles into the streets of Giverny. The cars would honk, and when the road was clear, Floralie would leap off the curb to the middle of the road, shouting, "Look! I'm alive, Tom. Look at how alive I am." But Tom would try and catch her by the back of her dress, crying, "No!" even though there wasn't a car in sight and nobody drove fast in Giverny. Floralie would fling bubbles across the street and tell Tom they were beautiful. He got angry at first, but when Floralie settled down on the curb with him again, he and Floralie laughed in spite of themselves, and Tom said, "It's not all so bad."

38

"You can't." Floralie staggered back from Tom's embrace. "Y-you just can't turn them in to the police," she repeated.

Tom tucked a handkerchief back into his pocket and laid a hand on Floralie's shoulder. "Floralie, these people kidnapped you . . ."

Floralie pulled away from Tom, stumbling into the head guard's chair. "But they *didn't* kidnap me. There's nothing dangerous about them. I came willingly to France—*I* led *them* here. And they're my friends—and they're more than that, too—they're our—"

"*Don't* do this, Floralie." Tom sighed.

"Just *listen*," pleaded Floralie.

But Tom wouldn't listen. He pressed his lips together and said, "Come. We're leaving."

"Not without them," insisted Floralie.

Floralie looked to Miss Clairoux and Mr. Tullier. Miss Clairoux nodded to her and said, "Go on, *ma chérie*. We will be okay."

"Go on, now," said Mr. Tullier.

Tom tugged at Floralie's elbow, but again, she pulled away. "No. Not without my friends. I will only come with my friends." Though her hands were shaking and her head spinning, Floralie gazed directly into Tom's eyes. "They are coming with me to find Mama *right now*. And if you don't allow it, I'll never forgive you."

"Floralie, I—" Tom's face started to melt again, and he choked, "I don't know where Mama is, and that's not a lie. I've never known."

"Well, *I* know. I've figured it out, and like it or not, I'm going to see her."

Tom's jaw went limp. "But that's not *possible*. Papa destroyed all records, all traces of her, every memory . . ."

"Yes," said Floralie. "But Mama didn't. She left her flowers behind. Don't you remember, Tom?" And ever so carefully,

Floralie uncurled her hand and revealed the eglantine flower.

Something like a ghost flitted across Tom's eyes. He took the flower, turned it once in his hand, then placed it back in Floralie's.

Floralie tucked it into her bag, then looked to Miss Clairoux and Mr. Tullier. "And we're not her only survivors," she breathed. "Mr. Tullier and Miss Clairoux—they're Mama's parents. Tom, they're our *grandparents*."

Tom's eyes widened. "I thought . . . But Mama never said . . . Why wouldn't she *tell* us?"

"Long story," said Miss Clairoux, and Mr. Tullier nodded.

Tom eyed Floralie. "Are you *sure*?"

Floralie nodded. "Absolutely."

Tom closed his eyes, took a breath, then turned to the policemen. "Let them go."

The policeman holding Miss Clairoux stammered, "But—but, sir—"

"I said, let them go," repeated Tom.

Mr. Tullier's policeman nodded and loosened his grip on Mr. Tullier. "As you wish," he said, but he turned his gaze to Nino, narrowed his eyes, and muttered, "but not the boy."

"Him?" piped up Floralie, turning to Nino. "Why not him?"

"*Parce que*," said the policeman, looking to Tom again, "while Floralie Laurel belongs to you, Monsieur Laurel, zat boy does not. Zat boy belongs to ze orphanage. Zat boy is ze missing Konstantinos Leventis."

Miss Clairoux's policeman let loose her arms and lunged for Nino.

"NO!" cried Floralie, and she clutched Nino's wrist. But the policeman was stronger, and he pulled Nino away, a sliver of Nino's skin coiling under Floralie's fingernail.

Floralie lunged for the policeman, but Tom caught hold of her waist. Floralie punched at Tom's hands, but his grip did not loosen. "I'm not losing him again!" she cried. "Not again, not him, too!"

Floralie grasped at the air as the policemen dragged Nino out of the office. "No! *No*, you can't take him." Floralie's voice cracked. Somewhere, as if a thousand miles away, Floralie heard Tom's voice: "*Hush, Flory, hush, hush . . .*"

As Floralie sunk back into Tom's arms, she realized that his words were not a thousand miles away. They were two years away. They were the same words he had whispered as the medics carried Papa's dead and drunken body out the door. They were the same words he had used as Papa laid Mama into the backseat of the taxi, the taxi that would take her away forever. And his hands, his hands were the same ones that had held her each time, except now they were three times stronger.

Floralie craned her neck to see the policemen tugging Nino

along behind them. When they reached the corridor's end, Nino was but a mouse-sized speck in the gap of the doorway. And then, he was gone.

Floralie spent the night pacing up and down Rue Claude Monet, waiting for her father to come stumbling, drunk, down the cobbles. When he did come, he said Floralie should never have got in the car with Mama.

But so often, Mama drove Floralie to the countryside. To the fields of lavender and tulips and pink-and-white-striped carnations, to the sunlit forests and the tall, tall mountains. And Floralie wondered to herself how she was supposed to know when Mama was her mother and when she was a stranger.

39

Tom gripped Floralie's hand the way he had when Floralie was little and they had taken a train ride up the Swiss Alps. Floralie had clung to the window, admiring the long drop down, but Tom had clung to her hand "just in case." There was no danger, and Tom's hand offered little safety; but still, he clung, and still, Floralie let him.

"So what now?" grunted Mr. Tullier once they were out in the rain again.

"L'Asile de Sainte-Rose pour les Femmes Sauvages," said Floralie. "That's where she is. It means the Asylum of Saint Rose for Wild Women. We'll find her, then we'll find Nino."

Tom wrapped his jacket around Floralie and spluttered, "But how do you kn—"

"There's a taxi!" Floralie cut him off, and she waved the taxi down.

"It's best to trust her, dear," advised Miss Clairoux to a befuddled Tom, as they clambered into the taxi.

The taxi traveled through the Paris streets, sloshing through puddles and clattering over cobblestones. Floralie's heart pirouetted faster with every turn the taxi took. If she were to paint this moment, she would paint it like Monet—wild, rushing, running colors. She would paint it the way salmon paint rivers in late-autumn evenings.

"We must be nearly there," said Floralie as they passed a statue of a saint with her hands clasped in prayer.

Indeed, the taxi turned one last corner and then rolled to a stop. "'Ere is ze place," said the driver.

Floralie gazed to a large, soot-stained building. Scarcely any lights were on, and iron bars sliced across the door's window.

"*Merci beaucoup*," said Tom, giving the driver a handful of francs.

The rain had slowed to a steady drizzle when Floralie, Tom, Mr. Tullier, and Miss Clairoux stepped out of the taxi. "You're sure this is it?" said Tom.

Floralie nodded. "I'm positive."

The four treaded up to the asylum, and Floralie took the rose-shaped door knocker. *Knock-knock-knock.*

A clattering came from inside as if someone were fiddling with an extensive amount of locks and chains. Finally, the door creaked open.

"*Qui est là?*" barked a woman from inside. She pulled the door open all the way, a dimly lit staircase rising into view. The woman was short, barely any taller than Floralie, but far stockier. Judging from her white apron and cap, she was clearly a nurse. She scowled at the looks of the four sopping wet, mud-spattered visitors.

Floralie cleared her throat and spoke in French, as dignified as possible: "I'm Floralie Laurel, and I'm here to see my mother."

"Oh," said the nurse. Her voice melted to a cloyingly sweet tone. "And who might your mother be, young lady?"

"Viscaria Laurel. She came here three years ago. She's tall with blond hair and—"

"No one here is named Viscaria," and the nurse nearly shut the door, but Floralie yanked it open, splinters pricking her fingertips.

"I meant Alice," pleaded Floralie.

Tom narrowed his eyes. "What—" he started, but Floralie gave him no time.

"Alice Laurel. Viscaria was her stage name from when she was a dancer."

The nurse's mouth twitched and said, "Well, there is an Alice Laurel—at least, her married name was Laurel, if I recall. She now goes by her birth name, Alice Clairoux. Does that ring a bell?"

Floralie nodded as Tom gaped at Miss Clairoux. "Yes. Yes, that's right," said Floralie. "May we come in?"

The nurse sighed. "Follow me."

The nurse led them inside, then bustled over to a small table. "And who do you have with you here?" she asked.

Tom, Miss Clairoux, and Mr. Tullier introduced themselves, and the nurse penned their names into a thick book atop the table. "Well," said the nurse, "you must act with utmost emotional stability when seeing her. We cannot have patients becoming upset. Understand?"

Floralie nodded vigorously.

The nurse slammed shut the book and led them up the narrow staircase. The floorboards squealed with every step, and Floralie could have sworn the shadows following them along the wallpaper were shaped like women, wild roses in their cheeks, poppies in their hair.

A long hallway stretched before them. On one side, it was lined with doors, and the other side, barred windows. The view of Paris looked strange from those windows. The whole of the city blurred together and colors collided with colors like a finger painting so even the lights dimmed to gray. Floralie shook her head; it was just the raindrops.

The nurse stopped at the last door and pulled a ring of keys from her pocket. They jangled as she searched for the right one, and upon finding a key with rust that matched the lock, she jammed it into the keyhole and twisted.

Floralie's feet went numb; her hands shook. She felt as if she were stepping into a dream. She had yet to tell whether it was a nightmare or a daydream.

"Alice?" the nurse whispered, peeking inside. "Alice, you have some visitors." She turned to Floralie. "Go on in."

It started with her talking to the moths. The fragile wings would flutter in and out of the streetlamp's glow at dusk, just paper things. Mama would let them tiptoe along her finger, then give each one a name and promise to fly south with them in the winter. One she called Daisy and whispered to her, "You're lovely. You're beautiful, you're small, and you're innocent. I hope nothing hurts you."

One evening, Mama and Floralie sat in the garden, lantern lit between them. Moths fluttered in and out of the flame. Most got away with no harm, but some would catch their wing in the fire, and spiral down to the soil. Mama dug graves for them. "People are like moths," she said. "Loving things that burn their wings."

40

A woman sat in a ghost-white nightgown at the edge of a bed. Her sheets were pulled so tight the bed looked more like a table than a bed. The woman did not look up when Floralie entered; she simply gazed off to the opposite wall, mouth closed, eyes hollow.

"Mama?" whispered Floralie.

The woman turned, said nothing.

"Mama, it's me. And Tom. We're here to rescue you."

Silence.

Floralie narrowed her eyes and took a step closer. She could hear the woman's breath—heavy. Mama's was light as feathers. Light as flowers. Floralie tore herself away from the woman and cut between Miss Clairoux and Mr. Tullier.

"Flory—" started Tom, but Floralie ignored him.

When she found the nurse outside the door, Floralie crossed her arms and said, "It's not her. I'm looking for Alice *Clairoux*, not whoever's in there," and she spelled out: "C-L-A-I-R-O-U-X."

The nurse smiled, a caramel-sweet, sticky, and sinister smile. "That is Alice Clairoux. Don't believe me? Get a mirror— you've got her eyes. Perhaps some things have changed since you saw her last."

Floralie bit her lip and stepped back into her room. She stared at the woman, sponging in her features. Green eyes—yes, Mama had green eyes. Pale skin—yes, just like Mama. Willowy figure—same as Mama. It had to be her . . . but why did she seem so different? It was like looking at a corpse of her.

Floralie was too preoccupied with the woman's eyes to feel her feet drift across the room, but there she was, inches from Viscaria. Her blond hair was streaked with gray and cascaded down her back—no, it used to cascade. Now it hung like a piece of laundry left out on the clothesline in a thunderstorm.

Floralie lowered herself onto the bed beside Viscaria. "Mama, it's me, Floralie," she whispered. Her throat clenched up.

"Floralie?" said Viscaria. Her voice was hoarse, but Floralie still recognized a hint of melody to it. Mama looked to Floralie, tilted her head.

"Yes, Mama, it's me, Floralie. I've come to rescue you." Floralie took Viscaria's hand. Frost-flower cold.

"I had a doll named Floralie," said Viscaria. And then her head turned for the door, and she called, "Margot?"

"Yes, dear?" said the nurse, peeping through the doorway.

"Margot Lady, do you remember my doll?" asked Viscaria. "My doll has come to rescue me."

"Of course she has, dear," soothed Nurse Margot, and she left the doorway.

"Mama, no, it's Floralie, Floralie Alice Laurel, your daughter."

"I have a daughter?" Viscaria's eyes grew large. "Oh my, when is she due?"

"Floralie—" started Tom. He edged close to the bed, but Floralie ignored him.

"No—no," said Floralie, "I'm already born, I'm here; I'm eleven years old now."

"Margot!" called Viscaria again. "Margot Lady, my Floralie Doll says I am to have a daughter who is eleven years old."

Nurse Margot returned from the hall and shot Floralie a glare. "You are *not* to distress the patient, young lady. If she becomes any more upset, I am afraid I must ask you to leave."

Floralie nodded and stroked Viscaria's hand. "Mama," she whispered, "don't you remember me? Look, I'm wearing your old ballet costume; you must remember ballet. And Tom, and your mother, Miss Clairoux, and—and Mr. Tullier—you were friends with him . . ."

Miss Clairoux and Mr. Tullier neared the bed. "Our daughter . . . ," breathed Miss Clairoux, clasping Mr. Tullier's hand.

"Viscaria?" whispered Mr. Tullier. He removed his hat and held it against his stomach.

"Tullier . . . ," whispered Viscaria. She narrowed her eyes, and then a hint of her vivacity sparked. "Do you water the willow tree for me?"

Mr. Tullier looked taken aback. He dropped his hat and fumbled for it before saying, "I—I—yes, I do."

"But not at the poppy dollhouse where Floralie Doll lives. My willow grows in the forget-me-not dollhouse, that's the one, yes? Who's that?" Viscaria looked to Miss Clairoux.

"That's Miss Clairoux," said Floralie. "That's your mother."

Miss Clairoux reached for Viscaria's hand and stroked it, but Viscaria made no sign of recognizing her. "Oh," she said. "Floralie Doll, how many dollhouses have I lived in?"

"I—I don't know, Mama," choked Floralie. "Look, I found this box from you, see," and Floralie withdrew the flower box from her bag. "Look, it's got your letter right here. You must remember writing that? And all these flowers . . . I've been trying to decode your message so we could be together again."

"My flowers!" burst Viscaria. "My Eglantine Doll flowers!"

"Eglantine?" Floralie looked from Viscaria to Mr. Tullier and back to Viscaria.

Viscaria ran her fingers along the dried flowers. "How is my Eglantine Doll? Is she still bright?"

"Gone, Viscaria," breathed Mr. Tullier. "My daughter is gone."

"Oh, that's right," and Viscaria snapped her fingers as if she had just lost a game of chess instead of a child.

Floralie looked to Mr. Tullier, confused. But Mr. Tullier did not meet her gaze. He stared straight on through to Viscaria. "Viscaria . . . ," he whispered.

"Yes, Tullier Doll?"

"I know you can't understand me clearly right now," he started, and with a crack, his knees gave way to the floor, "but I never got to tell you." He stared up at Viscaria and clutched her hand so tight his knuckles grew white. "You were more than a caretaker to Eglantine, and you were more than a caretaker to me. You are my daughter and Eglantine's half sister. And we both loved you."

Viscaria gazed straight through Mr. Tullier.

And then she turned to Floralie. "Floralie Doll," she said, "you will water the willow tree, won't you? When Tullier Doll is gone like Eglantine Doll? Will you do that back at the forget-me-not dollhouse? For me?"

Viscaria's hand slipped from the flowers as Floralie stood and backed away from the bed.

Floralie felt as if she had chalk dust in her throat. "I—I'm not really a doll—you must know that . . . don't you? This is just pretend . . ."

"Oh, I love pretend!" and Viscaria clasped her hands together. "What shall we play, Floralie Doll?"

Tears burned at the back of Floralie's eyes. She shoved aside Mr. Tullier and Miss Clairoux and flew out into the hall. The moment she caught sight of Nurse Margot, she screamed, "You did this to her!"

The nurse's cheeks went cherry red. "Please, you are *disturbing*—"

"I DON'T CARE!" bellowed Floralie. "I'LL DISTURB THE WHOLE WORLD FOR ALL I CARE! My mother's gone, and it's all your fault!"

Floralie felt Miss Clairoux's gentle hand on her arm; Floralie pulled away, sobbing even harder.

"Floralie—" Tom tried, but Floralie didn't want to listen. She wanted to shout and scream; she wanted to shatter the windows with nothing but her voice.

"You locked her up when she was meant to be free!"

"I assure you this institution has done no such thing!" insisted Nurse Margot. "Alice was half gone by the time we took her in, and good thing we did get her when we did, mind you. Now *be quiet!*" She turned to Miss Clairoux and said, "Madame, I'm sorry, but I'm going to have to ask you to remove the child from the building."

"I will *not* be removed!"

A pair of arms wrapped around her stomach. "Floralie— listen to me—"

"The only one who should be removed is Mama! She doesn't belong here—you don't know the first thing about her!" Tears streamed down Floralie's cheeks, and she let the arms swirl her away from Nurse Margot. Her fists were in some distant land, punching and hitting, but the body holding her did not flinch.

It was only when the body began to shake that Floralie looked up and realized it was Tom, and he was crying, too. Hard. Even harder than Floralie. His tears ran wild in Floralie's hair, each teardrop a bluebird with wings that never took flight, pecking nests out of knots that never housed anything but rain. Between sobs, Tom breathed, "*I'm so sorry.*"

Floralie wiped at her own eyes and choked, "You never cry."

Tom took a jagged breath. "I know. And that is why I'm sorry."

Footsteps echoed from down the hall.

"Who—?" started Floralie, but as she turned, her stomach plummeted.

A most peacocklike figure waltzed down the corridor, feather hat bobbing, shoes clacking, rings glittering. The vague aroma of prunes and sour lemons filled Floralie's nostrils. Grandmama had arrived.

"So it's decided," said Grandmama, pleasantly clasping her hands together as if they had just decided on where they were going to have their picnic. "She'll have a day in Paris with the children—supervised of course—then away she goes."

Papa's face drained of all color, but he nodded and said, "Sure."

Mama said not a word.

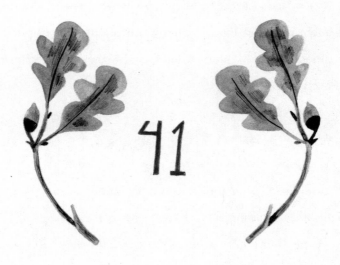

41

Tom gripped Floralie's shoulder. "No, no, no," he muttered as Grandmama came barreling down the hall. Floralie didn't think she had ever seen her grandmother *barrel*.

Upon reaching them, Grandmama scowled down at Floralie and Tom, but said nothing. And then, quick as sheers clipping rosebuds, Grandmama raised a hand and struck Tom across the cheek. "You have *disgraced* yourself." Her voice quaked with rage.

Grandmama yanked Floralie by her collar out of Tom's grip. "Don't you dare—" started Tom, but someone cut him off.

"Margot Lady?" It was Viscaria. "Margot Lady, where did my dolly friends go?"

Margot threw her hands up in the air. "Ah, *mon Dieu!* Out, out, out! All of you! Your little family reunion will just have to take place elsewhere," and she began to shoo Floralie, Tom, Grandmama, Miss Clairoux, and Mr. Tullier back down the staircase.

Floralie's collar pinched her neck, but she managed to glance back for one forget-me-not-sized moment. Viscaria peeked out from her room, and Floralie could have sworn she saw something bloom in the gardens within her eyes. But when Floralie looked again, there was nothing. It had only been a reflection.

"There is no excuse," Grandmama hissed to Tom as they strode down the rain-washed Paris streets.

Floralie pushed and pulled to wriggle free from Grandmama's grasp, but Grandmama held on with surprising strength. "And *you* stop making such a fuss, young lady! You'll be lucky if you ever see a city light again, no less a drop of sunshine," spat Grandmama into Floralie's ear. "If only I had simply taken her the day I came to visit, we wouldn't have had to go through this whole ordeal! I should have expected as much from the beginning—a *runaway* in the family! And you," Grandmama snarled as she rounded on Miss Clairoux, "just who do you think you are, taking off with her like that?"

"I am Delphine Alice Clairoux. And I am Floralie's grandmother."

Grandmama swatted at Miss Clairoux as if she were a housefly. "Impossible! *I'm* Floralie's grandmother, therefore *I* know what's best for her."

"No you don't," shot Floralie. "You don't know me at all. And Miss Clairoux *is* my grandmother. She's Mama's mother."

Grandmama returned her gaze to Floralie. "You are just like her, aren't you, Floralie? Like that Viscaria. Rude, obnoxious, naïve. If you had had a proper mother, she would have taught you at least the etiquette beyond that of a three-year-old. But no, your mother is growing more insane by the minute, just like you will someday unless someone whips you into shape."

Tears burned at Floralie's eyes again at the thought of Mama. Floralie remembered now, the conversation between Papa and Grandmama. *"She's marring our family lineage, John-Paul,"* Grandmama had said to Papa. *"Heaven knows what damage she'll do to our reputation once she's fully lost it. It's best to send her off."*

"Oh, stop sniveling, child," scoffed Grandmama. "It is no secret that woman lost it ages ago."

"That's enough." It was Tom.

Grandmama stopped mid-step. *"What* did you say?"

"I said that's enough. You are not taking her. I won't allow it."

"Well," said Grandmama. She brushed off her dress as

if Tom's words could spew invisible crumbs, and she yanked Floralie's collar even tighter. "And how, pray tell, do you intend on supporting both yourself and Floralie with nothing but a barely stocked flower shop to fund you?"

Tom pulled Floralie loose of Grandmama's grip and tilted up his chin. "We will just have to manage."

All color in Grandmama's face drained, and she looked from Tom to Floralie and back to Tom again, mouth agape. "Well then," she said and huffed, "so be it. If my presence is no longer wanted, I shall burden you with it no longer."

Tom wrapped Floralie up in his arms, turned to Grandmama, and said, "Lovely."

Grandmama's mouth twitched, but she said nothing. Tom took Floralie's hand, pushed past Grandmama, and led the way to nowhere in particular.

Mama went dancing on the rooftop under oak tree leaves. Vivacious eyes, she called down to Floralie, "This is how to be alive."

42

Twenty minutes of sloshing through puddles and a short taxi ride later, Tom, Floralie, Miss Clairoux, and Mr. Tullier ended up at a small café inside the Gare Saint-Lazare train station. Floralie listened to the chattering of many languages and breathed the tinny smell of train smoke.

The finality of Mama's fate settled into Floralie's stomach, her heart, her fingertips, like a moth relinquishing itself to a flame. The pain of it numbed her to the bone. She felt cold.

"I suppose we'll have to go back to England now," said Floralie to Tom as the four sat, sipping their tea (and in Mr. Tullier's case, coffee).

Tom nodded. "I suppose we will."

"And the flower shop—what will happen to the flower shop? And our house . . . surely we won't be able to afford it all now."

"That's my job to figure out. It's not your weight to carry, Flory. Here, have some of this." He tore his croissant in two and handed one half to Floralie. "You must be famished."

Floralie took a bite of the croissant, then laid it on her saucer. "It is, though—my weight to carry," she said. "I got us into this mess. I'm growing up, and you're not as old as you like to pretend you are, Tom. We've got to do this together."

"Floralie, please just let me be your guardian as Papa intended. I will be able to handle the house and the shop and—"

"If I might be so bold as to intervene," started Mr. Tullier. He gazed from Floralie to Tom, forget-me-not eyes twinkling.

Tom looked up. "Yes, sir?"

"You are not orphans anymore. *Please* tell me you realize that. I was just beginning to believe Floralie inherited my intelligence . . ."

"What?" breathed Tom.

"Of course," said Floralie. "But you don't have to, Mr. Tullier, we can find a way—"

Mr. Tullier put up a hand to silence Floralie. "You've got grandparents now." He coughed, adding, "Grandparents that *don't* try and lock you up in their dismal orphanage. We're sticking together."

"But your life—" said Tom. "You live here, in France. And, Miss Clairoux, you've got your library. We couldn't ask that sort of sacrifice from either of you."

"There's nothing sacrificial about it," grunted Mr. Tullier. "Do you know how long I've been mourning both my daughters? Eglantine and Viscaria?"

"Mr. Tullier," whispered Floralie. "You never did tell me about . . . about Eglantine."

Mr. Tullier shifted his eyes to his saucer. "Nothing to tell. She died as a baby."

"I found her ashes." The words hung in the air, heavy as a corpse.

Mr. Tullier snapped up his head. His eyes were bloodshot. "What?"

"Her ashes. Found them in Monet's paint box. Mama may have dug her grave, but you never buried her, did you? You never let her go."

Mr. Tullier closed his eyes, and Floralie wondered if he was flying to his wonderland. She wondered if he even still had a wonderland, and if he did, how long had it been winter there? But more important, were there yet buds on the trees?

"I—" Mr. Tullier's voice cracked. "*I killed her.* I killed my own daughter. The little light of my life . . . I destroyed."

"What?" breathed Floralie. "No . . . no, that's a mistake.

You would never, never, ever . . ."

Mr. Tullier nodded. "I did. It was an accident. Left her alone in my office for two minutes while studying a sprig of belladonna. Moment I came back, she was chewing on it. Do you know what belladonna is?"

"Poison," murmured Floralie.

"That's right. One of the most deadly flowers alive. And it was all for my book, my stupid floriography I was so *obsessed* with. I'm sorry I didn't tell you about the burned books. I wanted to get to know you and believed you would leave the minute you found out. I burned all the books after Eglantine died—except for the one your mother stole. She had been working as Eglantine's caretaker, after running away from Delphine. I paid her in ballet lessons and trips to Palais Garnier. She didn't even know I was her father, but my, how she loved Eglantine." Mr. Tullier smiled at that and added, "Viscaria called Eglantine her 'wildflower.'"

"'Wildflower,'" repeated Floralie. "That's what Mama called me. D'you think . . . ?" She dug through her bag for the box of flowers and, upon finding it, pulled Mama's letter out from inside. "It's signed *V.A.C.* With a *C* for Clairoux—her maiden name. Do you think this letter and these flowers weren't for me after all? Could they have been for Eglantine, before Mama even knew me?"

Floralie remembered the tiny knob on the side of the box,

the initials that read, E.F.T.—*Eglantine Floralie Tullier.*

Mr. Tullier smiled. "Perhaps," he said. "She certainly loved that little girl. I was going to let Viscaria go after that. After all, she was only there to take care of my child until Eglantine grew old enough, but Eglantine was not *going* to grow old. She was dead, and even my wife had died in childbirth; Viscaria had nothing to care for. But I couldn't let her go . . . She was my daughter, even if she didn't know it. I loved her. But I was selfish. You see, eventually, she grew fond of your father, John-Paul. She wanted to marry, but I disapproved of him and feared being alone. I would not let her leave, and so she ran away with him, bounding from England, to Turkey, to Paris, and finally, back again to Giverny. I never told her she was my daughter—not until tonight."

"Why didn't you tell her?" asked Floralie.

"Because I was a coward. I thought if I told her, she would leave me. I thought if I told her she would hate me for abandoning her, for having to live thirteen years of her life fatherless." He turned to Miss Clairoux and squeezed her hand. "For leaving her mother the moment I found out she was pregnant. I am a coward, Floralie. And I can never make up for that. But you can bet I'm going to try. Mr. Laurel"—he turned to Tom—"I will do whatever it takes to help your family. Our family. And, Floralie?"

"Yes?" Floralie looked up to the wizened face, wrinkles like scars, aching like thorn wounds.

"Do you want to live with me? Move to France? I can educate you. I taught children your age for many years, after all. I was a science teacher at a boys' school after years of working at a university. You can paint as much as you wish. You can have Monet's garden all to yourself. Would you like that?"

Floralie's heart fluttered. *Yes.* Yes, she would like that very much. Yes, her heart longed for that. Yes, her heart would fly for that. She nodded.

Tom shifted in his chair and glanced up to Mr. Tullier. His face had turned burgundy. "Oh, but—but, Mr. Tullier, we could never put you out of your way—"

"Quite the contrary," said Mr. Tullier. "Floralie is an excellent artist. I would be honored if she were to continue painting my flowers as I rewrite my floriography. She would make a superb illustrator."

Yes, yes, yes. The word coursed through Floralie's veins, thundered her heart.

"Well—" Tom looked from Mr. Tullier to Floralie. "Well—I'm sure she would, but . . . well, we *have* just been reunited . . ."

"Oh." Mr. Tullier's cheeks flushed. He bowed his head and stirred the bubbles out of his coffee. "Oh, but of course. I'm sorry. I shouldn't have mentioned it in the first place."

"Well—I am not a rich woman by any means—but if I can be of any help in raising Floralie, I would be more than happy," pitched in Miss Clairoux.

Tom replied, "That's very kind of you, but I think—"

"What about what *I* think? Does that count for nothing anymore?" Floralie's voice caught her by surprise.

Tom turned, took a breath, and said, "Of course it counts. What do you think, Floralie?"

Floralie bit her lip. "I love you, Tom. I love you, and I need you, always. I'll always need you. But I think . . . I think I want to paint. I want to go with Mr. Tullier."

Tears glossed Tom's eyes; he blinked rapidly to keep them at bay. "Very well. If that is what you wish."

A pang of guilt stabbed Floralie's stomach, but she nodded.

"If you've made up your mind, then, we had better gather your things from Whitterly End." Tom dabbed his mouth with a napkin and stood.

Floralie scooted back her chair and stood as well before saying, "But, you haven't finished your tea—"

"I'm not very thirsty. Come now; we've not a moment to doddle."

Miss Clairoux and Mr. Tullier stood as Tom began to stride toward the ticket booth, heels clicking against the tile and reverberating around the high-ceilinged station.

Mr. Tullier hurried to catch up. "Tom—" he called. "Tom, wait."

Tom turned, and for yet the third time that evening, his face was splotched with tears. "What is it?"

Mr. Tullier looked to the floor and gestured to Tom's leather shoes. "If I may be so bold, I daresay those shoes of yours weren't meant for flower shops."

Tom's mouth went slack. "N-no. No, they're what—er—what they wear at university. What's that have to do with anything?"

Mr. Tullier shifted his weight and looked intently at Tom. "If I could send you there—to a university—would you go?"

The corners of Tom's eyes wrinkled—but this time, not with worry. This time, they wrinkled with hope, perhaps even happiness. "In a heartbeat."

Mr. Tullier clasped his hands together. "Then it's done."

Tom's jaw dropped. Floralie's did, too, and in unison, they said, "You're serious?"

Mr. Tullier patted Tom on the back. "What're you interested in? Physics? History?"

"Literature. I've dreamed for years of studying literature," breathed Tom.

"Well, I happen to know that L'Université de Paris has a *stellar* literature program. I think you would fit in just fine there. And you can come home to Giverny anytime you wish. And besides that, any grandson of mine deserves a good education to match good genes."

The first day of school, the teacher said, "Oh, you're Thomas's sister! How wonderful."

Floralie laughed at that and then flew away to her wonderland.

43

After securing two tickets back to England for Tom and Floralie to collect their things, the four waited on the platform until a whistle blew and a scarlet engine emerged from the fog. A gust of wind nearly knocked Floralie off her feet as the train came blazing by, and then creaked to a stop.

As the doors opened and passengers trickled out, Mr. Tullier led Floralie, Tom, and Miss Clairoux to car 3B, carrying Floralie's bag.

"I think we can manage from here," said Tom, taking Floralie's bag. "We'll arrive at Giverny in three days' time. And thank you." Tom smiled, then turned into the compartment to find space for Floralie's bag on the luggage rack as Miss Clairoux went to sit on a bench a few paces back from the tracks.

"I'd best be getting tickets back to Giverny," Mr. Tullier said to Floralie, then reached into his pocket. When he pulled out Philomenos, Mr. Tullier winked and muttered, "Your vermin."

Floralie smiled and took Philomenos in her palm. "And, Floralie," said Mr. Tullier, forget-me-not eyes narrowed, "you're sure this is okay? Staying with me."

"Of course!" exclaimed Floralie. "I couldn't be a smidgen more pleased."

"Good," said Mr. Tullier. "I'm glad. So I will see you—"

"Wait—" interrupted Floralie. "I just have one question."

"Don't you always?" said Mr. Tullier with a laugh, and Floralie noticed there was a wholeness to his laugh that hadn't been there before. "Go on, then."

"Why did you write the floriographies in the first place? Why flowers? Miss Clairoux told me you were blind as a child, and once you could see, you didn't like the way the world looked."

Mr. Tullier sighed. "No, I didn't. I could see pain. I could see my little brother's knees bleed when he fell from his bike; I could see my older sister's tears the first time a man broke her heart, and I could see the light leave my father's eyes as he lay on his deathbed. But flowers, flowers are not made of pain. Flowers are beautiful."

"But if they're so beautiful, why did you refuse to describe them to Miss Clairoux?"

"Because I was young and stupid. I was no longer blind, but my vision was clouded by pain. So, after Delphine left, I went to work for Monet, who taught me much about beauty—it took me a long time to really see it. But my flower language was my attempt at fulfilling Delphine's wish, even after she left me. My floriographies, if used properly, could translate the emotions of flowers. They could explain flowers in a way the blind could see them. Let me ask you something: Did you know that near the end of his life, Monet began to lose his sight?"

Floralie shook her head no.

Mr. Tullier half smiled. "Well, during that time, he told me something. He was painting his tulips, cataracts and all, when he said it to me: 'Everyone discusses my art and pretends to understand, as if it were necessary to understand, when it is simply necessary to love.' Can you remember that?"

Floralie remembered reading that in *A History of Dreamlands*. She nodded.

"Good girl." Mr. Tullier tipped his hat at Floralie. "*À bientôt*, Floralie."

"*À bientôt*, Monsieur Tullier."

When Mr. Tullier had gone, Tom returned from the luggage racks and said, "Are you ready, Flory?"

Floralie stepped halfway onto the train, one foot on, one foot off. She bit her lip before saying, "You go on; I'll be there in a minute."

Tom nodded and stepped into the compartment. Once he was out of sight, Floralie called out, "Miss Clairoux!"

Miss Clairoux stood from a platform bench and hurried over to Floralie. When she came to the door, Miss Clairoux grasped Floralie's shoulders and chirped, "Why so glum, *ma chérie?*"

"I'm not glum," said Floralie.

"My dear," Miss Clairoux said, "I can feel. I can feel your bones beneath your skin, and they ache with melancholy. I can feel them trembling."

Floralie stroked Philomenos behind his ear. "It's just . . . Nino. He's back at that horrible orphanage. It's awful."

"I may be but a blind old maid, but in my humble experience, I have found that there is nothing more certain than the uncertainty of forever." A smile peeked through Miss Clairoux's wrinkles the way stars do clouds on stormy nights. "There is something else, isn't there, *ma chérie?*"

"Well," started Floralie. "There is one other thing. My mother's flowers. I suppose it doesn't matter anymore, but . . . I never did find out what they mean."

Miss Clairoux tilted up her chin and was silent for a moment before saying, "Describe them."

And so Floralie did, remembering the colors, shapes, and sizes of each and every flower. She scarcely got a quarter way through them when Miss Clairoux put up her hand. "No, *ma chérie*. Tell me how they *feel*."

And with that, understanding bloomed in Floralie like a laurel bud first realizing it has petals. First realizing the sunshine and the rain could only give it so much; victory grew inside itself. Except it wasn't quite *understanding*—it was *feeling*. Yes, that was the secret, was it not?

Floralie looked up to Miss Clairoux again. "Just . . . one more thing. Miss Clairoux?"

"Mmm?"

"You didn't buy a ticket. When are you coming back? To Whitterly End, I mean."

"Oh, I'm not going back. Goodness no. I've got a library to patch up. Whitterly End's library can hold its own without me. And"—she nodded in Mr. Tullier's direction, pale eyes twinkling—"I left a story in Giverny."

A laugh escaped Floralie, the tinkle of a bell lurking somewhere within it.

Miss Clairoux took Floralie's hand and whispered, "We will be together soon."

Floralie gripped Miss Clairoux's hand tighter, then pulled her old and fragile body into a hug. Tears burned at the back of

Floralie's eyes, but somehow, she was smiling, too. *"Merci,* Miss Clairoux," she whispered. *"Je t'aime."*

As the train chugged back to England and as Tom fell asleep behind a book (an analysis of three Shakespeare plays), Floralie opened up the box of flowers. She had learned enough in Mr. Tullier's garden to be able to recognize them now, even the more obscure ones: burgundy rose, mountain pink, mourning bride, lily of the valley, primrose, pink carnation, meadow saffron, and eglantine.

Philomenos curled up in the box's corner as Floralie carefully removed each flower and laid them on the empty seat beside her. She stroked Philomenos as he slipped off to sleep, his fur oddly cold despite the summer heat. She pulled a handkerchief from her bag and blanketed the mouse with it, then turned back to her flowers.

As Monet's quote echoed in Floralie's mind, each flower turned into a shard of a poem. And she realized Monet and Mr. Tullier and Miss Clairoux were right. Floralie didn't have to understand the flowers. She simply had to feel them.

Sunshine Lungs
By Floralie Alice Laurel

My sunshine lungs
Gasp for breath in sunless spaces,
Crawl out of their box,
Clear their throats of dust,
They speak for the first time
In long-lost tongues.

The burgundy rose is deep as the
Gap behind my wallpaper, letting sunlight through.
A mountain pink inside whispers, "You will soon
Climb high as me,"
Or is it my mother, mourning bride behind her ear
Blooming big as her kisses
Before a long good-bye?

Lily of the valley, bowed like a widow on her knees
Over a grave she once laid tears, but now leaves smiles
Soft as primrose,
Petals like child skin and fairy wings,
Ballet silk made of mermaid scales,
And watercolors weeping wonderland meadows

Because belief in the invisible is a talent
Often forgotten at the feet of carnation trees,
Pink with promise, "I will not forget you."
But all that lies beyond
Is meadow saffron singing sweetly,
"My happiest days are gone."

Except for eglantine, stubborn, wild, whimsical eglantine
Growing where she pleases
But mostly in stories so bittersweet
They hurt and heal at the same time.
And like poems filled with gaps

And wonderlands with mouse holes,
It is through our broken spaces
That light seeps in
And fills up our sunshine lungs.

She wrote the poem on her hands and heard the words in her head, but the voice was ... different. While Floralie knew, logically, she was the one making up the flower meanings, the meanings came not in her own voice, but another's. It was a familiar voice, a distant voice, a dream voice. It was her wonderland gardener.

Floralie and Mama lay on an old quilt in the garden, two sets of eyes filled with constellations. The night swirled around them, swaddling them like a blanket. Mama brushed her hand up to the sky, pressed her fingers against the Milky Way. "Even the sky has mistakes, darling. Beautiful, diamond-cut mistakes. Even the sky has scars."

She threw a henbane flower to the sky, and said, "That one's for imperfection."

44

In the morning, Floralie found Tom in the kitchen, head stuck in a cabinet, with a trunk half the size of Floralie behind him. Upon closer inspection, Floralie found the trunk to be piled high with everything from teabags to curtains to salt and pepper shakers.

Floralie stifled a laugh. "They do have tea in France, you know. And curtains."

Tom jumped, bumping his head on the inside of the cabinet. When he emerged, he was juggling three jars of honey. He turned to Floralie and babbled, "Where'd you come from? Never mind, gather some handkerchiefs from the laundry basket by the stairs. Wait—no, what am I thinking? Just bring the whole basket; you'll need stockings and dishrags, too," and he turned back to his cabinet.

So this suitcase was for *her.* Floralie knelt beside the trunk and pulled out a candlestick and a tin clinking with spare buttons. "Tom . . ."

"Huh?" Tom turned again. His forehead looked far more wrinkly today than usual, and his quicksand eyes were bloodshot.

"I've already packed." It wasn't completely true, but not entirely false either. She'd packed her paints and toiletries, and thought out which clothes she would bring. Really, there wasn't much else she needed.

"Oh," said Tom. His shoulders seemed to shrivel as he dropped the honey onto the counter and leaned back against the wall. "Already? But—but, I'm sure you haven't organized your shoes—or—or folded your linens properly. And how will I know if you've forgotten something if I don't know what you've already packed? Fetch your suitcase; we'll just have to repack together."

Floralie sighed and replied with a hug. Caught off guard, Tom stumbled back before wrapping his hands around Floralie's head, stroking her bird's nest hair. "Tom," whispered Floralie. "I'm going to be okay. And you're going to be okay. You can visit me anytime you like." She smiled and added, "And just imagine you: a university student!"

Floralie looked up and spotted a sneaking tear in Tom's left eye. As it slithered down his cheek, Floralie brushed it away, giggling as her finger traced ridges of stubble. "When was the last time you shaved?" she said, laughing.

Tom strained his face into a smirk and said, "When was the last time you brushed your hair?" And both held close to each other, letting loose laughter, tear choked, but joyful. *Laughter,* Floralie thought, *was very close to sunshine.*

When Floralie pulled away, she wiped her face on her sleeve and said, "I'm going to the shop attic to give Philomenos breakfast, make sure I didn't leave anything there. But I'll be back for lunch."

As Floralie ascended the staircase behind the little flower shop, she felt oddly the same as she had when ascending the staircase of her old home in Giverny. Scents lingered in the air, scents Floralie had become so accustomed to, she had forgotten they existed—fosteriana tulips and soil, mothballs, old wood, paper and poems. And she had never noticed it before, but the higher she climbed, the narrower the steps became. Nearly doll sized.

A tad unnerved, Floralie skipped to the top lickety-split,

opened the door, and pulled on the light string. But as the bulb flickered to light, Floralie had to keep herself from shrieking. She stumbled back, catching herself on a crate of irises, and clutched her heart.

"Thought you'd g-got rid of me, d-did you?"

Floralie surveyed the boy up and down. Raggedy clothes, mousy hair, grimy hands. It was as if he had never left. "B-but—what—you—*how*?"

"I think y-you stutter worse than I do." A crooked smile broke Nino's mouth, but this time, his lips did not bleed; he had been speaking more.

"I just—I don't understand," said Floralie.

"They s-sent me back to the orphanage," explained Nino, "and, naturally, I escaped again. N-nothing new. When'd you get back?"

"Last night."

"Oh. You didn't find her, d-did you?"

"No," breathed Floralie. She watched a leggy spider skitter across the wood floor and said, "I did." The numbness crept back into Floralie's fingertips as she remembered Mama's vacant eyes.

"Oh," said Nino. It was the sort of "oh" that let Floralie know she didn't have to explain any further. Not now anyway. Not yet.

"But I'm going back—to Mr. Tullier's. I'm going to live with him. He's going to teach me, and I'm going to paint. I have a real family now."

Nino's eyes lit up. "Floralie, that's great!" he exclaimed. "Really, really great."

"You're telling *me*!" Floralie laughed.

"Oh—have y-you seen it yet?"

"Seen what?"

"The sign," said Nino. "There's a f-for sale sign up at the g-gate of your grandmother's orphanage."

Floralie's jaw dropped. "*No!*"

A wry smile flitted across Nino's mouth. "*Yes.* I s'pose after I went missing twice, the authorities weren't about let it st-st-stay open.

"Where's Philomenos?" Nino asked. "He d-did come home with you, didn't he?"

Floralie nodded toward the mouse hole. "Yeah, I brought him back. I let him in here last night so he could sleep in his own bed—wouldn't stop squeaking and squirming in mine. But, Nino . . . I don't think he's been well."

"Wh-what do you mean?" But Nino gave no time for Floralie to answer. He laid his head on the ground before the mouse hole and called into it: "Philomenos? Philomenos, c-come on out."

Not a sound.

"Philomenos!" Nino hollered, louder this time. He looked up at Floralie for a moment and said, "Hand me some paper. There should be some in my pack."

Floralie spotted Nino's bag a few paces off. She knelt beside it and pulled from it the tattered leather notebook. Nino snatched it, flipped it open, and tore a piece from inside. He then crumpled it up, making as much noise as possible. "Philomenos!" he called again. "Philomenos, I've got paper! Come out, you can have all you want," and he flicked the wad of paper into the mouse hole.

Still, no mouse.

"He must be st-stuck. He always comes to paper," said Nino. "Help me tear down some wood."

Floralie's eyebrows jumped an inch. "Tear down some *wood*? Are you completely mad—"

"*Please.*"

Floralie sighed, but nonetheless crouched beside Nino and slipped her fingers into the mouse hole. The wood inside was loose and, unsurprisingly, rotting; it made her stomach squirm. She clawed at the wood, felt it chip away, debris collecting beneath her fingernails. Between the two of them, Floralie and Nino widened the mouse hole perhaps three inches before the wood became harder, thicker.

"I don't think it'll chip anymore," said Floralie, but Nino was not in the mood for giving up.

Nino plunged his hand into his pocket, fished around, and pulled out a nail. He then poked the tip into another nail in a board of wood and screwed it out. He repeated at the other end, again on two other boards, and then loosened them from the wall. They fell with a thud between Nino and Floralie, sending spiders scattering to their corners.

"*Wow.*" The word escaped Floralie's mouth hardly with her consent.

"That's a lot of paper," breathed Nino, for inside the rotting mouse hole was a palace of crinkled paper, dust bunnies, and stolen trinkets.

Floralie's lungs felt too stunned to produce sound, so she pulled a fountain pen from Nino's pack and wrote instead. *This must be Philomenos's wonderland.*

The day Mama left, Floralie wrote her first letter. Her first poem. It went like this:

> The lamplighter killed the moth last night
> Sun at his heels, stars in his hair,
> Shadows chased him up the ladder to
> His chink of hallowed light
> Unraveling the godforsaken wicked night—
> That is not what killed her

This light, this brilliant, beautiful
Hallowed light
Was hers.
Belonged to her quick beating heart,
Lit for her warmth-seeking wings,
Danced with her skin paper-thin
Gleamed and glowed and glistened
For her, only for her
She cared for it.
She slipped under the glass
And was already

Ash
By the time
The lamplighter came back that dawn
As snuffer-outer this time around
And the flame slipped into ashes
Into ashes into ashes
The night is not what killed her

The moth
Never cared for the night.

45

Nino looked Floralie in the eye and smiled. Gingerly, they crawled inside the mouse hole. The hole was deeper than Floralie would have thought possible, and much taller. Specks of sunlight peeped through cracks in the ceiling, dancing like fairies across the paper floor. Shreds of newspaper hung around the cracks, fluttering like ghost curtains with the breeze.

Floralie squinted in the dimness, dust collecting on her eyelashes. A pile of chestnut fur curled up in a page of an old book caught her eye; Nino saw it, too. "There he is!" exclaimed Nino, scooting over to Philomenos. "You had me so worried, Phil—" Nino's voice cut short.

Floralie held her breath. "What is it?" she said after a moment.

Nino gave no reply.

"Well, say something," pushed Floralie. "What's wrong?"

Nino turned. His head was cast down, but his face was scrunched into carnation-sized wrinkles. And in his palms, he cradled the mouse, limp and lifeless.

Words would not do. Words rarely "do" in these situations. Floralie slid over and wrapped her arms around Nino, his chin on her shoulder, and hers on his head. Nino smelled of dirt and too-old fish, but Floralie paid no mind. Neither moved, and neither spoke for quite a long time, not until Nino pulled away and laid Philomenos back into his paper bed.

Floralie stroked his fur with one finger. He was ice cold. "I'm sorry," was all she could manage. "I . . . I was supposed to take care of him. It's my fault."

"*No.*" The fierceness took Floralie by surprise. It was not a tone Floralie had yet experienced in Nino's voice. Nino squeezed shut his eyes, then opened them again. "It's no one's fault. He was old."

"It was the turpentine." Floralie felt as if someone had slammed her chest with a brick.

"What?"

"I didn't want to believe it before, but I'm sure of it. Philomenos only started acting strange after running through a violet patch in Mr. Tullier's garden with spilled turpentine. I was painting, and . . . it just happened. It's my fault." Floralie chanced a look toward Nino, and then back to Philomenos. "Are you mad? You should be mad."

But Nino shook his head. He took a pen from his pocket and unwrinkled one of Philomenos's papers. He began to scribble in the corner, and then stopped short, eyes wide.

I'm not mad. I couldn't be mad. Not at someone who has given me such

The words cut off there, but Nino had circled thrice a word printed on the old paper: *bonheur.* Floralie knew it to be French for "happiness." The word was framed by a watercolor illustration of a sprig of small pink flowers and forest-green leaves. The page was titled in spidery script, *Armoise*, which Floralie had learned at Mr. Tullier's to be the French word for the flower "mugwort." Beneath the illustration was a paragraph in French elaborating on the flower. Upon closer inspection, Floralie realized that every word was handwritten. Beside the page number in the corner, five words were scratched in tiny print: *La Floriographie Complète, Sylvestre Tullier.*

"This is it," Nino breathed. "It was here all along."

Floralie's heart drummed against her chest as she fingered another fragile paper. This one read, *Primrose.* This flower's definition was far more complex than the mugwort's. It read, *The sadness that accompanies a child's imagination when others cannot believe in the unseen. The sadness of leaving childhood behind and separating imagination from reality. The sting of truth. Longing for belief.*

"Impossible," muttered Floralie.

"What?" said Nino.

"It's just like the poem I wrote about primrose."

She laid the primrose page down again as Nino asked, "Wh-what poem?"

"The one I wrote on the train back from Paris. Here," and she rolled up her sleeve for Nino to see her "Sunshine Lungs" poem. "See?" she said, after Nino had read it. "The primrose definition . . . I mean, I wrote it differently, but it's the same thing—childhood belief and imagination and sadness. Same themes. Strange, no?"

Floralie unwrinkled another paper. This one was for lily of the valley. The definition read, *The return of lost happiness.* Floralie could hardly believe her eyes. "This one, too, just like my poem, only simplified."

Floralie uncurled four more pages; more flower definitions. These read,

> Burgundy Rose: *For someone who is completely and utterly unaware of the vast beauty within him- or herself.*
> Pink Carnation: *I will never forget you.*
> Meadow Saffron: *My happiest days are gone.*
> Mourning Bride: *Unfortunate attachment; I have lost all; the way losing something hurts more for having loved it; caring about things that disappear.*

"Philomenos must have the whole book here," she said, unwrinkling another definition. This one read,

> Mountain Pink: *You are aspiring.*

And that made Floralie smile very much indeed.

Nino began to leaf through the papers as well. Shiny objects glinted in the dim light, and Nino said, "Look. There's tons of stuff here. Philomenos must have stolen all this stuff . . . but from where?"

Floralie turned to Nino and glanced down at the pile of trinkets before him. Her eyes widened, and then . . . tears. "*Me.*"

In some faraway place, Nino's hand landed on Floralie's shoulder. "What do you mean?" he said. "Are you okay?"

Floralie gave no reply. She knew these trinkets. These were dollhouse trinkets. A tin of Parisian mascara, half used. A silver comb, daisy-blond hair knotted in its teeth. A rusty needle tucked into a spool of thread, pointe-shoe pink. A makeup brush, still powdered with blush. Floralie's own drawing, a tiny sketch of a daffodil she had made four years ago. Everything was from Mama's Palais Garnier dressing room drawer.

"We must have taken them when we moved," said Floralie. "Before Mr. Duncan moved into the attic, we kept boxes of things up here because we had no time to sort everything when we arrived."

"So Philomenos must have got into this box and stolen everything," finished Nino.

Floralie nodded. "That's how he got Mr. Tullier's book. It belonged to my mother."

"But what about your f-flower box? You found that behind your wallpaper. H-how d'you think that got there? It seems impossible," said Nino.

Floralie shrugged, remembering Miss Clairoux's story of Mr. Tullier's blindness being cured, no matter how impossible it seemed. She laughed and said, "Angels, perhaps."

And then Floralie wept. And wept. She wept harder than she had at her father's grave, at her withered wallpaper, at her mother's asylum, tears filling up the hollowed mouse hole. She let her sadness loose. She was not afraid. And Nino waited, and when Floralie was ready, he listened.

I don't exist to her, she wrote. *I've been stupid. The last words I said to her three years ago were, "Good-bye, Mama." The last word she said to me was, "Who?"* The letters grew shaky as Floralie's fingers quivered; she gripped the pen tighter. *How was she supposed to remember my name, when she couldn't remember her own?*

Nino did not write for a long time, but when he did, he wrote, *I don't know. But I think it's your story. It hurts, but it will heal you. Stories are pesky like that.*

Floralie giggled at that. *Nino,* she wrote. *Will you come with me?*

What? wrote Nino.

To France. Come live with me, me and Mr. Tullier and Miss Clairoux.

Nino grinned, yellowed teeth, crooked mouth. He took Floralie's hand in his and wrote, *Yes.*

Floralie and Nino spent the rest of the morning sorting through Philomenos's things, compiling the pages of Mr. Tullier's floriography. For hours, not a word could be heard from the little mouse hole, for words are of little importance next to stories. And some stories unfold in gaps between stories, inside the broken spaces of mouse holes and poems. And Floralie realized now: She was the gap in her mother's poetry. Lost and forgotten, it didn't mean she didn't exist. It meant she had space. Space to paint, dream, wonder. Space to flourish.

As she sorted with Nino, Floralie flew to her enchanted garden. And when she landed with a thud on the ground, she found the grass was green with springtime, flowers blooming beneath her knees, a sprout of a willow tree growing tall before her very eyes. When she stood, the weight of her arms took her by surprise; she was carrying something. A familiar silver box.

Floralie pulled open the lid. It was filled with gray ashes, and dropped in the middle was a smooth white stone engraved with the words, JE T'AIME, MA FLEUR. 1902–1903.

The growing willow now towered over Floralie, enclosed her in its leaves. Something else had appeared, too—a shovel. Floralie knew what she was here for. She picked up the shovel, knelt at the bottom of the willow, and dug. And when the hole was deep enough, Floralie placed the box of ashes inside, whispering, *"Good night, my wildflower. Good night, Eglantine."* She filled the grave with dirt and watched as a flower grew, five pink petals surrounding a sunshine-yellow middle.

A splash of water hit the eglantine flower.

Floralie looked up to find her gardener there, watering can tilted and giving life to the flower. But the gardener was different now. She was not the unreachable, shadowy figure she had been before. And when she looked into Floralie's eyes, the gardener laughed, a laugh like bells, and eyes like gardens.

The gardener's water splashed Floralie's hands, washing them of dirt. And as it did, Floralie laughed, too. *"Hello, Mama."*

ACKNOWLEDGMENTS

Without the help of many people, this book would not be a book. Therefore, I extend thanks to Jenna Pocius, Charlie Ilgunas, Courtney Fahy, Sonali Fry, Rob Wall, Dave Barrett, Anne Heausler, Nadia Almahdi, Crystal McCoy, and the rest of the wonderful team at Little Bee Books. Thank you to my fantastic agent, Jaida Temperly, and everyone at New Leaf Literary. Thank you to Laura Noakes, Myra Goldberg, and Janet Karman, who helped shape this book. Thank you to my teachers who inspired me: Karen Sylva, Claudia Heller, Luann Duesterberg, Janet Armentano, Lori Whyte, Bridget Flynn, and Kirstin Peltz. Thank you to my family and friends who keep me sane and encourage me, especially Chaz Moser and El Gagnon. Thank you to my students for amazing me every day. And thank you, dear reader: I offer you a rose.

Floriography

the return of lost happiness

you are aspiring

the sting of truth

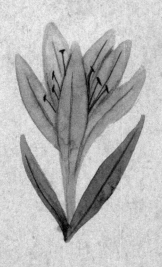

my happiest days are gone

the language of flowers

for someone who is unaware
of the vast beauty within

I wound to heal

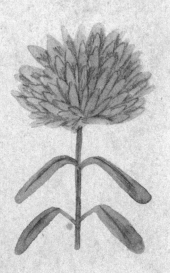

unfortunate attachment

I will never forget
you